A Love to Call Home

BREANNE ANDREWS

Redbud Blossom Publishing

Cover design by Josephine Blake, Covers and Cupcakes, LLC
Edited by Jessica Barber, New Life Editing Solutions
Proofread by Laurie Sibley
Formatted by Audrey Blenheim

https://authorbreanneandrews.com/

Dedication

*For my husband—thank you for becoming my very best friend &
supporting my dreams
For my children—being your mother is my greatest joy, thank
you for all the love & laughter
I love you all.*

Chapter One

driana watched her son Isaac blow out the candles on his birthday cake. Marveling at how fast the years had flown by, she clapped along with the gathering of friends and family as the last candle was extinguished.

It was impossible, in these moments, not to get wrapped up in nostalgia and wonder over how those depressed, sleep-deprived early days with a colicky baby had blossomed into something happier and easier than she'd imagined. Though, she supposed easier didn't seem quite the best word choice. Single motherhood had both strengthened and matured her, but it was not easy. Without her family's help and support, she knew their story would be much different.

Isaac looked from her to his abuelo. "Time to cut the cake now!"

He made a karate chop, popped up out of his chair, then bounded over to where Adriana stood next to her dad. Isaac gave them both a high five. She shoved the nostalgia aside, focusing instead on the present. Isaac's happiness was the sunlight radiating warmth through her days. Today, he was exuberant. She hadn't noticed any indication the constant attention was wearing on him. There were many ways Isaac was much like her. His outgoing and energetic personality was not one of those ways.

"Great job with that candle, mijo," her dad said.

The term of endearment was commonly heard in their family. Her parents had grown up in homes where Spanish was preferred over English. In turn, they'd raised their children to speak both languages in equal measure.

"I was really careful not to spit when I blew out the candles," Isaac whispered, a serious expression on his face.

Adriana smiled down at her son, trying not to laugh. "That was very thoughtful of you."

Isaac's birthdays had been much smaller affairs in previous years. Four days earlier, they had celebrated his fifth birthday with a simple meal of breakfast for dinner, one of his favorites. The subject had come up amongst her family that evening while she stuck a single candle in a small stack of blueberry pancakes. She wasn't surprised he'd remembered that conversation.

Ruffling Isaac's hair, Adriana encouraged him to head back to his seat so he could be served and eat with his guests. Then she walked over to the punch bowl and began spooning the fruit-flavored drink into small cups.

Her mom distributed slices of cake onto yellow paper plates while her sister, Marissa, added scoops of chocolate chip ice cream for each child. Their younger brother, Gabe, whirred each serving airplane-style to the kids at the table. Parties with her family usually involved this level of group effort. Even her sister-in-law Danielle had contributed by making the colorful, two-tiered creation. She could already envision future birthdays for Isaac following this new tradition.

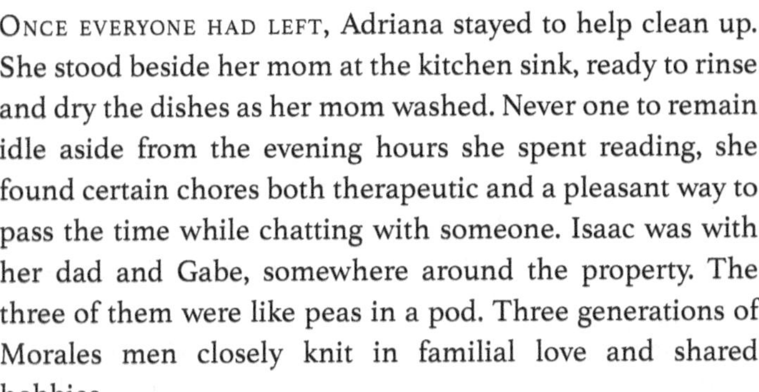

ONCE EVERYONE HAD LEFT, Adriana stayed to help clean up. She stood beside her mom at the kitchen sink, ready to rinse and dry the dishes as her mom washed. Never one to remain idle aside from the evening hours she spent reading, she found certain chores both therapeutic and a pleasant way to pass the time while chatting with someone. Isaac was with her dad and Gabe, somewhere around the property. The three of them were like peas in a pod. Three generations of Morales men closely knit in familial love and shared hobbies.

Her mom squeezed dish soap into the filling sink, a fresh, citrusy aroma wafted through the air. Adriana breathed it in, a sense of contentment settling over her. Things were good and her heart was happy. Yet, there was clearly something her mom wanted to address. She'd noticed her mom's not-so-subtle glances all day and had chosen to ignore them.

"Mamá? What's with the long glances?" Adriana prodded, finally pushed to address whatever was on her mom's mind.

"I've been worried, that's all. How are you doing?" Her mom confessed quietly in Spanish, before she shut off the water and slipped on a pair of dish gloves.

Considering her mom's words, Adriana sifted through the current month in her mind. Once the realization hit, her lighthearted mood diminished. Tomorrow was the third anniversary of Brett signing over his parental rights.

Adriana's shoulders fell as she frowned. "I . . . I guess I lost track of what day tomorrow is."

Brett had never been involved in Isaac's life. He hadn't wanted to be a father, nor had he wanted her to keep the baby. She spent much of her pregnancy and Isaac's youngest months feeling miserable and abandoned. Once the heaviest of that anguish subsided there was still always the wondering and hoping Brett would come around. He never did, not in any positive way.

Eventually, faced with too many fears and possibilities, with a disappointment and heartache that only increased over time, years of neglect turned into a permanent reality when she'd offered him a way out. She hadn't seen or heard from him since. Brett had signed willingly, without a backward glance, as if it wasn't a life-changing event. Adriana had grieved the decision like a death, while simultaneously feeling relieved he would never show up again and rattle their lives.

It was not supposed to have worked out that way, but life rarely worked out as you planned. Or didn't plan, as the case had been. Her behavior and state of mind in the months she'd been with Brett were very unlike the person she'd been before and since. Their relationship had been her first serious one and trouble from the start. Instead of seeing warning signs, she compromised again and again for the sake of someone who never valued the effort. She had been ridiculously hopeful that their dreams would work toward a harmonious mingling but there was only ever emotional turmoil. Becoming a mom under those circumstances had taken a hefty toll.

Yet, it had also given her the greatest gift—her son. Adriana had always imagined starting a family that looked much like the one she came from. At the very least, she certainly had never seen herself raising a child without a husband. She believed in every decision she'd made for Isaac, but letting Brett sign away his rights piled on more guilt. That guilt had been a living, breathing thing that paralyzed her for months after those papers were finalized.

For her, it always came back to one simple truth—Isaac

was what mattered. Every reason to do better started and ended with him. That determination had pushed her forward and allowed the healing process to begin. She worked hard to create security and stability in Isaac's life because she needed it as much as he did. One day he'd ask challenging questions, and he deserved honest answers. She dared to hope she could erase any glaring obviousness of an absence in their lives.

"Adriana? Talk to me."

Her trip down memory lane was interrupted by her mom's concerned voice. What could she say? This was the first time the anniversary hadn't cost her days of lost sleep and renewed dismay over her life choices and how negatively they'd impacted not just her, but more importantly, Isaac. Out of self-preservation she must have blocked out today's date.

Her mom abandoned her attempt at washing the dishes, choosing instead to focus intently on her youngest daughter. Her hand gently rested on Adriana's arm.

"I shouldn't have said anything, mija. I'm sorry." She drew closer and hugged Adriana.

Adriana returned the embrace, trying to soak in the comfort she was offering but feeling hollowed out instead.

"Está bien, mamá. It's okay. Really. I'm not upset with you. It's only natural you'd wonder," Adriana replied.

"It's hard for me to see this date approach every year, to know how you blame yourself. Brett made his choice. It's an unchanging reality that you can't blame yourself for."

"I know."

Adriana slipped into that old, familiar thought loop, the one that played out every scenario, wondering if there was something she could have done differently. It was a waste of mental effort.

She sighed, "Maybe there's this subconscious part of me

that's ready to move on, and the rest of me just needs to catch up."

Her mom gave her a loaded look as she reached for another dish to scrub. She had never been good at disguising her feelings. If the subject of Brett's absence was tired, the more recent encouragement for Adriana to stop swearing off dating was a close second. Though usually it was her sister wearing her out with the subject. She was losing count of how many times she'd had to defend her choice to continue not dating. Especially to Marissa, who adamantly reminded her that she was too young to make such proclamations over her life.

"Not that kind of move on." She refrained from rolling her eyes.

Her mom tsked, unapologetic. "I just want to know you're happy and settled. I worry about you. I worry you're lonely."

Adriana tucked her arm in the crook of her mother's and leaned into her, interrupting the scrubbing she'd been doing. "We are happy, Mom."

Her mom patted a wet gloved hand on hers. A sigh full of conflicting emotions escaped her lips.

The truth was, Adriana wouldn't even know where or how to begin with a relationship, anyway. The thought alone was uncomfortable. Her family's traditional beliefs aside, she preferred the comfort of living the life she'd created in their shadows, the one without the risk of further abandonment and failure. She and Isaac had found contentment, the ability to thrive together. That was enough. In fact, it was more than she could ever ask for.

ADRIANA PLACED a collection of condiments on the rotating tray in the middle of her parents' dining room table. Her siblings would be arriving soon for family night, just as they did every Wednesday. It was a commitment held in high regard among the Morales household, even before most of them had moved out. She peered out the window, and grinned at the sight of her dad, decked out in layers, supervising the smoker as snow fell just beyond the covered patio.

"Hola?" Thomas's voice boomed across the foyer. She heard the door shut, and a moment later, he and Danielle came around the corner of the family room.

"Hola, tío!" Isaac popped up and waved from the couch, where he'd been watching a movie.

"Hey, chiquito!" Thomas replied in his loud voice, a smile beaming across his face, as he went over and lifted Isaac up in a big squeeze, Isaac's little boy giggles muffled in his uncle's arm.

Putting him down just as their dad walked into the room, Thomas exclaimed, "Pops!" Then immediately enveloped him in a big bear hug, like he hadn't seen him in months instead of just the other day. Her family was definitely a hugging family.

Danielle smiled warmly at both men as she continued toward the dining room, her hands full with a container of whatever she'd made for dessert. Adriana could hear Gabe bounding down the stairs. As he came around the corner, Marissa walked through the front door, immediately followed by her husband and their twins. A boisterous ruckus of greeting ensued immediately.

"I have some great news," Thomas said as soon as things quieted. "The food truck finally has a permanent location to call home!"

All at once, their voices increased in volume and filled

the space again. Words of celebration and encouragement were offered with a peppering of curious questions.

"We'd love to offer you more solid work hours, if you're available, Adriana." Danielle's voice was beside her, breaking through the noise as Thomas began addressing the questions.

"I'm still interested," Adriana assured her. "We can discuss days and hours later?"

Danielle nodded, looking pleased.

Thomas and Danielle had opened their food truck a couple of years ago, frequenting festivals and setting up in various temporary locations during peak lunch hours. A home base had always been their goal, and it was finally being realized.

Helping with the food truck, alongside Danielle's growing catering business, was currently a side job—part-time work that had always been extremely part-time. Adriana had done a lot of odd jobs these last few years, finding things that allowed her to spend ample time with Isaac and still make ends meet. Work on her family's farm and homemade goods shop had been the primary job since she had moved back to the farm she'd grown up on.

A permanent location that offered a steadier work schedule could mean money to put aside for going back to school and finishing her degree. This development seemed like an opportunity to take a step in a new direction. It was difficult for her to consider anything for herself. Isaac was always her utmost priority. Reenrolling in classes at the community college would benefit both her and Isaac, though.

"Why don't we sit down and discuss this more over dinner. We're letting the food get cold," their mother said, gently.

Gabe reached out his hands toward Isaac and the twins. "Let's go wash up."

Adriana's attention followed them to the kitchen sink. Isaac stepped up on the stool first and held his hand out for a squirt of soap. Isaac was closely attached not only to her parents, but her siblings as well. That fact always renewed the gratitude she felt over their current situation. It fostered that steady security that was so vital.

She liked things as they were and made no apologies for being protective of the comfortable familiarity enjoyed in moments like this. Of course, as Isaac grew older, his world would continue to expand. Change was inevitable. Avoiding it was easy for now, but that would not always be the case. Worry knotted her shoulders whenever she thought about it.

Chapter Two

Nathan took a deep breath and let it out slowly, trying to ignore how the chill in the air stung his face and lungs. It felt like the first he'd taken in a lifetime. Weariness hung like a thick, wet blanket, but the heavy feeling lifted a degree as he stepped off the last step of the boarding ramp. Gratitude and relief soaked into him. It was over. He'd made it through another deployment.

Snowflakes fell around him as he made his way across the tarmac. It was springtime, but this was mountain country. The weather was unpredictable and moody. Thankfully it hadn't delayed their arrival. The return home was a lengthy process and delays weren't uncommon. The days it took to reach this point required a practiced effort of patience. Most of the time, his training made him capable of stomping out any restlessness it caused him. He was antsy, though. The comforts of home were so close.

Bussing into their headquarters from the airfield, he noticed stray posters on the tall chain-link fences. Most of the words and designs had smeared down the now-frozen paper. They'd probably been completed and strung up during a sunnier day not long ago. Some of the posters were blowing loose from their ties. His chest tightened. Watching them reminded him too much of the blowing tents and flapping fabric surrounding the combat outposts he'd spent the last year living and working in.

Nathan closed his eyes, blocking out the reminders of where he'd just come from. He'd been doing this too long and been on enough deployments that the memories could knock him over if he let them. He let the present moment ground him—the stuffy air, the vibration of the bus's wheels against asphalt, the chill coming from the window.

He lifted his gaze toward the mountain range until the scenery in his mind changed. These mountains were a backdrop for many happy times with people he cared about. His high school years were spent just a couple hours north of where he was now stationed, and his family still lived there. On any given day, they were only a short drive away—a fact Nathan didn't take for granted. Thinking about their support and how much it meant to him wound his thoughts in another inevitable direction—on his ex, Lindsey.

She had dumped him with the ever infamous "Dear John" letter only weeks into the deployment. The unexpected contempt and sullen tone of her letter had been a blow to his morale for months. Their relationship had been rocky before he left. Nathan took part of the blame, because as his focus continued to drift toward deployment, her resentfulness worsened. He was thousands of miles away before he even left. It always happened that way, no matter how hard he tried to remain present.

This deployment hadn't been as bad as some of his previous ones, but the heavy weight of trouble at home settled over him like a dense fog. He was too far away from her to fix things. And that was as much a problem as the issues between them were. The lack of consistent contact was out of his control. Still, she used it as an instigator for her complaints.

He didn't have the capacity in any form to deal with what he saw that letter as—a tantrum demanding attention. A final ultimatum to the motive she'd been working toward, the one he'd thought she would eventually realize was futile —getting him to leave the military early. This was his career choice, and that became a problem for her.

He wondered if it always had been. Her talks of their future often left out the military in roundabout ways. Nathan's hadn't. There wasn't another alternative for him, at least not one he could readily see on the horizon. Her tendency toward dramatics pinched a nerve, but he hadn't wanted to break up with her and confidently believed they would work it out. That dismissive optimism had been a mistake.

He sighed, leaning his head back and closing his eyes. Being unattached suited his life better than he wanted it to. Having something strong and lasting, building a family of his own . . . well, he'd be lying if he said that hadn't always been the eventual end goal. Maybe God had something else in mind. Either way, he wasn't sure anymore if having both the career he loved and the family life he coveted were going to work out like he'd expected.

His parents had done it. They were still happily married and not the only success story to which he could point. The possibility of having it all had been just around the corner. Hadn't it?

A nagging thought settled in his gut at that moment. It was the loss of an idea, of the dream of it all, that stung more than the loss of Lindsey herself. He didn't know what that said about him, that he could be with someone for over two years and not really miss her at all. That could just be the betrayal talking, he lied to himself. And that lie comforted him enough to shut out those questions and focus on the moment ahead.

NATHAN STOOD IN FORMATION, waiting for the homecoming ceremony to come to an end. He could feel the anticipation, especially from those in uniform with him. Everyone was growing restless. It was palpable in the heated building.

He had noticed more of those posters when his group had walked into their position. So many emotions pulsed through those images and words. In the sea of faces before him were spouses and significant others enduring this life in a variety of ways. Some of those relationships might not make it. Some would not only make it, they would strengthen. How did one know if a relationship could withstand this life? Because despite being raised by two of the steadiest people he knew, he hadn't a clue how he kept missing the mark.

He'd spotted his parents and sister, Heather, almost instantly. They were directly in his line of sight, the three of them sitting close together on the fold-away bleachers. His mom and sister held a decorated sign between them, wide smiles brightening their faces. His dad was as stoic as the soldiers around him, but Nathan could still detect the pride and relief behind that carefully guarded expression.

Finally, the last words were spoken, and they were released. His family came toward him immediately. He'd barely made it halfway across the floor before his sister careened into him with a giant hug. He returned her tight squeeze. When she pulled away, her body stuttered in an effort not to sob. She had always been an easy crier, never ashamed to show her emotions or sensitivity.

"Hey kiddo, it's okay. I'm home." He smiled reassuringly, ruffling up her hair.

He knew she probably hated him calling her kiddo, her twentieth birthday was only weeks away, but old habits die hard, and she never complained.

She shoved his hand away good-naturedly. "Hey!" she said, sniffling.

He smirked mischievously while she attempted to rearrange the curls he'd mangled. Despite the seven-year age difference, Heather and Nathan were close. He couldn't really remember a time it had been any other way. He had looked out for her since the day she was born, and as the years passed, they became friends instead of just siblings.

His mom reached for him next, her cheeks wet with tears. "Thank God you made it home safely again. This day couldn't get here fast enough," she choked out, barely above a whisper.

He knew her heart was heavy for every family who couldn't say the same. His mom was moved to action by that compassion and frequently found ways to serve organizations and families in the aftermath of such heavy loss. She always said it was ideal for her because she understood military life from varying perspectives and called her experience God-gifted insight.

She held him a moment longer, her reluctance to let him go obvious. Finally, patting his arm, she made way for his father, who was handing Heather a travel pack of tissues. Nathan's dad scooped him up into a bear hug, adding a couple of emotional pats on the back.

"It's good to have you back on US soil, son." His dad's voice betrayed some emotion, but his eyes were dry.

It was easy to see how deployments weighed on his family, he'd never taken pleasure in that aspect of his job. Was he being selfish hoping for a lasting relationship? Did he really want another loved one going through this? Some said it was a terrible idea to marry and bring a family into the equation. He usually disagreed. When he imagined a wife standing on the other side of a deployment waiting for him, his heart ached with yearning. This was the life he chose. He couldn't control the challenges that came with it, but the right person could choose him despite that, couldn't they?

At least he'd always have his family, and they understood better than most. Nathan and Heather had grown up with their parents both in the military for a time. His dad had stayed in until retirement. Military life today looked different from what he'd grown up around. Still, some things were the same. Flexibility and resilience were invaluable traits. Attitude mattered. If you couldn't change a situation, you had to roll with it and hopefully find the positive along the way.

"I stocked your fridge and pantry for you earlier today. We thought we could go grab a bite to eat though. Would you be up for that?" his mom asked, searching his face.

He wondered what she saw there. If her own expression was any indication, he wasn't hiding how bone tired he was as well as he'd thought.

"I am. I'd just like to shower and change before we go."

Food had certainly been on his mind when he thought of home. He'd been looking forward to having the luxury of unlimited food choices again. Though what he really looked forward to was his mom's home cooking, not the restaurant options available. That would come soon enough if her comment about stocking his kitchen meant what he thought it did.

As they considered where to eat, Nathan couldn't help but look around the crowded room. He saw the families still gathering around their soldiers, wiping eyes and repeated hugs that never quite seemed to be enough. He saw laughter and looks of amazement over babies and children that were new or had grown in the time apart. Patrick Davis, his best friend, had his arm around his girlfriend, a pretty blonde Davis had met online before he moved to this post. And Daniel Walsh listened in rapture to the young daughter in his arms, telling him a story while animatedly making gestures with her arms, the thick braids on her head bouncing in time to her movements. His wife and their other daughter standing beside them.

He saw a few of his soldiers huddled together, a small collection of loved ones between them, and he saw some of the guys with no one at all walking toward the exit together. He couldn't tell what they were feeling at that moment. He only knew he'd need to make sure they were dealing okay, finding a good headspace.

"Give me a minute. I'll be right back." Nathan touched his mom's shoulder gently, meeting the questioning gazes of his family before jogging over to the soldiers he'd seen walking alone.

Would they accept the invitation to dinner? Probably not, but if nothing else, he wanted them to know they'd been noticed. They were seen and more than welcome.

Chapter Three

full tray in hand, Adriana approached a table of soldiers. The men were crowded together between the two benches on either side. Perched on the end opposite Adriana was a woman, the purple scrubs she wore were in stark contrast to the muted shades of camo surrounding her. It was hard to differentiate most at the table, grouped together as they were. Their uniform masked differences she otherwise may have noticed, and the patrol caps shaded their eyes and hid most of their hair. As she drew closer, she noticed one of the shorter soldiers nudge another next to him. Taking a deep breath, she fortified herself for whatever was coming.

It was decided early on that she would work the tables during their busiest hours. Initially, she had pushed back. But whatever Thomas and Danielle needed for this venture to succeed was important. More important than her tendency to avoid stepping outside her comfort zone. The very one she knew those men were going to challenge in a matter of seconds.

"Hi, I have a few orders here. Let's see, two number ones?" She gave the nudged soldier a quick once-over. His light blue eyes were in stark contrast to his nearly black eyebrows and sun-touched skin. She looked first at the rank patch on his cap, then the last name attached to his uniform jacket—you learned a thing or two living so close to a military base all your life. His last name was Connors.

Two other guys reached up to take the containers of food from her. Reading their name patches required more direct staring than she was comfortable with, so she readjusted the tray and looked back at the ticket.

"I also have a number two and four?"

Connors spoke up, though he hadn't quit staring at her. "I'm four." He smirked as she placed his food on the table in front of him just as he reached for it.

The guy next to him, the one that had noticed her first, took the other meal. His last name was Gregg, his eyes were dark, and his fair skin was dusted with freckles. He was the same rank as Connors.

Focusing on the job at hand, she spoke up again, "And I have a number five and six tacos?"

"We're the tacos." The woman spoke up, gesturing between her and the man next to her. She wore a gold wedding set on her ring finger. The way they sat together, arms entwined, made it obvious they were a couple. The last name on his top was long and unreadable from her angle.

The man on Adriana's opposite side had his forearms leaning against the table. He'd been turned away from her when she'd first approached. Now his elbows were propped up and his light-brown eyes fixed on her.

"Five," he said, lifting a finger.

She handed over the order of tacos. Then looked his way again. His expression was serious, preoccupied, even. Nothing like the jovial mood of Connors and Gregg, the two elbow nudgers directly across from him. Never in the mood for that kind of attention, her thoughts toward them had grown more annoyed by the second, but the instant she looked at him, something shifted.

His eyes scanned her face and what was left on the tray. He was noticeably attractive—in a way that seemed more a fact than personal opinion. This awareness furthered her discomfort, and her annoyance increased anew. She looked down quickly, too distracted to catch the name on his uniform, then grabbed his food and placed it in front of him.

Looking around the table, she fixed a polite smile in place, feeling anything but genuine.

"Is there anything else I can get for you?"

Connors, the blue-eyed smirker, spoke up. "Yeah, uh, I was wondering if I could get your number?"

Adriana didn't want to look at him. Her gaze flitted between him and the others at the table. If she could simply teleport herself elsewhere, she would have. In a heartbeat.

"Dude." The soldier next to the woman said under his breath. He'd fully turned toward Adriana's direction to address Connors and she caught the name on his patch —Villalobos.

She tucked the tray under her arm and tilted her head with as much sass as she could muster. Letting her body language set the tone, "How about anything that's actually on the menu?"

Connors wasn't deterred. "Come on, I'll let you show me a good time."

She heard groans erupt around the table—from embarrassment or annoyance, she couldn't tell. Someone across from him must have kicked him under the table because Connors jumped and protested in that direction.

"Hey, I'm just shooting my shot," he replied to no one in particular, barely seeming chagrined.

Villalobos's wife looked like she might throw her container of salsa in Connor's direction. Villalobos was shaking his head, a hand on her arm.

It could have been amusing to witness the little things happening around her if she wasn't the object of the chaos. The feel of everyone's eyes on her made her twitchy. She worked hard to keep her face expressionless and her eyes from focusing too closely on any one person, especially Connors. The guy didn't need an ounce of encouragement. Adriana didn't want to spend another moment attempting stellar customer service.

"Enjoy your meal." She forced out a polite smile before turning and walking purposefully back toward the food truck. She could hear multiple voices speak in low forceful tones as she made her escape.

She was nearly ready to step into the food truck when a woman's voice called out.

"Excuse me?"

Adriana turned her head slightly then stopped when she realized the woman in the purple scrubs, Villalobos's presumed wife, was following her.

She stopped. "Yes?"

"I meant to ask for more napkins back there." She gestured behind her.

"Oh, of course." Adriana dug in her apron then handed a small pile of napkins to her.

"Thanks. Not that you needed it, but you had a table full of guys ready to come to your defense back there. They wouldn't have let things get out of hand. Connors showing off is nothing new. He's kind of an idiot."

Adriana raised her eyebrows and nodded, flattening her

lips together in acknowledgement. She thought she'd managed it well enough.

"Anyway. Thanks again." The woman smiled then turned and walked away.

Adriana sighed. She stepped into the food truck without looking up toward the direction of the tables, happy the entire situation was over and hadn't become even more awkward.

Thomas, who'd been handing a to-go order to a customer as she walked back into the truck, pointed out most unhelpfully, "Some guys at that table are staring after you."

Adriana grabbed a rag to clean the tray more forcefully than she meant to, taking a deep breath as she tried to shove away her frustration. It wasn't that big of a deal—she shouldn't let it get under her skin.

Thomas looked at her for a long moment before slanting his eyes back in the direction of the table in question, his fists on his hips. "Are they giving you a hard time?"

"One of them asked for my number."

Thomas relaxed his stance and chuckled a little. "It was bound to happen eventually with all these soldiers and college guys around. What did you say to him?"

Adriana wasn't amused. "I told him I wasn't serving up anything not on the menu."

Thomas laughed. "So, I take it you don't need me to handle things for you?"

Adriana couldn't help smiling a little as she shook her head. The comeback had been wittier than she'd believed herself capable of. Turning off unwanted attention from men wasn't something she usually needed to practice, which suited her just fine. Marissa always accused her of having an aura of disdain that kept any potential admirers scared off. Whatever seemed to keep her either invisible or unapproachable was perfectly acceptable in her mind.

She recognized that for some guys, that so-called aura was more a challenge than a barrier. Brett had been like that. She'd practiced blending in on purpose even then, and he'd not been deterred once he set his sights on her. She'd been a fool for that sort of confidence more than once. It had sucked her into thinking it somehow meant a guy thought you were special. Now it was a harbinger of doom —experience had been a thorough teacher.

ADRIANA WAS STAMPING paper bags in the catering van late the next afternoon while Danielle was running an errand. The van was set up similarly to the food truck with more frills and style.

After a brief time, a small family had huddled amongst one of the picnic tables. Her eyes focused just past them on a soldier walking from a black pickup toward the food truck. Thomas had been right about one thing—this was a popular spot for the soldiers with the post being so close. She realized it was the soldier from yesterday, number five, the attractive one with the light-brown eyes. He went straight toward the food truck window, his stride purposeful and confident. He was alone this time. Sighing, she continued her task of stamping bags and hoped he didn't have a sweet tooth.

At the sound of approaching footsteps, she raised her head. Well. So much for hoping. He was closing in, paper bag in hand. Resting the stamp against the edge of the ink pad, she stood, smoothing down her apron before looking up to meet his gaze. He stopped in front of the window, somehow managing to look as if he was standing at attention while also altogether relaxed.

"I hear this is the place to come for a churro cupcake." He smiled and looked on as he waited for her reply. It was a smile that didn't quite reach his eyes yet softened their intensity.

"This would be the place." She busied herself with getting a container ready.

Without looking at him, she asked, "How many would you like?"

He was quiet for a moment, as if considering. "Let me get three," he finally replied.

She took her time, using the tongs to move each cupcake carefully from the case to the box. Their creamy frosting was sprinkled with a few thin, crunchy strips of scratch-made tortillas covered in cinnamon and sugar.

"Is this your bakery?" he asked. She could see him in her periphery. He'd put his paper bag on the counter and leaned against it to watch her while she worked.

She shook her head, still not meeting his gaze. "I just work here."

"And at the food truck?" That was an obvious answer, wasn't it? Unless maybe he'd already forgotten her?

She nodded. "Yes."

"They're owned by the same people, right?"

"Yeah," she replied again, still not looking at him.

He asked too many questions. If she were more forthcoming with information, maybe he'd stop, but that wasn't her natural tendency and making conversation with strangers wasn't easy for her.

Finishing up, she finally glanced back up at him. "Is there anything else you'd like?"

"No, thank you," he replied, shaking his head. He pushed off the counter and glanced around them.

His expression was unreadable. Yesterday at the table, it had seemed so disinterested and unaffected, like life bored him. Today she changed her mind. He wasn't bored or unaware—in fact, he seemed overly aware. She didn't like feeling singled out in that awareness. Placing the tongs in their usual spot, she rang up his items and gave him his total.

"You served my table yesterday." He made the statement simply, as if just making an observation.

"Mmhmm." Her stomach fluttered nervously.

"I wanted to apologize for that," he continued, his expression one of genuine remorse, as if he'd been the one to make her uncomfortable.

Her eyebrows creased together. Why was he apologizing?

Then he clarified, "Connors asking for your number and being obnoxious."

He must have mistakenly believed she was confused because she didn't remember. Maybe she pulled off not caring better than she'd thought. While the unwanted advance had been exasperating, she hadn't expected an apology from anyone.

He waited for her to respond, and when she didn't, he continued, "I should have known he was going to say something more and put a stop to it sooner."

She finally found her tongue. "Did you encourage him?"

"No. Of course not. Unfortunately, he doesn't require encouragement."

"If you didn't encourage him, you have nothing to apologize for. You can't anticipate everything someone might do."

He shook his head, his expression even more serious. "That's not the way I see it."

He handed her his card, and she went to work getting it swiped through their system while wondering why he was so insistent on taking the blame. Wait. She didn't care. She wasn't going to argue with him about it. She had zero interest in understanding his reasons or commiserating together over another guy's overexuberance.

"Don't worry about it. I'm capable of handling myself." She looked up, handing him his card, hoping her tone helped him understand she was not a damsel needing saving or protecting. Besides, if she did, that's what her brothers and dad were for—they didn't leave much room anymore for anyone else to take up the mantle.

His head bobbed in a nod of acknowledgement as his eyes searched her face, like he was trying to puzzle something out. What that was, she could only guess. Danielle came around the corner as she ripped the receipt from the machine.

"Hi there! I'm Danielle Morales, one of the owners."

"Hello. Nathan Prescott." He reached out and shook her hand.

Adriana watched as his attention shifted toward Danielle. She sighed quietly. Finally. Except instead of turning away, she found herself examining him—the patches on his uniform, the short brown hair exposed under his hat. His strong jawline. She averted her eyes toward Danielle.

"I see Adriana has set you up with some of my specialty churro cupcakes," Danielle said, gesturing to the pastry box Adriana had placed on the counter by his bag of food.

He looked from his box to Adriana, his gaze lingering on her before he turned back to Danielle. Adriana began finding things to preoccupy herself with, determined not to acknowledge another thing about him.

"Yes, they look delicious."

Danielle beamed. "I hope you enjoy them—they are one of my best sellers."

"That's what I've been told on more than one occasion. It's nice to meet the face behind the bakery."

Adriana couldn't believe what a cheesy comment that was. Under her breath, she quietly exclaimed, "Ayy..."

They both looked her way briefly, causing her to look away and cringe a bit. Oops. She needed to get away from the window. There was no point standing here. She really should just go back to the truck.

"Thank you," Danielle replied. "I enjoy getting the chance to talk to our customers."

Given her tone, Adriana could tell she was beaming even more—if that was possible. She knew Danielle ate up the compliments, no matter how cheesy, if they were genuine. She really did love engaging with her customers, and she paid attention to details in those interactions, making them feel noticed and appreciated. It was something Adriana noticed and had started trying to do herself—making customers aware of the little things you remembered about them. Most people liked that.

"Your place is becoming a fast favorite around post," the soldier admitted.

"We're thrilled to hear it. My husband used to set up there on occasion."

"I remember. It's been a long time since I've seen him out there."

Adriana couldn't help but notice he continued to glance her way repeatedly, as if he expected her to join in at any moment.

"Well, I should go," he finally said, taking his items from the counter. Adriana busied herself folding the rag that really just needed to be tossed in the wash bin.

"Thanks for your help, Adriana."

She looked up, glancing again at the patches he wore

before letting her eyes meet his. "You're welcome, Sergeant Prescott."

It took him a beat to turn and walk away. He looked like he wanted to protest something. Once he'd turned, Adriana tossed the rag where it belonged. Unable to ignore him, she glanced back toward his retreating form as he headed to his vehicle, her annoyance freshly sparked.

Danielle walked back around and into the van. "He was nice. And cute." She tilted her head at Adriana. "Why are you giving him stank eye?"

Adriana turned fully toward her sister-in-law. "I didn't like him."

Danielle shrugged. "Why? What's not to like?"

Adriana turned her head toward the direction he'd gone once more. He was in his truck. She couldn't tell if he was looking toward her or just in this general direction. Looking back at Danielle, she rolled her eyes and ignored the question.

Danielle was smiling like someone who sees the dessert they've been hoping to grab still in the case for the taking. "I hope I didn't interrupt anything. It looked like he would have liked to talk to you more."

Danielle didn't meddle, but she did like to tease in that good-natured way of hers. Adriana shook her head in a gesture that let her sister-in-law know she thought she was being silly.

Danielle kept on. "Two words, sis: body language. I was watching him. It was so obvious. You, on the other hand, were as aloof as ever. I think he may have left disappointed."

"Good." Adriana said, raising her eyebrows and twisting her mouth into a sardonic smile.

Danielle let out a low laugh.

Adriana went back to the food truck to finish out her shift. If he was disappointed in her lack of interest, it would serve as notice that she was not a woman tickled by the attentions of any man, one in uniform included.

He did wear that uniform well, though. His presence had provoked something she'd long thought dead. Even mentally acknowledging that spark of attraction was vexing. What was it about . . . Nope. She stopped herself mid-thought, refusing to let her mind take off in that direction. Poking at that detail too closely was unnecessary. If he came back, she'd make sure he knew how little he interested her.

Chapter Four

Adriana pulled into the driveway of a sprawling rustic craftsman-styled home located on the western outskirts of the city. She put the car in park as her best friend Kristin came bounding down the front porch. She bounced up and down by the driver's side door. Adriana pulled the keys out of the ignition and stepped out, unable to keep from grinning ear to ear.

"It is so good to see you!" Kristin exclaimed, her voice pitched high in excitement.

Adriana laughed, squeezing back. "It's good to see you too. It's been a while."

Kristin squeezed harder, rocking her side to side a couple of times before releasing her and grabbing up Isaac, who had unbuckled himself and come out of the car during their reunion.

"Wow, Isaac! Look at how much you've grown."

She gave him a big hug, then a flat-palmed touch to the top of his head as if measuring his height. Isaac smiled before thanking her for the birthday gift she'd sent him and launching into a story about his parties.

Adriana glowed at the sight in front of her. She was so happy to have her best friend close again. Kristin had just moved back to the area after taking a teaching job at one of the local schools. She was staying with her mom and stepdad while she looked for a house of her own.

Kristin and Adriana grew up together. They'd attended the same schools until high school. When Kristin's parents divorced, she moved up north with her dad and younger sister, Libby. The two best friends had made time for one another as much as they could but between college for Kristin and motherhood for Adriana, life had gotten in the way more often than not in recent years.

Making their way into the house, Adriana was greeted with a hug by Kristin's mother, Joyce. They chatted, Isaac as much a part of the conversation as the adults, and Kristin made her way to the kitchen island. Adriana's lips twitched with affection for her best friend—she'd always had the gift of hospitality, even when they were young, and she was no doubt busying herself with preparing a snack and refreshments for her guests.

Adriana hugged Joyce again, excusing herself to follow Kristin to the back patio. As she stepped outside, she smiled at the sight of two iced coffees and a plastic cup of lemonade on the patio table. Foregoing the array of snacks, Isaac rushed straight toward a play set that Kristin's stepfather, Vic, had built for his grandchildren.

"Are you up for going out for dinner this evening?" Kristin asked as she plopped down on a cushioned patio chair.

"Just the three of us?" Adriana asked, grabbing one of the iced coffees before sitting in the chair next to her.

"Well, I invited Patrick and Libby."

"How are things with you and Patrick now that distance is not a factor?" Adriana asked.

Kristin's face lit up, and immediately she began telling Adriana how well they were getting along, how amazing Patrick was, and about the time they were spending together.

"I think he's the one. I really, really do," Kristin said, sighing happily.

Adriana smiled at her, "I'm happy for you both. You've been together awhile, and now you can grow even closer."

Kristin smiled and nodded. "I'm looking forward to it so much. I wasn't sure I'd get there. All the guys I dated in college were just . . ." She shrugged. "Meh."

Adriana had doubted Kristin's relationship with Patrick at first. Meeting someone online seemed terribly risky. She'd been wrong. Fortunately, she'd had the foresight not to overshare her worries. Kristin had come down to see Patrick and introduce him to friends and family, so Adriana had been around him a couple times before he'd deployed over a year ago. He really did seem like a great guy, and most importantly, he was good to Kristin.

"I have big plans that I want you to be a part of," Kristin began.

"Oh?" Adriana wondered.

"I want to start hosting gatherings as soon as I close on my house." She'd sent regular updates to Adriana about the cute house she'd found close to the school. "Game nights, cookouts, getting a group together for the festivals and such around town. It's the perfect time of year to plan these things, don't you think?"

"Sure," Adriana said hesitantly. "I'm not sure how I work into the equation though."

"That should be obvious. I want you to be part of all of it."

Adriana wasn't biting. "I don't know. . ."

"Don't look at me like that." Kristin used her bossy-best

friend tone. "It'll be good for you to get out more. Besides, it'll give us the opportunity to spend even more time together." Kristin's smile stretched across her face, and she wiggled her shoulders in a little seated dance.

"Well, you know I'm not one for going out or . . ."

"Crowds of strangers? Yes, I know. But I'd keep it relatively small. Low-key hanging out, getting to know some new people. Good, healthy fun."

"I have plenty of fun," Adriana countered.

"Of course you do. I'm talking about you getting a little time away occasionally. Add something new and different to your life with me, your trusty sidekick, helping you along on the ride. What do you say?"

Adriana squinted. Sidekick? Kristin, though incredibly loyal was never really the sidekick. She was the main character. That was why they were perfect as best friends—she stood out so Adriana could blend in. "I don't know. I want to hang out with you more, but I thought that would look a little different from what you have in mind."

"We will do the usual stuff you're thinking of, but having you at these other things would be so fun too. Come on, Adriana, you've got to let go of this flawed idea you have."

"Flawed idea." Adriana snarled a little at the word. "What does that mean?"

"This notion that mom life means a dull social life."

"I do not have a dull life. My life is full." She resented such a statement.

Adriana knew her best friend—Kristin had a plan going, and she wasn't one to back off from what she wanted easily. Kristin didn't usually poke at much when it came to Adriana's choices, though looking back at the past years they had been in closer proximity, Kristin did challenge her tendencies toward staying secluded from certain things. She supposed neither of their roles had changed.

"That's not what I said. I'm only pointing out it's okay to remind yourself that you are young and single and not just a mom."

"I don't need a reminder. I make the choice not to include all those things. I don't want to do any of that . . ." She waved her hands around as if to indicate all the things unsaid. "Single lady stuff."

"I get that. I really do. I'm not suggesting you start dating or meeting guys. I'm just saying." She shrugged. "You kind of hide from anything that doesn't involve work, your family, or being a mom." Her look was knowing, free of judgment, and full of love.

Sighing, Adriana put her hand out to grab Kristin's. "I know you mean well. My life is full though. It's full in wonderful ways. I do fun things. I have my family. I have work that I enjoy. I'm busy right now too, with Isaac out of school."

Kristin squeezed her hand. "You are kind of making my point for me. You know I think you're an amazing mother, right? Isaac is beyond blessed to have you and the family he has. But all that would still be true if you weren't so singularly minded."

Adriana pursed her lips. Spending time with Kristin was important to her, and compromising a little was not an unreasonable ask.

"I am excited to add more time with you into my days."

"Does that mean you'll come around when I plan these things? It would mean a lot to me to have you there." Kristin clapped quietly. Smiling widely, she wiggled her shoulders in another little dance. Her expressiveness was full of a spunk that always made the air around her feel lighter. Adriana sometimes forgot that these days.

"Yes. I can do that. Sometimes," she said, putting a finger up to hold back the excitement bubbling across from her.

"And so long as it doesn't involve setting me up with anyone. Ever."

Adriana trusted Kristin explicitly, but that was a non-negotiable condition she felt compelled to make clear.

"Absolutely. Cross my heart, I would never do that." Kristin was as serious as Adriana was.

Chapter Five

Nathan had eaten at Sol de Montaña more than any other place since returning from deployment. The food truck was on his way home from work, though he usually preferred doing his own cooking. It wasn't convenience that steered him in that direction so often. No, it was a certain attractive brunette that made these frequent stops more appealing than his quiet kitchen.

Each time he came by, he was greeted with warmth and amiable conversation, with one exception. Adriana had been distant—her politeness appropriate for customers, but barely stretching beyond the friendliness Thomas and Danielle openly expressed. Despite her indifference, Nathan didn't deny it was a pleasure to see her whenever she was working. She was gorgeous in a way she seemed either completely unaware of or inconvenienced by. He wanted to discover what was beyond that beauty.

Watching her with Connors, and even that day she'd been at the bakery van, had made it clear she had no tolerance for flirting. He wasn't trying to flirt, though. Not really. In whatever capacity those small stretches of time allowed, he wanted to get to know her. Discovering whether they were compatible was the objective, if only he could get her to see him as less of a threat. Because for whatever reason, every good-natured attempt fell flat. Most people had a better response to him. It wasn't conceit that made him sure of that, simply the fact he was often told he was likeable and easy to talk to.

He noticed her look up from where she was working as he got in line. When he smiled at her, he swore her eyes tightened at the corners just slightly before she focused again on the customers in front of her.

"You're inside today." Nathan stated the obvious idiotically when it was his turn to order, then groaned inwardly. He was going to win her over in no time with that dazzling commentary.

"Yes," Adriana said, leaving it closed for further engagement. Nothing new there.

Clicking her pen out, she focused on the pad in her hand. "What can I get for you?"

Always all business. He looked over at the menu again, though he already knew what he wanted. "I'll try the number one today."

"Would you like your usual drink?" she asked with a quick glance.

He'd always ordered the Jarritos Tamarind bottled soda. He couldn't help but smile. She was paying more attention than she let on, and he watched as she seemed to consider what she'd said. The delay in his response prompted her to finally look up at him again.

"You remember my drink order?" he finally asked.

She held her bottom lip between her teeth for a moment and squinted at him. "I have a good memory. Sergeant Prescott." She added the last bit with an eyebrow raise.

He laughed a little, nodding and looking down then

back up at her. Of course, that's all it was. She was clearly just doing her job. "Yeah, the usual would be great."

"It'll be ready in a few moments. Would you like it to go?" she asked as he paid her.

"Yes, thanks." He moved over to the side, looking over at her again.

She looked in his direction before she turned away from the window. Maybe she wasn't repelled by him after all. He turned toward the parking lot and watched as cars came and went. Adriana interested him, but he didn't want to be just another clueless moron pestering her while she was working. His presence during the whole debacle with Connors may have made him seem even less appealing. Which was unfortunate. Connors was obnoxious and made everyone around him obnoxious by association. Nathan wasn't that kind of guy even if he might keep company with that type sometimes. It was just the way things went working with a bunch of guys that came from such different walks of life. Too many of them were more than a little rough around the edges or just idiotic. There wasn't a way around it.

Before long, she was coming out of the food truck to hand him his order, a damp rag tucked in her elbow. Her hair was pulled back, as he'd always seen it. For once, she didn't look away as she drew closer. Her beautiful, dark brown eyes took him in, and he allowed himself a moment to do the same. She had on a dark blue top that barely scooped below her neckline. Her curves were enticing even with an apron tied around her waist. There were a few rings on her fingers, but as he'd noticed that first day at the table, her left ring finger was bare.

"Here you are." She handed him a bag and his drink. "I put some salsa, utensils, and napkins in there. Is there anything else I can grab for you, Sergeant Prescott?"

The way she addressed him was amusing. He didn't

think he'd ever both disliked and enjoyed the sound of his title quite like when she said it. This was no good at all. Letting her get under his skin would not do—one-sided as it was.

"Sounds like you thought of everything. I do have one additional request though. If you wouldn't mind?"

She tilted her head and looked at him suspiciously. "What's that?"

"That you'd just call me Nathan."

Her mouth twitched up like she almost wanted to smile. Then she moved to walk away, nodding agreeably while her face said something entirely different. "Of course. Have a great day then."

She gave him that super polite customer service smile of hers before turning toward the eating area, rag in hand, without a backward glance.

"You too." He lifted his bag up in an almost sarcastic farewell gesture that went entirely unnoticed.

He could take a hint. The message she was sending seemed obvious enough, even if he wasn't sure he had a good read on her. Maybe he was delusional, but he hadn't failed to notice how many times she looked in his direction.

NATHAN AND PATRICK were grabbing a quick takeout lunch before getting back to work, and once again, Nathan found himself pulling into the parking lot of the food truck. That familiar excitement sparked immediately, despite how clear it was that his attempts were not and would never be appreciated. A couple of weeks had passed, and nothing had changed with Adriana.

Patrick looked up from the booklet he was studying. "Ah.

Yes, I'm hungry! I'll just quickly grab our order so we can get back."

Nathan had unbuckled, unable to refrain from acting on the ridiculous thrill that shot through him the minute he saw this place. Patrick had called their order in ahead of time, so there really was no reason to linger besides the inconvenient attraction he felt for Adriana.

It was reminiscent of a high school crush when you couldn't wait for class to start just for the opportunity to see that one special person and exist in their periphery. He hadn't felt this way in a long time. Not even with Lindsey. Things had started differently for them, though. She'd pursued him. He'd been uncertain he wanted a relationship. Before long they'd just sort of drifted right into one. Happily. Until it wasn't anymore.

He tapped his fingers against the door's arm rest in agitation. He didn't like thinking about Lindsey anymore, and he hated his mind's automatic attempt to compare her with Adriana.

As Patrick reached for the door handle, he added, "You know . . . I didn't mention it earlier because I couldn't remember if it was the right place, but Kristin's best friend's family owns this place."

Nathan immediately snapped to attention. He turned to look at Patrick as he was about to shut the door. "Wait a sec. Kristin's best friend owns this place?"

"Her brother and sister-in-law," Patrick corrected, tucking his book in the side pocket of his uniform pants.

Patrick had noticed that he was leaving to go out more and had teased him about his habits changing now that he didn't have Lindsey to impress. Nathan had taken it in stride, not wanting to reveal the truth of the matter yet— that he was essentially looking for ways to see a woman who had captured his attention but wasn't the least bit interested.

Nathan sat there staring at his best friend, wondering if Adriana was the woman in question. In all the times he'd visited, he'd only seen one other person there besides her, Thomas, and Danielle.

"I'm going to go grab our food," Patrick said, looking at him a moment longer before shutting the door and walking over to the line in front of the window.

Nathan watched to see if Adriana was around. Sure enough, she stood off to the side of the food truck, handing a couple of full paper bags to one of the waiting customers. She looked as she always did, put together and focused on working. As she began to turn, he watched Patrick somehow get her attention. He saw her smile and approach him. They talked for a moment, and it was clear she was comfortable with him. Even from this distance Nathan could tell they had a familiarity. It sparked a hint of jealousy. How long might it take for her to be comfortable with him? He recognized things were different with Patrick. She knew him outside of work and from a trusted source. Nathan realized what had just been presented to him—a connection between them. The possibilities lit up in neon.

She walked away, returning a couple minutes later with their food, handing it to Patrick, and exchanging a few more words with him.

When Patrick got back in the truck, placing the food between them, he looked over at Nathan. "I was hoping I could convince her to take a moment away. I wanted to introduce you two."

"We've actually met," Nathan admitted.

"Oh?" Patrick paused for a second. "I guess since you keep coming here, I should have figured you'd have seen her around."

Nathan huffed out a little laugh as he pulled out of the parking lot. "Yeah."

"Hold up. Is she why you keep coming here?" Patrick said, shock clear in his voice.

"The food is really good," Nathan countered.

Patrick smirked. "No wonder you've been eating out so much." Then his demeanor changed. Nathan could tell Patrick was suddenly not so optimistic about this discovery.

Nathan's eyebrows twitched together. He wondered what that was about, but Patrick would tell him when he was ready.

"What do you know about her?"

Patrick hesitated. "Not much. We've only spent a little time around one another. She's quiet. Honestly, I'm a little surprised she talked to me so much today."

So, that stand-offish behavior wasn't reserved just for him. That warm, hopeful feeling he'd felt just moments before strengthened.

"I can tell you she comes from a big family. Kristin took me to this giant cookout once. She said they do it a few times a year. You'd swear the whole town was there, but it's just their family and a handful of friends."

Getting to know Danielle and Thomas these past few weeks, he could picture exactly what Patrick was describing. He wondered how Adriana fit into her family's dynamics. Was she quiet or livelier and more outgoing amongst friends and loved ones?

"There's something else." Patrick's tone caught Nathan's attention. If he'd thought he was less than optimistic before, he sounded more like he was giving fair warning now.

"I hope it's her stellar food service interesting you, because she does not date."

Nathan glanced sideways at him as he turned toward the gate into post.

Patrick sighed. "And Kristin is very protective of her. You

know those events Kristin's been talking about doing as soon as she moves into her house?"

"Yeah?"

"Well, letting on that you've got a thing for Adriana might be a quick way to get your invitation rescinded."

Nathan did not want to get on Kristin's bad side. They got along, he liked her, and he thought she was great for Patrick.

"I know. It sucks, man, and I know you'd be cool, but she's already asked me not to invite anyone I think might make a nuisance out of themselves."

"Don't invite Connors then," Nathan said, as they pulled up for their turn to show their IDs to the guards at the gate. Knowing it would require more explanation, he launched into the story of the first time he'd ever seen Adriana as soon as they made their way toward headquarters.

Patrick was both as annoyed and amused as Nathan had been by Connors's antics and by Adriana's response. It wasn't the first time they'd seen Connors act that way, but honestly, it was the first time Nathan had seen him shot down so thoroughly. It had been unexpected, even with as down to business as she'd appeared from the moment she stepped beside their table.

"In any case," Nathan added, "I don't think Kristin has much to worry about. Adriana is more than capable of handling herself."

"No kidding. I think Kristin's more concerned Adriana won't come around. I get the impression it wouldn't take much to keep her away."

Nathan could understand Kristin's concern. "She is guarded, that's for sure."

Patrick nodded.

Nathan wondered aloud, "I don't know. Something tells me it's more than just being shy, but I can't figure her out."

Patrick's hesitation felt loaded. There was something more he needed to say. Nathan waited, pulling into a spot in front of the building where they spent many hours when they weren't out on training exercises or details. When he didn't say anything else, Nathan shut the engine off and gestured with his hand.

"Out with it. What aren't you telling me?"

Patrick rubbed the bridge of his nose. "Well, yeah. I believe some of it is just who she is."

He stopped talking, grabbing for their bags of food. Nathan tugged them closer to his side. "And?"

"Maybe ask Kristin for more details."

"I'd rather not. You told me that would be a bad idea, anyway." Something important fed her reluctance—that much was clear. What he didn't understand was Patrick's hesitation.

"Yeah . . ." Patrick cleared his throat. "She's a mom. Protectiveness is in their nature, isn't it?"

"Kristin?" That didn't sound right, but Nathan wasn't following, even with the obvious direction Patrick was headed.

"No." Patrick laughed. "Adriana."

Nathan huffed out the breath he'd been holding. "She has kids?" he said, more to himself than Patrick. "She's not married or anything, right?"

Patrick shook his head. "A son—I think he's five—and no, she's single. Remember? She doesn't date."

Nathan looked out the windshield and frowned.

"Sorry, man. At least you know now, right? Before you've considered getting invested in seeking out a relationship with her."

Patrick was right. They were strangers. There was no reason for him to feel invested whatsoever in getting to know her. This was just an infatuation. Maybe a rebound infatuation. Was that a thing? Yeah. It could be a thing.

"Can we go eat now?" Patrick asked, impatiently. "You can grill me about it more inside."

Nathan took the bags as he opened the door and stepped out. "Yeah, yeah. Let's go."

As they walked, Nathan tried to process everything. He had not been expecting that news. It had crossed his mind there might be another guy. Turns out there was—just nothing like the scenario he'd imagined. Her status as a single mom would certainly color every decision she made, including who she let into her life. Anyone given that privilege would have to prove their worth. They would need to earn her trust before they gained her affection, then the boy's as well. That was weighty.

Given what he'd witnessed about her, she was not ready to allow someone that opportunity. She was closed off, and it was possible that was less a personality trait and more due to her circumstances. Painful experiences could do that to a person, and Patrick had said the dad wasn't involved. Nathan wondered what that meant. Did her ex not fit into the equation at all? Either way, it might be best to take Patrick's advice and leave things alone.

Chapter Six

Adriana and Kristin stepped back from the entryway wall, both tipping their heads to the side.

"What do you think? Does it work?" Kristin asked.

Kristin had spent the beginning of the week moving into her house. Now it was time for all the little details and decorating. Isaac had gone on a fishing adventure with her parents and siblings. The trip was something Adriana would typically have joined, but her mom had encouraged her to spend time with Kristin. She'd been at her house ever since, helping her make decorating decisions.

Adriana hummed thoughtfully. "It's close."

She looked over at her best friend, who had brought her thumb to her mouth, worrying a nail against her front teeth. Moving closer to the wall, Adriana gestured. "Maybe something here and here?"

Kristin nodded. "I think you're right. It's a shame I'll have to go back out and find a few more pieces to finish the look." She smiled coyly at Adriana.

"Yes. Truly a shame," Adriana agreed.

She grabbed the painter's tape while Kristin sorted through various shapes and sizes of paper so they could mark the positions they had in mind. After they finished, she stretched then handed the tape to Kristin.

"I should go. I need to finish shopping for Sofia and Elijah's birthday presents."

"Their birthday party is next weekend, right?" Kristin asked as she closed the handheld toolbox her dad had gifted her as a housewarming present. Kristin had been proud to show off the practical gift, lovingly handling each item when she'd shown Adriana.

"Yeah." Adriana grabbed her purse off the hook by the door, securing it across her shoulder. "You and your family are still coming to dinner this Sunday, right?"

"We'll be there." Kristin nodded.

"Are you bringing Patrick?"

"He's leaving for a camping trip of sorts tomorrow morning."

"Of sorts?"

"Yeah, a few of the guys he deployed with planned this rafting and hiking thing. They aren't supposed to return until Monday night."

"Well, if he makes it in early, he's more than welcome to come. He can bring them if he wants."

Kristin smiled. "I'll keep that in mind and let you know if that works out."

Adriana nodded, then gave her best friend a farewell hug. "I'll see you then."

ONCE AT THE BOOKSTORE, Adriana browsed the children's section. While hovering over a table of dinosaur books, she picked up a couple that had caught her eye. Taking her time to sift through the pages, she considered them before choosing another to look through. There were a lot of great choices at this table, and Elijah's fascination with the creatures made one of these books an absolute necessity.

Suddenly, a prickly feeling settled over her, an awareness of someone watching her. Looking around as nonchalantly as possible, she glanced at a few people around her in the children's section. None of them seemed aware of her presence at all. Maybe she was just imagining it.

Picking up a book, she flipped the pages back and forth without really seeing them. Her mind was distracted now. She couldn't shake off that feeling. Curiosity won out, and, in an attempt not to look obvious, she lowered the book to chin level and looked toward the large clock on one of the wide pillars in front of her. Pulling her eyes off the clock, she paused. Comic books and graphic novels for younger readers filled the short shelves that faced away from her, dividing the children's area from the rest of the store. A man stood there. He was turned partially toward her, his head down. A comic book was spread open between his hands. He seemed familiar.

Bouncing her eyes off him, toward the clock, and back to her book again, she realized she did know him. It had thrown her off at first, seeing him hatless. Between that and the lack of the uniform he wore anytime he came by the food truck, she hadn't immediately placed him.

As her line of sight moved back to the shelves he stood at, her stomach flip-flopped. He'd brought his gaze to her. Those searching, intense eyes focused on hers, and it was obvious he'd recognized her. In the moment they looked at one another, he seemed to quickly decide on a plan of action. Putting down the comic book, he made his way toward her.

Being forced to make awkward small talk made her

cringe. She quickly looked back down as he approached, tightening her hold on the book and fighting the desire to race out of the store. There was no way she could pretend she hadn't seen him. He could be here for a while, and she couldn't just leave without finishing her shopping. That would be silly. Placing the book down with exaggerated care, she forced herself to look at him as he stopped on the opposite side of the table.

"Hi, Adriana. I thought it was you." He seemed to hesitate, as if he'd only just now thought through the decision to come over.

She attempted a smile, knowing it was probably strained. "Hi, Sergeant Prescott."

He put his hands partially in his pockets. "I'd really like it if you just called me Nathan."

His request was casual, like he might follow it with a shrug, but his expression was expectant.

Being contrary felt more out of spite by this point.

"Very well," she agreed, without immediately acquiescing.

His answering smile made her believe he was satisfied with her answer. "I apologize if I was staring. I recognized you but debated coming over to say hello."

She'd not expected him to be so forthcoming.

"So, what brings you to the children's section?" she asked, gesturing toward the shelves he'd been standing at moments ago.

"I noticed you when I was walking by on my way to the guidebooks. The comic book browsing was just a cover while I decided whether to come say hello." He looked at her apologetically, rubbing the back of his neck.

"Ah," she replied. His honesty discombobulated her. She wasn't sure what to say in response. He didn't feed her lines or flirtatious nonsense. Even with all the ways he tried to make conversation at the food truck, it hadn't really been like he was coming onto her so much as trying to genuinely engage with her. That realization made him feel much less threatening than a situation like this would generally warrant.

A moment of awkward silence slid past. They were just staring at one another. Her gaze traveled down to the books —she was desperate to pick one up, just to have something to do.

"And what now? Now that you know I'm who you thought I was?" The question had just tripped right out of her mouth. She had no idea why she asked him that. The silence had been uncomfortable. That must be the reason she was encouraging a conversation with him at all. Walking away at this point would be rude, on top of awkward.

His face relaxed and his eyes danced with the full smile he treated her to. That smile made him look approachable, like someone you wanted to be around. Well. There was no taking it back now.

"That's a good question." He looked down at the books on the table in front of them, then back at her. It always felt like he was trying to figure her out, observe something she gave away about herself without even knowing it. "For starters, I wonder, what brings you to the bookstore?"

"Oh." She hesitated, looking off to the side before sliding her gaze back to his. "I'm shopping for my niece and nephew's birthday coming up this weekend."

"What type of book are you looking for?"

She looked down at the one she'd just had in her hand.

"For my nephew—he's really into dinosaurs right now— I was thinking one of these books would work." She pointed at the few she'd found. It was the most forthcoming she'd ever been with him.

He came around to her side of the table, stopping closer

than arm's length from her. Before she could even consider it, she took a step away from him to get more space. He looked down at the books she'd pointed out, ignoring her movement, and picked them up. Flipping through each separately, he made some little noises, the ones people made when they were pondering decisions. Little hums and "ahhs." He even nodded a couple of times. She watched him, studying his expressions and movements.

A heightened awareness seemed to drown out their surroundings. His hair was longer on top than she would've guessed, still short but sort of . . . unsuccessfully tamed in multiple directions. Maybe he ran his fingers through it a lot? Out of stress, perhaps? His muscles in the arm closest to her flexed at his movements. She breathed in deeply and let out a slow sigh then looked quickly away. He was still looking at the books. Thank God. She did not need to be caught noticing him. Details about men weren't ever on her radar—not like that.

"Great choices," he finally said. "Personally, I like the interactive aspects of this one." He pointed to the second book he'd browsed through.

She nodded. "I really like that one as well." She pointed to another. "But this one has wonderful, detailed illustrations. It has my favorite pictures out of all the choices."

She looked back up at him. He searched her face, interest alight. Almost distractedly, he picked up the one she'd pointed to and opened it to a random page. He made an agreeable noise. "They are good."

He flipped through a few more pages before putting it down. His gaze lingered a moment at the books on the table before he turned toward her slightly. Crossing his arms, he leaned his side against it.

"I have an idea," he said, as if mulling over his thoughts aloud.

She maneuvered herself to face him more directly, raising her eyebrows and waiting for him to continue.

"Want to toss a coin for it?" He smirked, reaching into his pocket. He pulled his hand out, opening his palm. A quarter, two dimes, and a penny rested inside. He picked up the quarter between his thumb and forefinger.

Her lips curved into a smile she couldn't fight, and she laughed a little in amused disbelief. Who was this guy? He didn't do or say what she expected.

"Okay, let's do it." She nodded, having no explanation for why she was still standing here entertaining any of this, except that his playful manner made it too easy to feel agreeable in ways she didn't typically.

He placed the other coins back in his pocket and planted his feet in mock seriousness, prepared to toss the quarter.

"Wait." She held out her hand. "Which side will be what?"

He nodded, considering. "Good question."

After a second, he said, "Tails for the illustrated, heads for the interactive."

She nodded once in agreement. He tossed. The coin flipped perfectly, and he caught it, keeping it hidden. He looked from the covered coin to her face.

"Moment of truth," he said in mock seriousness. "Ready?"

She breathed in dramatically and nodded, caught up in the game he'd created. "Yes. It's now or never," she deadpanned, playing along.

He uncovered the coin. The quarter rested heads up.

"Well, there you have it," she said. "Interactive it is."

She picked up the book, the one that in the end she truly believed her nephew would appreciate the most. It had been a more enjoyable method of choosing. Smiling down at it, she realized she'd just shared a moment with Nathan she'd not had with anyone outside of her well-established and secure circle. That just didn't happen to her by choice. Suddenly unsteady, she tried to calm the fluttery feeling in her chest. She was still in control here. This was fine. Totally fine.

NATHAN WATCHED ADRIANA hug the book close and tucked the quarter in the pocket opposite the one he'd pulled it from. He worked on taming the goofy grin plastered on his face. Her ability to play along surprised him in the best way but he didn't want to be so obvious about it.

"I won't tell if you'd rather take the other one," he said.

"Oh no." She looked up at him seriously. "The coin has spoken. The toss must be honored."

He laughed and nodded. When he'd first spotted her, he'd stopped in his tracks, doing a double take. Her dark hair was loose, falling past her shoulder blades in long waves. It was the first time he'd ever seen her hair out of its usual bun or braid. He had briefly considered just walking along without acknowledging her. The reasons for doing so centered on his conversation with Patrick and the suspicion that any greeting from him wasn't likely to be well received. Thankfully, that thought hadn't stuck.

"Is there anything else you need a helpful coin toss for then?" he asked.

Her smile widened. The amusement twinkling in her eyes brightened everything about her. He hadn't seen her smile at him once without hesitation before this moment. A jolt of attraction shot through him, unwilling to be ignored.

She looked down at the items tucked in her arms. "No, I think I'm done today. Thank you though."

"It stands at the ready if you change your mind."

He waited for her to look up again and grace him with those beautiful, expressive brown eyes. He couldn't stop staring at her. She made so many facial expressions. Every expression, he'd wonder if she was aware of it. Her face and body language, all spoke in high volume. Still, what he'd believed days ago was frustratingly accurate—he wasn't entirely certain he was ever reading her right.

He thought he made her nervous. It was in the way she'd stepped away from him, the way she seemed to monitor his movement and closeness. She didn't trust him in the slightest, that much had always been obvious. It made this moment seem like a gift.

"Well." She looked around. "Now that I have everything I came for, I should go."

And just like that, the moment was over. He wasn't sure how to keep her, get more conversation out of her without stretching past the limits to where she'd close off again. "It was great to run into you."

She smiled at him. "Yeah . . ." She hesitated, almost as if something surprised her. "It was. Thanks again." She gestured at the book in her arms before placing it in her shopping bag.

He watched as she turned to walk toward the cash registers. After a few seconds of hesitation, he strode after her, closing the distance quickly.

"Adriana?" he called out just before reaching her.

She turned, a look on her face that he recognized well. "Hmm?"

"Would you maybe want to grab coffee or lunch sometime?" he asked. Rushing for a reason, he added, "It would be a great opportunity to discuss how the coin fares? I feel strongly invested in the outcome."

Her eyebrow raised as she studied him. "Oh? So, this . . ." She considered a moment. "Meeting . . . would ease the suspense I'm sure you must already be feeling?" Her expression was skeptical even as she entertained his request.

He nodded exaggeratedly. "Yes. Exactly. I'd appreciate your thoughtfulness in this matter."

"In that case . . ." Her hesitance lingered and in that moment, he felt as if he was finally reading her exactly right.

He wanted her to be more certain of him, wanted to earn that trust. "What if when I come by the food truck next time, maybe you can take a break and sit with me?" he asked, hoping to find a compromise that would be acceptable.

Several emotions flashed across her face.

"Maybe," she said simply, more unsure than disagreeable, like she was still trying to decide whether to tell him to get lost. "That might work."

He made to turn and walk back toward the heart of the store. "Until then?" he asked.

She watched him move away from her. "Until then . . ." she agreed slowly.

He waved and turned from her, commanding himself not to look back. Let her think this was all just casual. Two acquaintances shooting the breeze.

It wasn't entirely untrue, except that he didn't do casual well. At all. He might take his time, but when he knew what he wanted, he was serious and committed to seeing it through. Working toward that end goal, bit by bit.

Until he could figure out what the end goal was, he'd get really good at casual. She might not know yet just how much they were getting ready to see one another. He looked forward to whatever came next, another chance to figure out the puzzle that was Adriana.

Chapter Seven

Holding a shallow box with bags of food, Adriana followed a young mother toward a van in the parking lot. She'd offered to help with the large to-go order because she understood the weary expression on the mother's face. This week had stretched out endlessly. She was beyond tapped out, socially more than anything. It was tough sometimes to balance obligations, family, and her need for solitude. She was looking forward to her days off from Sol de Montaña.

Relaxing her tense shoulders, she adjusted the box and attempted to open the passenger door. The cardboard wobbled, and thick strands of her ponytail whipped around and skimmed her face. Adriana sighed and quickly straightened the box, then reached out for the door again.

"Here, let me get that for you." A man's arm shot into her field of vision, opening the door.

She stepped back and took a deep breath. All that previous tension slammed into her again, along with another gust of wind. Her eyes trailed up the man's arm to his face as he stepped in front of the opened door. Nathan smiled at her. *Could this day just be over already?*

A puffy cloud hid the sun, softening the brightness. It was then that she noticed his eyes weren't at all the brown she'd thought they were. They were like walking through the Rockies on an early fall day—shades of vivid light brown blended with bursts of deep-green and gold. Stunning and complex and . . . his eyebrows raised in question. Oh. She'd spent too much time just looking at him.

Shifting her gaze down to the trays of food, she closed her eyes and sucked in a gulp of air. "Thank you." She offered a quick smile before focusing on her task once more.

The last thing she wanted to do was drop this order. Nathan continued to stand in the way of the door, blocking the wind from shoving it back toward her. Once the order was secured in the seat, she looked back toward the woman, who was gently instructing the oldest child how to buckle herself while she worked on getting the baby strapped in his car seat.

"Your order is all secure, ma'am."

The woman looked up, relief apparent on her face. "Thank you so much." She finished with the buckle, then rifled through her purse. "I really appreciate you offering to help me."

Adriana shook her head. "I'm happy to help. Have a great day."

Nathan shut the door as Adriana stepped away. She looked around. His truck was parked at a perfect vantage point to have noticed her struggling. No wonder he'd arrived so suddenly.

She only gave him a quick glance before walking back toward the food truck.

He fell into step beside her. "Do you have some free time to take a break?"

Adriana had known this moment would come. She'd agreed, hadn't she? It wasn't busy yet. She doubted her brother would mind if she took a short break. He would wonder about it, though. Oh well. The sooner she told Nathan the outcome of their little game, the sooner she could move on. She'd worry about her family later.

She looked up at him. "Let me make sure Thomas doesn't need me for anything. Would you like me to put in an order for you?"

"Oh, that isn't necessary." He waved her off. "I think the guys in my squad have a problem."

Her steps halted for a second. "A problem?"

In response to her concern, he hurriedly clarified, "No—not like that. I have a pickup order as well. I meant we all might be more than a little addicted to the food here."

She closed her eyes and shook her head, laughing a little. That was a relief.

They'd stopped walking. What was it about him that made her forget her place? She was not supposed to feel relaxed or find it so easy to smile at him.

"If you want to sit, I'm going to let Thomas know. I'll make sure he has your order ready by the time we're done," she said as she forced her smile to relax.

Nathan nodded, turning toward the covered seating area.

Adriana made her way toward the table a few minutes later, a cup of ice water in each hand and a brown paper bag tucked in the crook of her elbow. Nathan stood as soon as he saw her approaching and held a chair out for her. The gesture nearly made her stumble. She looked into his impressive hazel eyes. He hadn't looked away from her once, nor had he taken his seat again.

"Can I take those?" he asked, gesturing at the cups of ice water in her hands.

Feeling out of sorts, she handed them to him then placed the brown bag on the table, refusing to look back up until they'd both sat down again.

"What's in the bag?" he asked, leaning forward.

"Sopapillas. Thomas and Danielle are introducing them to some of the combos."

Her brother and sister-in-law had mentioned the decision to add them as part of the menu earlier that morning. Bringing them out now had been Adriana's idea. The dessert was a sly way to, hopefully, redirect some of Nathan's attention.

"Can I eat one now?" Nathan asked, peeking into the bag.

"Of course." She waved him on.

He wasted no time digging in. "These are amazing," He said between bites.

She smirked as she watched him. Success. She may not know Nathan well, but she knew the power of good food.

He held one of the sugary pillows of dough out to her. "Do you want one?"

Adriana shook her head. "I'm good, thank you."

"It's tempting not to share these with the guys." His grin was mischievous.

She laughed a little, then took a sip of her water and tried to swallow down the sense of giddiness that raced through her. It had nothing to do with bringing out the dessert early and everything to do with the man sitting across from her.

"So, tell me how the coin fared. Did we make a good choice?"

"We did. The coin chose well. My nephew was thrilled. I have it under good authority that it's a popular bedtime pick."

She'd thought of Nathan as soon as Elijah began

ripping the tissue paper out of the gift bag, and if she was being honest, even before then. It made that certainty settle in, the one that told her she needed to cut this off. Now.

"I'm glad I didn't steer you wrong."

His smiles were contagious. Sitting across from him like this, the ease she felt in his presence triggered feelings she didn't want to examine. Those feelings bubbled to the surface, threatening to ruin her careful intentions to keep most people at a distance—attractive men that were fun and easy to talk to especially. As if she had ever encountered a man that caused this uproar of emotions. Nathan was an exception, and not one she appreciated.

"Do you like to read?" Nathan asked, seemingly out of the blue.

"Yes."

"I thought so. It seems only a person who appreciates books would be so particular about picking just the right one for someone they loved. Especially a young child."

Hmm, she'd never thought of it that way. Her family enjoyed reading. Books were frequently part of gift giving, even children's gifts. They were also a part of some of her warmest childhood memories.

"It's sort of tradition," she replied, but immediately changed course. "Do you like to read?"

He brushed his hands together, sprinkling cinnamon and sugar on the ground beside his chair. His eyes searched her face before he replied. "Depends. I don't mind reading. Mostly military stuff, history, and guidebooks, things like that."

"Guidebooks about what?"

"Hiking, fishing, outdoors stuff . . ." he rattled off, thoughtful, then offered more details. "My mom and dad encouraged me and my sister to study and read about things that interested us. They also used to play radio theater during long road trips."

"Radio theater?" she asked, clarifying. "Like stories with added drama and sound effects, right?"

He smiled, looking pleased she knew what he meant. "Exactly that."

"Sometimes . . ." Her alarm chimed loudly in her apron pocket, thankfully interrupting her.

Saved by the bell, quite literally. She'd been about to say she and Isaac had listened to a couple of those. He was too easy to talk to.

"Sorry." She reached into her pocket and turned it off. "That's my five-minute warning."

It wasn't that Isaac was a secret, really. But they'd never talked about her personal life. With barely a thought, she'd been about to speak of it as if he already knew intimate details. That alarm had been the perfect reminder of the decision she'd made before.

He looked at her, amusement shining in his eyes. "You set an alarm for yourself?"

She shrugged. "I set a lot of alarms and reminders for nearly everything. It helps me not lose track of stuff."

He was looking at her that way again—like he was on the brink of discovering all her secrets. A smirk teased one side of his mouth. He leaned back and crossed his arms.

"What?" Adriana laughed nervously, her face growing warm under his scrutiny.

"You fascinate me," he admitted, breaking his silence.

She suddenly felt jittery, like the caffeine she'd had that morning had just now kicked in and on overdrive. How was she supposed to respond to something like that?

Chapter Eight

Nathan watched Adriana react, her expression bewildered. He wondered if she was enjoying this break as much as he was and how he could convince her to go to dinner with him sometime. Thomas walked over, carrying a large bag, and placed it on their table.

"Here's your order." He looked at Nathan, his expression scrutinizing but not unfriendly.

"Thanks, I appreciate it." Nathan acknowledged him with a nod. He hoped to convey more than one message with that gesture—one older brother to another. He wasn't here to make trouble.

Thomas and Adriana exchanged a look before he walked off. Oh yeah. He was definitely checking in on her. Nathan closed the bag of sopapillas, then looked at his watch.

Adriana placed her hands flat on the table, as if bracing herself to stand, but she didn't make any further movement. "I need to get back to work."

"I do as well. Thanks again for dessert and for spending your break with me." He grinned at her.

She smiled back, catching her bottom lip between her teeth, as if to control the reaction, and he wondered how much less she'd fidget if she realized it only commanded more of his attention.

Nathan wasn't ready to leave, as much as he knew he had to. He brought his right hand to the left chest pocket of his uniform and tapped it lightly with his fingers. Her willingness to sit with him made him wonder...

"I almost wish you had another decision that my trusty coin could help with."

She tilted her head, her expression curious as she glanced at his fingers still resting on his pocket, "Almost?"

Here goes. It was time for straightforward honesty. Adjusting his cap, out of habit rather than necessity, he confessed, "Well, I'd just properly ask you out on a date if I thought you wouldn't turn me down flat."

Her eyes widened a touch, her solemn focus completely on him. "It's better you didn't."

"Why? Because you aren't interested?" he inquired, trying to read the ever-changing emotions flitting across her face. Because he'd seen how quickly she could punch out a well-timed rejection, he was going to need for her to come right out and say exactly what she felt. Her behavior with him, while flighty, didn't always seem like complete disinterest. It was like the way a deer watches an approach, ready to run at the slightest provocation.

The skin between her eyebrows creased a little. He wanted to reach out and smooth it with his thumb. It took a beat before she replied, "I would n—" She shook her head slightly. "You don't even know anything about me."

Her objection sounded full of disbelief. He didn't

respond, though he wanted to argue back that dating was an obvious cure for that problem.

"There are important things . . . You'd change your mind if you did." She was stumbling over her words.

Was his asking her out such a shock?

"Try me," he challenged.

Her avoidance tactics were reflexive. That playfulness she'd shown earlier and at the bookstore was gone. Had he been wrong in assuming they'd made progress toward friendlier territory?

"If it's so important that you believe it'll potentially change my mind, why not give it to me straight?"

Adriana balked at him. Nathan knew he was pushing. She was always sidestepping him. He wanted to challenge that tendency instead of letting her off the hook so easily.

"You're being presumptuous." Her forehead creased in an accusatory frown.

Thinking they'd been headed toward new territory had been a reach. Adriana was still firmly tucked behind that thick wall of hers. She was going to have to let her guard down a bit more for them to get anywhere. What he couldn't figure out was how to help her see he was someone she could trust.

He propped his elbow up and leaned his chin on his knuckles, not finished yet. "Let's have it then. What do I need to know?"

She shot up, her chair teetering behind her. Nathan hadn't expected it, and he almost flinched. Her expression softened—anger released in exchange for something that looked more like uncertainty. It was a quick switch, and he waited, hoping she'd sit back down.

"I don't owe you further explanation." Her voice was quiet, firm.

She turned toward the food truck. Nathan was up and

out of his chair before she could fully pivot. His stride was longer than hers, and in a couple steps, he was around the table. Reaching out, he gently touched the back of her elbow.

"Hey," he said softly.

She turned slowly, looking down toward where he'd made contact before settling on his face. There was a lull in their usual lunch crowd today. A couple of customers were gathered at the window browsing the menu. Thomas's gaze was locked on him and Adriana. Nathan didn't want to cause a scene, but he refused to feel guilty for acting on the belief that Adriana needed someone to push on her defenses, shake her up a little.

"You're right. You don't. I didn't mean to be a jerk. I'm just trying to get to know you."

That crease was back between her eyebrows.

"At the bookstore . . ." He rubbed the back of his neck, running his hand up to the top of his cap and resting it there. "I thought we'd had a good time." He'd also thought they'd passed the hurdle he was currently falling face first over.

A small smile tugged at her lips, one shoulder lifted in a little shrug. "That was a nice moment."

Every step forward was a hesitant tiptoe. So hard to earn and too easy to take back. All those shifting emotions she tried to hide weren't lost on him. The reason behind all of it was another matter.

She sighed, looking away again before shaking her head and continuing. "Earlier when you asked me if my response was because I wasn't interested?"

She said it like a question, so he nodded, waiting.

"Well, it is. That is, I don't have an interest in a relationship. With anyone."

There it was. He had the answer his heart had

demanded. Nathan wanted those details she refused to share, but he couldn't force her to let him in. He wanted an opportunity to tell her that if this was because of what Patrick had revealed, that didn't change his mind. Her secretive behavior was frustrating because he didn't understand it. Like those locked diaries Heather used to request for every birthday, Adriana's heart was off-limits.

Taking a deep breath, he let it out slowly. "And what you said earlier . . . you don't want to elaborate on that?"

She shook her head, avoiding eye contact. He could tell her they had mutual friends, except the timing felt wrong, as if he was wielding it against her. He should have mentioned it before everything else. In the rush of the moment, he hadn't thought it through, and now that moment had passed. Things might get more than a little awkward soon.

"Okay. I respect that."

He'd back off, give her more space. Something convinced him she was worth the patience and the effort. Besides, time was on his side for now. They'd have more chances to get to know one another. Though he might need to do some damage control first. When Adriana realized how closely they were connected, she was not going to suddenly flip a switch and make things easier on any of them. Patrick had warned Nathan, and he'd tossed caution out the window for a bid at her trust. What was that decision going to cost him?

Nathan and Patrick were at the gym working out. Between sets, he'd updated Patrick on things with Adriana.

As they were walking toward the exit, Patrick's face scrunched up, and he swung his head in disappointment.

"Man, I told you she's not available. This after I decided not to tell Kristin."

Nathan stopped at the water station to fill up his bottle. "You didn't tell her anything, not even that I knew Adriana?"

"No. I thought it would be better not to for now, since Adriana clearly hadn't brought it up either, and I told you to lie low."

"You didn't really though."

Patrick pointed at Nathan as he took his turn at the station. "Oh, but I did. Everything I told you was me saying to back off. If Kristin gets wind of any tension between the two of you, who do you think she's going to stop inviting? As much as she likes you, dude, it isn't going to be her best friend."

He was right. Nathan had been certain he was going to have more opportunities to prove himself as someone Adriana could trust, but if he didn't start by being someone Kristin could, this wasn't going anywhere. They made their way to the front door and headed toward the parking lot.

"I'm sorry, man. You're right, I didn't think about my actions putting you in a bad spot. If it means anything, I'm backing off."

"You'd better. You'd better play it cooler than cool," Patrick said, his tone semi-serious. Nathan knew the intention behind it. This wasn't Patrick giving him a lecture.

"What's the deal anyway? It's not like you to rush off and ask anyone out."

His impression wasn't wrong. It had taken months of Lindsey's not-so-subtle flirtations before Nathan had really taken their relationship potential into consideration. And before her, it had been years since he'd pursued anything serious. He'd dated, sure, but he'd been too wrapped up in constant training, deployments, and his goals to put much effort into it.

Nathan shrugged. "There's just something about her."

"Look, despite giving you a hard time, I know you. This can't only be about Adriana's looks, and I know it isn't some vain attempt at a hookup."

"Well, no. Of course not. I mean, don't get me wrong—she's beautiful and I'm attracted." Nathan stopped, scratched his head, and tried to put into words what he was feeling. He wasn't sure he could explain it, barely understanding it himself, but every time he was around her, he felt it like a spark igniting down to the core of his being.

"There are other females that fit those parameters you might have better luck with," Patrick said, slapping Nathan's shoulder and shoving him forward good-naturedly.

Nathan wasn't exactly putting himself out there, and he had no desire to. He didn't plan on getting a dating app or social media, and lurking at the typical singles locations had never been his thing. Most women he'd dated, he had met through friends and mutual acquaintances. Noticing Adriana had just sort of happened. He hadn't been looking for it.

"I don't know what else to say, man. I try to tell myself it's stupid, then I catch myself thinking about her, wondering about her. What she likes, what she doesn't. What might make her really laugh. Not just that little one she breathes out with her mouth closed, but an honest to goodness laugh, like I got her to do today before it all went south."

Patrick was looking at him with his eyebrows raised, and Nathan knew he was giving away too much of his feelings, yet he continued. "Or at the bookstore. That was fun. I want to know what made her loosen up, and I want to get her there again."

Patrick shook his head, like he was giving a bad diagnosis. "You are way more involved than you've previously let on."

"I'm not, I'm just interested. So, there's only one thing I need to know," Nathan said.

"What's that?" Patrick asked, squinting at him.

"Will she be at Kristin's this weekend?" Nathan walked backward in front of Patrick.

He tossed his sweaty pullover at Nathan's face. "You're supposed to be playing it cool. After what happened, you'd be lucky if she didn't leave once she sees you."

Nathan caught the pullover. "Give me a break. You know me better than that. Besides, I'm holding out hope she doesn't, and I'm working on Plan B."

"Oh yeah? And what's Plan B?"

"Friendship," Nathan said, tossing the pullover back in Patrick's direction as they reached their vehicles.

"Friendship? After everything you just told me, is that all?"

"Of course. Come on, it's not that serious." Nathan wanted to believe in what he was saying.

Patrick laughed sarcastically. "Yeah. Sure."

"Do you think Adriana is going to tell Kristin about me?" Nathan wondered.

Patrick shrugged. "Who knows? I'd say you're in the clear for now."

"Good deal." His lack of consideration was not a mistake he'd make twice. If he was given the chance, he'd show Adriana just how great of a friend he could be.

Chapter Nine

Adriana and Marissa were overseeing their usual weekly preparations of the farm's store front. Isaac and the twins were just outside the door, lost in whatever make-believe game they had cooked up to pass the time.

"Thomas mentioned your reoccurring visitor at Sol de Montaña," Marissa said nonchalantly as she organized jars of honey on a shelf.

Adriana pulled her gaze from the children to scrutinize her sister. "What?"

"Yeah. Mom and I know all about this guy."

"What guy?" Adriana put her hands on her hips. "There isn't *a guy*."

"There is. Don't try to be sneaky. Thomas said there's a soldier that comes multiple times a week."

Adriana turned away from her sister and wrinkled her nose. Why had Thomas said anything at all?

"Well, there's nothing to know. He is hardly worth mentioning. We have several repeat customers, especially from the post."

"Sure. But he's the only guy asking about you whenever you aren't there." Marissa came back to stand beside her, her smile full of the sort of shenanigans Adriana would always strive to avoid. "I got the impression Thomas and Danielle have become rather chummy with the guy. Thomas didn't seem bothered by his frequent visits, anyway."

Somehow, she'd missed this budding attachment. All of it must have come about before the last time she'd seen Nathan at the food truck. Thomas hadn't been feeling so chummy then, that was for sure. She didn't think Nathan would be so quick to seek her out now. Right? Her stomach twisted.

"Well, of course not. He's a paying customer." Adriana rolled her eyes. "Don't dig for something that isn't there."

"Oh, come on. Who is he?"

"Why don't you ask Thomas and Danielle? Since they are so"—she used her fingers to make quotation marks—"chummy."

It was Marissa's turn to roll her eyes and mutter under her breath in Spanish before responding more clearly. "Trust me, Mom and I jumped all over it. I want to hear your opinion, though. His name is Nathan, right?"

Adriana opened another box, pulling more jars of honey and jam onto the table for sorting. She stopped to give her sister a pointed look. "Sergeant Prescott is just a soldier that likes the food we serve."

Marissa laughed. "Ohhh, Sergeant Prescott, huh?" She nudged Adriana's shoulder with her own.

Adriana shooed her back. "Quit." She shook her head but couldn't help but smile. Her sister was impossible.

"Seems as if he likes *you* even more than the food," Marissa said.

"Maybe he did. He knows where I stand." She looked at her sister and shrugged.

"Oh?" Marissa's face lit up with interest. "What do you mean? Did he ask you out?"

"He tried. I've made it clear that I am not interested."

"You're so difficult." Marissa groaned. "Is he a creep? Ugly? Rude? Smelly? What is it exactly that has you turned off? Because if none of that fits this guy, maybe he deserves a chance."

Adriana frowned. He was absolutely none of those things, but she didn't want to admit she had noticed anything about him. "I am not dating. There is enough on my plate and—"

"Yeah, yeah," Marissa interrupted. "You aren't interested. Blah, blah, blah." She turned her back on Adriana, taking jars back and forth to the shelf.

They had fans going, but it was warm in the little building. Adriana's skin felt sticky. Marissa's discontent wasn't upsetting. This back and forth had been going on between them long enough that Adriana didn't bat an eye at it most of the time. Her sister was always going to think this was somehow part of looking out for her.

Brushing the hair that had fallen out of her loose ponytail away from her face, Adriana puffed out a breath. Nathan and their last conversation flitted through her mind. He had never been that pushy before, and it had provoked her. Her mood that day certainly played a part, but all that aside, she couldn't trust herself around him. He made it too easy to get lost in conversation and warm feelings. The best thing she could do was make sure he knew he was just Thomas's customer. She was there to do a job. Nothing more.

~

Elijah and Sofia had stayed over with Isaac Friday night, so Saturday before heading over to Kristin's, Adriana took the three of them over to Marissa and Logan's house for round two of their first sleepover of the season.

Kristin had planned a wide range of finger foods for the gathering, and Adriana had offered to help with prep and anything else she might need to get ready for her guests.

While mixing dips for raw vegetables and chips, Kristin told her all about setting up her firepit in the backyard and having the space for a volleyball net to go up as well. The backyard was modestly rectangular, with a wide patio perfect for grilling and outdoor eating.

"Tell me about the people you've invited," Adriana asked, covering the ranch dip and placing it in the refrigerator to chill.

"You know some of them; Libby, Jacob, Mya, Patrick."

Jacob was Kristin's stepbrother and Mya was his wife. Kristin had always looked up to Adriana's family and the way they stayed so close. She could see how this might be somewhat like a recreation of the gatherings they had— ones that Kristin had been a part of nearly as long as the two of them had been friends.

"I also invited the other third-grade teachers at my school. I don't think any of them can make it this time, though." Kristin placed the onion dip in the fridge next to the ranch and the salsa Adriana's dad had sent with her. "Patrick is inviting some of the guys from work."

Adriana knew this would probably be the case. She'd mentally prepared herself to deal with a collection of potentially single soldiers. Hopefully Patrick's friends were better behaved than the elbow nudgers, Connors and Gregg, who still came by the food truck on occasion.

"Have you met them?"

Kristin nodded while shrugging. "Most of them. Two are

married and bringing their wives. There were a couple names I wasn't familiar with that he mentioned bringing because, as he said, 'they need an alternative to finding trouble or too much isolation.'"

"Huh," Adriana replied. "Is Patrick like the older brother of these guys or what?" She meant the question kindly.

"Yeah, especially the guys he's in charge of. I think Patrick and his best friend treat it like a personal mission or something—to be someone these guys can turn to and count on. Someone setting a good example."

"From what I know of Patrick, that doesn't surprise me." They'd pulled out washed vegetables and began cutting them. "His best friend is a soldier too?"

"Yeah. They met in basic and have been close ever since. He got stationed here a couple months after Patrick. I am not trying to set you up or anything, so don't take this the wrong way, but I think you'll like him. He's a great guy. He's someone you could be comfortable around, like you are with Patrick."

"Helloooo!" Libby's voice gave away her presence as she came around the corner into the kitchen.

"What did you do to your hair?" Kristin asked, holding a chunk of one side out to examine it.

Libby's short, light blonde hair had a few thick strands of red and blue peeking through at the nape of her neck.

"Isn't it great? We were playing around with colors in school today, and I decided to go patriotic."

"Fourth of July is a month away." Kristin laughed. "But it fits you well."

Libby tilted her head and smiled with her eyes closed. "Thank you. I brought these eclairs from the bakery and Mom's buffalo chicken dip." She handed Kristin the containers in her hand. "What can I help with?"

"I'm going to put you in charge of getting the burger toppings ready while I cook bacon for the baked beans."

ADRIANA WAS FILLING the ice chest that would go outside with canned drinks. Kristin was pulling the baked beans out of the oven. The kitchen smelled like the sweet, sticky goodness of beans and bacon baked with brown sugar. Libby had gone out back to set up chairs and clean the tables.

"You know. . ." Adriana spoke without looking at Kristin. "There are a lot of soldiers that show up at Sol de Montaña."

"I figured. Patrick has mentioned picking up lunch there occasionally."

Adriana continued once she'd added another bag of ice. "I've seen him there. He always picks up an order, but there's some that stay and dine on site."

It took a few long seconds of silence before Adriana looked up at Kristin from her position bent over the ice chest. She was eyeing Adriana while blowing on a bean-filled spoon.

"I was wondering if any of them were someone Patrick might bring. How weird would that be?"

"Has something happened?" Kristin asked.

"I'm just saying it would be a funny coincidence."

The thought had been in the back of her mind, growing louder by the minute. Actually, it would not be funny at all. Maybe a lot of soldiers were protective and felt overwhelming responsibility for each other. Yet, it was the way she'd remembered Nathan apologizing for Connors that had snagged against what Kristin had said earlier.

"There's probably thousands of soldiers living around us." Kristin lowered the oven to a warming temperature and stuck the beans back in. "You might have a point, though. Let's see, I remember last names better because that's all Patrick uses." She started listing off last names. At the end of her list, she paused. "Then, of course, there's Prescott and Walsh."

Adriana's stomach dropped at the familiar name. Kristin couldn't know anything about Nathan if she was acting this unaffected by mentioning him. Surely, it was the same guy. Though Prescott was probably a common name. "Prescott and Walsh?"

Kristin clarified, "Yes, Nathan Prescott is Patrick's best friend. Daniel Walsh is another great guy. He's married. His wife, Cassie, is witty but a total sweetheart. You'll like her. They have two little girls. Do any of those names sound familiar? Would you know if any of those soldiers had come by?"

Adriana stood, shutting the full ice chest. "Um. In fact, I do recognize a name. He comes to the food truck a lot."

"Who?" Kristin asked, intrigued.

"Patrick's best friend."

Kristin's eyes widened. "I can't believe I'm just now hearing of this."

"Well, to be fair, it was . . ." She'd been about to say nothing, but in saying so, she'd be outright denying a crucial truth. It was not just nothing. If their moment at the bookstore had never happened, she could chalk it all up to an unmentionable disturbance. She'd never have considered telling Kristin about the random soldier chatting her up every chance he got, because doing so would make it a bigger deal than she would ever make it.

Her best friend blinked and shook her head. "I wasn't talking about you, silly. I'm shocked Patrick and Nathan haven't mentioned it to me! Patrick knows who you are. It seems logical he'd be aware of Nathan's preference for your family's food and would have introduced you two or something!"

She was worked up, and yet she had a point. How had it failed to come up in the weeks that they'd known one another? She recalled Patrick mentioning he wanted her to meet someone when he'd come by for a pickup order. Had the someone been Nathan? And if so, why had Nathan himself never mentioned it?

Kristin shrugged. "Oh well. Maybe he didn't know. I guess guys are just different about that stuff. I would have told you something like that." She moved to stand next to one side of the ice chest. "Here, grab that side and we'll get this beast to the patio."

Adriana lifted her side and shuffled backward toward the patio door, but all the while those questions tumbled around in her mind, increasing her anxiety. Seeing Nathan in her best friend's house was going to be strange. There was no way around that.

Chapter Ten

"Hey, guys!" Kristin greeted Nathan and Patrick excitedly as they walked into the open front room.

"Hey," Nathan said with a smile and a quick wave before she was scooped up by Patrick.

They weren't inappropriately affectionate, but it was still quite mushy. He turned his attention toward the kitchen. On the other side of the wide island that separated the two spaces, Adriana stood intensely focused on arranging vegetables around a large platter. Her hair was down again, the front pieces pulled away from her face and cascading past her shoulders in long, layered waves.

Patrick stepped into his line of sight. Leaning over, he swiped a carrot from the platter. "Hey, Adriana."

Adriana looked up with a smile, "Hi."

Her eyes slid over to Nathan and like a shade coming down, her expression closed off again. They hadn't seen each other since earlier that week when he'd made the mistake of asking her out in that roundabout way. He hadn't expected the girl from the bookstore, but the dismissal still chafed more than he cared to admit.

"Well, you two," Kristin said, coming to the rescue. "I'd make introductions, but I've recently been informed you've already met." Kristin gave both Nathan and Adriana a pointed but unserious look.

Adriana remained impassive as Patrick chuckled. Nathan didn't miss the nervousness of it. He didn't allow himself to react. Not responding first seemed the smartest choice. Kristin knew something—what, though? Adriana was still here, and he wasn't getting thrown out, so whatever had been said wasn't bad enough to rescind Kristin's good graces. Not that he'd done anything so terrible to warrant that.

Patrick spoke up. "I think this occasion still calls for an official introduction. Adriana,"—he gestured toward Nathan —"I'd like you to meet Nathan Prescott, the best guy I know."

Kristin smiled widely at her boyfriend, then followed his lead. "And Nathan, this is my best friend since grade school, Adriana Morales."

Nathan smiled and shook his head a little. They could be such dorks, but it worked because Adriana was smiling back cheerfully.

The doorbell rang just as Kristin's sister popped her head in from the back door. "Hey there, boys! Sis, can you come out here for a sec?"

Patrick offered to grab the door as Kristin exchanged a quick look with Adriana before she turned and went toward Libby. As soon as Kristin turned away, Adriana was once again enthralled in vegetable placement. Nathan stepped forward cautiously, trying to gauge how she'd respond to his nearness as he moved toward her. He was almost convinced she was completely ignoring him for how little attention she gave him.

"Hi," Nathan said once he was standing directly beside the bar, opposite from her.

She looked up, her deep brown eyes absent of their earlier wariness. Her mouth tilted up on one side, just barely. Encouraged, he continued making his way around the edge of the bar, quicker this time. He did not stop until he was a few steps away from her. Then he reached out his hand.

"It's a pleasure to meet you, Adriana Morales, Kristin's best friend." Nathan waited, hoping to tease another smile out of her.

She gave him that look women do so often—his own mother and sister prime examples. The one that says they see right through your little game, but then she smiled. It was cute how obviously reluctant she was to do so.

"Hi, Nathan Prescott, the best guy Patrick knows. I'm happy to meet you."

That simple touch, her soft hand gripping his briefly, sparked a deeper craving inside of him. He imagined using the opportunity to tug her into an embrace instead, then almost laughed at the response he pictured her having.

She'd called him by his first name, another unexpected victory. His playfulness had paid off in more ways than one —she was happy to meet him? Call him a glutton for punishment, but that hope was ignited again.

As everyone stood or sat around the open patio, Nathan tried to ignore Adriana's presence. It was easy until she moved or spoke, then it was like a radar pinged. He fought against the itch to turn and look in her direction every time, and yet his awareness of her seemed to only increase the more he resisted.

When it was time to eat, they took seats around tables set up outside. Walsh had saved Nathan a seat next to him, diagonally across from where Adriana sat between Kristin and Elena Villalobos. Elena had been there the first time at the food truck. Both women recognized one another immediately, and Elena wasted no time trying to strike up a friendship with her.

Nathan gave in to the pull he'd been feeling since he arrived, letting his eyes drift Adriana's way throughout dinner and afterward while everyone lingered at the tables. He noticed how she floated on the outside of conversation, how it wasn't just with him that she seemed more interested in what was said to her than in contributing anything about herself. He noticed when her gaze would dart his way. Particularly after he'd heard mention of her son. He'd been in a friendly debate with Seth Fontana, one of his soldiers, over who'd been the better player during softball the night before.

As they sorted out teams for a game of backyard volleyball after dinner, Nathan noticed Adriana choosing to sit out the first round. He took his cue to do the same. She'd pulled some chairs away from the table, placing them around the outside of the game space. Nathan grabbed one, bringing it closer to where she sat.

He caught her following his movements and let a breath pass before he spoke. "Do you like volleyball?"

She looked toward the game that had just started, stretching out her legs as she leaned back. "It's fun. I haven't played in a long time. It's one of Kristin's favorites. Did you know she played in school?"

Nathan shook his head, then glanced at the game, where Adriana's focus continued to wander. "I didn't. What about you? Did you play any sports, or do you enjoy any now?"

"In elementary school, but not since."

"So, what do you like to do?"

"You ask a lot of questions."

"You give really short answers."

"What about you, Nathan? What do you do for fun?"

Fine. He'd play along and let her reluctance slide. For the moment. He listed a few of the more active things he enjoyed.

"Your turn," he said pointedly.

She considered. "I go camping with my family. I read, but I don't have a lot of free time for that."

"Why is that? Working too much?" he asked.

He watched as she took in a deep, slow breath. It was as if she was resigning herself to something unwelcome.

"Well, no. My son keeps me busy. Most of my free time is spent doing activities I can do with him, things he prefers." She looked up at him, mouth tight.

Finally. He let the silence build between them, waiting for her to add more.

"You must already know. It's been mentioned multiple times today." Her eyes didn't break away from his.

He'd only heard it the one time at the table, and it hadn't been widely discussed. Deciding on the truth, he responded, "I've known."

Her eyebrows drew together. "You've known?" She lingered on that last word, her eyes darted toward the game again. "How is that?"

He shrugged, shaking his head, then adjusted his chair, facing her more fully. He couldn't care less about the game at this point or about anyone noticing his focus was nowhere on it. "It came up when Patrick realized I already knew who you were."

Her mouth twitched, and he could see that same irritation she'd shown at the food truck simmering beneath the surface. Knowing who he was must be very new for her still. How else had she failed to connect the possibilities?

"Did you know the other day?"

Nathan continued to choose candor. "Yes."

"You let me believe you had no clue about my life. Let me storm off, and what? The whole time, you just failed to mention it?"

He sighed. "I wasn't trying to force anything out of you. I wanted you to want to tell me."

"You could have just called me out on it. Why not just do that?" She darted her eyes back to the game before settling on him again, and he did the same.

He noticed Kristin stealing glances their way, compelled himself to let in the noises of the game again, and sat back before they drew more attention.

"I told you already. There was no reason to do that."

It was like she'd said, no explanation was owed. He'd recognized that even before she'd made it clear. Just as he recognized right now that she easily had control of how tonight had gone—more than he did. He was willing to bet if she'd simply said the words, Kristin would have seen him out of there. They were best friends, and regardless of how Kristin felt about him, that was just what best friends did.

"Hey, Nathan! Come on over here and take Fontana's place," Patrick called to him before Adriana could respond.

Nathan looked over at his best friend. Kristin stood next to him, watching them. That was a hint if ever he'd been given one. He looked back at Adriana. She was watching him, her expression unreadable.

"I guess I'd better head over there."

She nodded, her mouth pursed in what he could only

perceive as annoyance, and he suspected it was directed at him.

As he prepared to serve, he noticed Adriana walking toward the other side of the net, giving Libby a high five as they exchanged places.

AFTER HIS TEAM won the game, Adriana made her way over to him. He looked around, but everyone else seemed to have their attention elsewhere. She was approaching him first? Unexpected.

"Good game," she said, looking up at him, arms crossed over her chest. She stopped close enough to speak quietly. "I'm not mad that you knew. I just don't like . . ." She shook her head, sighing. "Honestly, I'm not sure where I was going with that."

He thought he might know. He saw it clearly. She didn't like being out of control of things. Nathan put his hat back on since he'd taken it off while playing.

"So, tell me something about him. His name is Isaac, right?" Nathan asked, figuring he'd finally get the privilege of hearing her open up about something important.

It took a beat before she replied. She was looking at him like she wasn't sure what to expect from him. "Yes. He turned five in April."

Then she surprised him by adding with affection, "He's energetic and sweet, loves being outside, and all the typical stuff boys his age do."

Her face lit up when she talked about Isaac. It seemed obvious from Nathan's limited knowledge that she adored her son and enjoyed motherhood, even given her circumstances. He wondered again what the story was with the father. That was not something she'd be willing to discuss.

Not yet, but he planned on doing what he could to get them closer.

Her body shifted, and she turned partially away from him. "Anyway, I wanted you to know everything is okay."

"Does this mean you'll talk to me more?"

"Whoa. Let's not get carried away." A coy, little smile tugged at her lips as she turned and walked away from him.

He watched her walk away, then looked up and shook his head, laughing to himself. Yeah, they'd get there.

Chapter Eleven

After everyone else had left, Adriana watched as Kristin poured hot water into two mugs, the herbal tea instantly releasing the smell of spicy citrus. Adriana and Kristin took their mugs to the living room, placing them on the coffee table while the infusers steeped.

"I forgot to tell you, I went to meet with the registrar yesterday," Adriana mentioned as they sat down on the couch.

"Do you think you'll start classes soon?" Kristin asked.

Adriana shrugged. "I don't know. I'd like to have a little more saved up before I commit. I don't want to have to rely on my family any more than I already do."

She filled Kristin in on what had been discussed at the meeting. The cost was more than she'd expected. The price tag had increased in the years she'd been out of school, but there was nothing to be done about it. If this was what she wanted, it was time to take steps forward, however small they needed to be.

"You can take out some loans. Not much, just something

to cushion whatever costs you're concerned about," Kristin suggested.

"I'd rather not."

"I know. I do think it could be the perfect time for you to start. You have some time to spare, Isaac's still young, and since you still essentially live with your parents, it's easy for them to continue helping out as they've done. I'm also here now to help more, you know."

"Because you have so much extra time?" Adriana looked at her with skepticism.

"For you and Isaac, there's always time," Kristin said matter-of-factly.

Adriana appreciated Kristin's offer to help. She'd hoped to do this on her own without relying more on those that had already done so much for her and Isaac. It wasn't something she'd voiced out loud, afraid it sounded ungrateful. It was time for her to start standing on her own more. If she couldn't manage that, then maybe she didn't deserve to reach for these goals at all.

Taking a deep breath, she let it out slowly. Or maybe she didn't have to be so stubbornly set on things working out a specific way. Letting her mind sift through the possibilities of starting classes this fall when Isaac would also be back in school, Adriana pulled out the tea infuser and laid it on the little dish Kristin had set out.

Doing the same, Kristin settled into the cushion, with her steaming cup. "On an unrelated note, you seemed tense earlier. Was Nathan bothering you?"

Adriana sat back, putting her bare feet against the edge of the coffee table. "No. We were talking about Isaac. It seems Patrick had already told Nathan about him."

Kristin cringed. "Patrick isn't winning any points with you lately, is he?"

"I'm not mad about it. At first, maybe. Mostly at Nathan."

She'd wondered how long the two of them had been aware of the connection and was still trying to decide how much it really mattered.

"At Nathan? Why?" Kristin asked.

Adriana grabbed a throw pillow with one hand and tucked it in her arms while carefully maneuvering the cup she held.

"He's had some obvious opportunities to have mentioned it. It's a long story. I didn't tell you before because up until today, Nathan was nothing more than this random guy."

Kristin gave her an inquisitive look. "I've got plenty of time for a long story."

"I'm getting there," Adriana said, soothing her friend's impatience.

She began her story, focusing on the facts more than any of her feelings. Kristin let her talk, interrupting on occasion to quietly exclaim or ask for clarification.

When she was done, Kristin took a deep breath. "I know why you didn't tell me anything sooner. Still, I wish I had known. I hope today wasn't too awkward for you."

"It was fine. Really."

"I've said it already, so you know I think Nathan is great, and I want to include Patrick's friends. However, my word still stands. If he's a problem, just let me know."

How could Adriana put Kristin in that position or insist on keeping someone from her events for no other reason than they'd dared to show interest in her? That would be selfish and immature. If Nathan had been a creep about it, it would have been a different story.

Kristin continued, "Although, I can't get over that he tossed a coin to help you pick a book. That's adorable. Makes it impossible not to root for the guy."

Adriana glanced at her sideways, raising her eyebrows.

She needed Kristin on her side. She was happy with the direction her life was going and romance was not included in that path.

Kristin read her expression effortlessly. Scooting closer, she leaned into her. "Can I at least root for you two to become friends?"

"Can I really stop you?" Adriana asked, mostly teasing.

"No." Kristin chuckled. "Just don't forget, I've got your back. Always," she reassured her.

"I know." Adriana leaned into her as well.

As much as she trusted Kristin and believed in the strength of their bond, she saw that Kristin's love for Patrick had already extended to caring about Nathan as well. The lines of her interests were no longer so easily drawn.

It wasn't a concept her best friend understood well, but there was no room in Adriana's life for anyone new. Especially anyone that looked at her with expectation and interest like Nathan did. Never mind her own temperamental emotions where he was concerned. Before today, she'd been convinced distance was the best way to handle him. Now she didn't know how to navigate the depth of their connections or what to think about the advantage he'd had. He'd known about Isaac and that she was Kristin's best friend. Before she could shut him out, boundaries were crossed that couldn't be reinforced.

Sure, ignoring him was always an option, but doing so and following through with the agreement to be here for Kristin pulled her in two separate directions. One had to win over the other. Life was as it should be, she couldn't change direction now.

Chapter Twelve

Nathan looked up from the file he was flipping through as Patrick approached.

"Hey, Kristin's on her way. She's bringing us some leftovers from dinner the other night."

"Oh?" Nathan barely looked up, focused on the sheet of paper he was looking for, a past counseling he'd done on a soldier.

"Yeah, you want to head outside to the benches? We can wait for her there."

"Uh. Sure. I can meet you out there in a few."

When Nathan arrived at the tables, Kristin was already sorting through a giant insulated bag. Patrick stood beside her, opening a bottle of Pepsi.

Nathan plopped a pastry bag in the center of the table. "Here, my mom left these cookies at my place. Oatmeal Scotties and peanut butter chocolate chip."

"Oooo, I love peanut butter chocolate chip," Kristin said. She handed both Nathan and Patrick a meal prep container stuffed with food.

As soon as they all sat down, Kristin fixed Nathan with a stare. "So. You know we have to talk about Adriana, right?"

Nathan asked, "What do you want to talk about?"

"Hmm. I don't know . . . how about the coin toss?"

Nathan couldn't help himself. He smiled. As soon as he did, Kristin's own mouth lifted.

"She told you about that?"

"Yes. That was really cute."

Nathan shrugged, trying not to make a big deal out of it. He looked down at his food. Kristin was studying him, and he needed to work at playing off how Adriana made him feel.

"You like her, don't you?" Kristin leaned forward.

"Is that what she told you?" Nathan countered.

Patrick was watching the exchange quietly, not yet injecting his opinion or knowledge.

"Not exactly. She told me a lot of things. Like how she's pretty sure you kicked that soldier under the table when he was being obnoxious and how you come to the food truck—a lot." She laughed. "She mentioned you love all the cinnamon and sugar treats Danielle makes and how long it took for her to call you by your first name."

Nathan studied Kristin. She seemed amused and almost gleeful. Adriana had noticed more than she let on. He'd suspected her to be observant, to notice what she pretended not to and now he knew for sure. What was more unexpected was that Adriana had shared so much, and not only shared it at all, but apparently hadn't done so in a negative light. Or if she had, Kristin was choosing to see past it for something else. Nathan didn't think that was it.

"Yeah. What was up with that?"

Kristin shook her head. "Who knows? Adriana likes to compartmentalize. Honestly, Nathan? I'm surprised she's given you the time of day at all. The whole bookstore thing?

Never would have believed it if I'd heard it from anyone else."

Nathan wasn't the least bit surprised by this revelation.

"She also told me you asked her out, and she turned you down." Kristin cringed a little and Nathan did too, inwardly.

Patrick spoke up, "Despite her turning him down, do you think she might like him too?"

Kristin looked between the two of them and shook her head. "Hmm . . . maybe? I don't know. She is still just as adamant as she's always been about not dating. She has her reasons, you know?" Kristin continued.

Nathan shook his head. "I don't know. Not really. Care to enlighten me as to why? I'd like to better understand."

Kristin shrugged. "I don't think I should really be the one to do that, sorry. I will say this—she has walls miles high and endless justifications holding them up." She sighed. "Nathan, I think you're great, but I cannot play matchmaker. Also, as her best friend, I'm going to tell you it's better to leave things be."

"Well, I say she should give our man here a chance. I think he could change her mind. Maybe we need to get them around one another more," Patrick plotted.

Kristin tilted her head, giving Patrick an affectionate look. "I think she'll come to realize Nathan is one of the good ones. I just don't think that'll make much of a difference in her decision. She won't let it."

"It's not that serious," Nathan said simply, taking a bite of slider. He'd let his emotions get away from him before, given away too much.

"Hm," Kristin said thoughtfully. "Before all this coming to light, I'd hoped the two of you would become good friends."

"I think we can. It's what I want too," Nathan agreed.

"We all hang out and have a good time. Seems like the perfect plan."

Patrick looked skeptical but Kristin beamed. He could tell she was glad he'd been on the same page as she was. He'd be willing to bet Adriana would approach each future visit to Kristin's parties with caution. Especially if she thought he would push against that firmly planted protection of hers. Though he wasn't above a little good-natured nudging, it was time to let her take the lead. If there was a possibility for any relationship at all, it was her choice more than his right now.

Chapter Thirteen

Adriana had assured Kristin nothing needed to be done about Nathan. She'd meant it, but she was still holding on to her original goal of limiting her contact with him. Knowing he was going to be at dinner tonight had made her second guess her decision to come.

All through dinner he'd easily been part of the conversation. On the occasions she spoke, he seemed to lean toward her, and he always had questions that made ignoring him out of the question. It irked her.

While most everyone else had headed outside, Adriana had stayed in to clean up the dishes left in the sink. If Kristin caught her doing it, she'd swiftly shoo her out of the kitchen, but the activity was therapeutic. The scrubbing motion and flow of the water relaxed her, calming her thoughts.

She heard the back door open and looked up. Nathan walked over with another dish and an empty pitcher. She met his gaze and an unexplainable feeling bubbled up.

"Here you go," he said, placing them by the sink.

"Thank you." She refocused on the dish she was rinsing, avoiding his stare.

"Need help with anything?"

He stayed in her line of sight, leaning against the countertop, and she could feel him watching her as she worked.

"No. This won't take long."

He moved again, but instead of leaving as she thought he would, he simply adjusted his stance — leaning his backside against the counter. She turned her head to watch him as he crossed one leg over another, then looked at her. He wasn't wearing a hat today. His hair looked shorter than the last time she'd seen it, and it still had that oddly attractive combination of messy and neat.

"I've been thinking of our situation." He gestured around them. "And I think it only makes sense that we should be friends." He shrugged, casual and cool, so unaffected. How did he do that?

She abandoned the scrubbing, hoping she was succeeding at keeping her expression neutral. "You want to be friends?"

"I wouldn't have said it otherwise," Nathan replied patiently.

"You barely even know anything about me. How are you sure being friends is a good idea?" She'd gone back to focusing on the dish.

"The getting to know you part is sort of how friendship works. I'm not that intolerable, am I?" He was teasing her again, as if he liked to rile her up a little.

She worked her lips between her teeth. After taking a second, she sighed. "It's not that. As cynical as this sounds, I'm terrible at making new friends. It's why the only friend I have is Kristin."

She considered her family as friends too, which would

probably further the point she was trying to make, but she refrained from adding to her argument.

"I know you believe that, but I don't buy it. Everyone seems to enjoy your company, despite whatever you think you're lacking." He paused, then added, "I enjoy your company."

She shut the water off and grabbed a towel, then turned to face him more directly. He didn't break eye contact. She felt both flattered and annoyed by his observation. Would nothing she said flip a switch on his feelings? She was going to have to come right out and say what was on her mind, and that annoyed her too.

"After you essentially asked me out, and I turned you down, shouldn't we leave things as they are? No label?"

Their best friends were in a serious relationship. She didn't want to further complicate things for any of them. Everything about this already felt complicated enough.

He pushed off the counter and took a step closer, sliding his hands in his pockets. "What I'm trying to say is you don't have to worry about that. Seems to me, we have a good foundation to start from, all things considered. If you're open to the idea of being friends, I am as well. I won't tell you to trust me because we don't know each other that well. It'll take time, but I intend to prove that you can."

His intensity unbalanced her. Why did he want her trust? Why was what they thought of one another important to him? She focused on the floor, wringing the towel. His hand reached out and grasped the towel, freezing her movements. She looked up at him. His hazel eyes searched her own before smiling down at her warmly. Did he know how powerful that smile was?

"I'm a great friend." His voice was low.

"Oh? Are you?" Adriana responded with sass. They both

continued to hold the towel, and she was fully aware of the warmth radiating from his hand. She let her eyes linger on him.

He nodded just slightly. "Try me."

The back door slid open, and she let go of the towel, stepping backward. He looked down at it in his hands, almost as if he'd forgotten he'd grabbed it at all. Libby came around the corner.

"Hey, you two." She gave them a strange look. "We were wondering where you went."

Oh. How long had they been inside?

"I was just cleaning up some dishes," Adriana said while Nathan said, "I brought in some stuff from the table."

They sounded so guilty. Avoiding time alone with him should be a no-brainer, so how did she manage to get pulled into these moments with him? Why did he still seek her out at all? Only friends? Yeah, right. She really was going to have to see it to believe it.

Ignoring that nagging desire to flee, she calmly asked, "Is there anything we need to grab?"

Libby looked between them again. "Nope. We've got it all."

Nathan had folded the towel and placed it back on the counter. He gestured toward the door. "Ladies first."

Adriana walked between him and Libby. As she stepped outside, she stopped and turned to look at Nathan. He almost ran into her and reached out reflexively. She didn't miss how he stopped himself, how his hands were just shy of touching her back before he jerked them down.

She followed the movement before looking at his face, then as if thinking out loud, she decided to let him know she'd give him the benefit of the doubt. "Kristin thinks you're great, and I trust her judgment, so I'll work harder on sparing you my excellent side-eye skills."

He laughed, and it made her smile. As she turned away from him, she pretended not to notice Libby's shocked expression. She really wanted to dislike Nathan. While it felt crucial, it had also proven impossible.

Chapter Fourteen

As summer flew by, Adriana's time had stretched to accommodate fall classes in addition to her usual jobs. Their days had changed a lot with the shifting of the seasons. She was busier than ever. The little free time she'd had was now nearly nonexistent. She and Isaac were in the garage gathering Nerf guns for a game out in the yard before dinner when her phone pinged. She walked over to check it as she stuffed extra Nerfs in her pocket. It was a text from Kristin.

Can I come by for a bit?

Adriana sent her a reply.

Of course!

Be there in about thirty.

Adriana and Isaac had just finished a third round of

Nerf wars in the side of the yard when Kristin's red Volkswagen bug pulled up into the long drive.

"Kristin's here!" Isaac exclaimed.

She ruffled Isaac's hair. "Go say hi but then we have to pick up these Nerfs."

"Okay." He bounded off the short distance to Kristin's parked car. She jumped out and spun him around in a big hug. "Hey, buddy! How are you?"

"I'm great! Mom and I were playing Nerf wars! I need to clean up now! You should come play with us sometime."

"I'd like that." She smiled down at him as she put him down. She smiled over at Adriana, who was picking up a few Nerfs that were littered around the driveway. As she made her way to her side, Isaac bounded past, picking up a few in the garden at the property boundary, looking like he was on a mission.

"Hey," Adriana said. "What brings you by?"

"Thought I'd come see you for a bit," Kristin said, shrugging nonchalantly, but she was buzzing with energy Adriana couldn't put her finger on.

Adriana looked at her, eyebrow raised. "Is everything okay?"

"Well . . ." Her weird energy erupted in a giant smile as she held out her left hand. "I'm engaged," she screamed excitedly.

Adriana's mouth dropped. She raised her hands up in the air and started dancing then closed the short distance between them and hugged her best friend. They both were nearly crushing each other in excitement.

Finally pulling apart, Adriana saw Isaac looking at them. She laughed at his expression of uncertainty and amusement then turned back to Kristin. "Let me help Isaac get these Nerfs cleaned up, then why don't you come up and tell me all about it?"

"Definitely! I'll help you." Kristin said, the energy still buzzing through her in obvious excitement.

When they were done, they went upstairs, and Kristin spilled all the details of her engagement story while they sat at the dining room table.

"Can you stay for dinner?" Adriana asked after some time had passed. "I need to get it started."

Kristin nodded. "Sure!"

While Adriana pulled ingredients out, Isaac asked Kristin if she'd come check out his new treasure collection. This was in reference to the summer's stash of rocks, dried flowers, and leaves, among other things, stored in a shoebox in his bedroom.

As they walked out, Adriana considered all that was about to change and all that had transpired since the beginning of the year. It had been a few weeks since she had seen Patrick and Kristin together. She had to admit she missed it. They had a contagious dynamic. Kristin, already full of energy and spunk, was somehow both more grounded and bubblier with him around. Adriana appreciated how good Patrick was for her best friend and how easy he was to get along with.

Sometimes it made Adriana wistful. Would there ever come a time in her life when she'd happily welcome something like that for herself? And when she did feel ready, would she find it? It didn't seem possible that there was a man out there perfectly suited for her or worth compromising her no dating rule. It was hard to picture making that kind of change in her life. She didn't have Kristin's capacity for openness and besides that, guys like Patrick were rare. Her thoughts wandered to Nathan of their own volition. She saw him much less than she had those first few months after they met. Still, this wasn't the first time he'd crossed her mind.

Their interactions had been limited lately and usually at the food truck, not at Kristin's. Spending time with her best friend involved other things since she had only made it back to one other gathering. Nathan hadn't been there. At the time, she'd felt a confusing mixture of relief and disappointment though she'd since reigned that in. Work and life on her family's farm was busy. Another successful summer harvest season had kept her distracted along with her work at the food truck and plenty of time spent with Isaac.

Kristin made it back, smiling widely. "He's got quite the variety in there. I love that you taught him how to press the flowers he picks."

Adriana smiled fondly. "I wanted to find a way to save some of the wildflowers he'd bring home for me. Once he saw me do it, he wanted to try it on his own."

Kristin leaned against the counter. "Need any help with dinner?"

"No, I'm just about done with the preparations, then I'll pop it in the oven, and it'll be done in a bit. So, have you thought about when you'll have the wedding yet? The theme? Any of that?"

Kristin sighed dreamily. "Oh, I don't know. I've never really had much of an idea in my head, besides knowing I want a small gathering in a church, at a location where neither side of my family feels like one or the other is being favored due to proximity. Just all that." She laughed. "And I don't need or want a lot of time to plan. Patrick and I have already talked about it. We want a late spring wedding. That time frame works with the school year ending. Besides, it's my favorite season and perfect for the bright colors I'd prefer. Also, I want you as my maid of honor." She squealed, her smile even bigger than usual.

"Oh, Kristin. I'd love to, but what about Libby?"

"Libby is with me on this. She knows she means everything to me. We're sisters, and yes, she is one of my closest friends, but we've both always been on the same page about this."

"Well, of course I accept. I just wanted to make sure . . ."

Kristin came around and hugged her. "You're always doing that. Second-guessing your place. Please don't." She squeezed, and Adriana squeezed back.

"I'm so happy for you, Kristin. I know you've been hoping for this."

Kristin sniffled. "Thank you. It almost doesn't feel real, like I need to pinch myself or something." She laughed, her voice wobbly.

Isaac came over to get a drink of the water he'd left on the table and looked between them. "Are you happy or sad, Kristin? You have tears."

"I'm so happy. These are happy tears."

He came over and patted both their arms with each hand, as if to comfort and share in their joy. The gesture made Adriana's heart swell. This moment and Kristin's joy was the warmth this cold day needed.

It had been a long couple of weeks. Keeping up with everything going on and the addition of the new things she'd put on her plate had brought some challenges. There was believing you were prepared to face something unfamiliar, and then there was actually facing it. While Adriana felt ready to tackle all of it now that she knew what to expect, she sure could use more moments to breathe.

Before Kristin left later that evening, she said, "We're planning a little dinner celebration soon. You'll come, right?"

Adriana didn't hesitate. "Of course."

"I know your work and class schedule, but let me know if there's any evening that absolutely doesn't work otherwise."

"Shouldn't I be planning all this?" Adriana asked.

Kristin shrugged. "I really like doing this stuff. I promise I will tear my hands off some tasks just for you later, though."

Adriana laughed. "Just say what and when. I'll talk to you tomorrow?"

"Yep." Kristin gave her and Isaac a hug, then headed down to her car.

Adriana's tendency to stay closed off hadn't been wiped away in one fell swoop. She'd been doing the same thing for so long, and like muscle memory, deviation from the norm was going to take practice and intention. Life allowed her to continue much as she'd always done with little push otherwise. She took a deep breath.

With a wedding came a new chapter for Kristin and Patrick, and this reality was going to make proximity even more likely for Adriana and Nathan. Sure, one day Nathan might change duty stations, but that didn't negate what she knew to be true in the moment they were living. It was time to make good on the agreement she'd made with both Nathan and Kristin months ago. Her stomach fluttered. Breathing in, she forced it to settle. It was a friendship. Nothing earth shattering. He was just a decent guy who happened to be part of the group of people she spent time with occasionally. That's all. She could do this.

Chapter Fifteen

Nathan hadn't been completely honest when he'd asked Adriana to be friends. It wasn't like he could simply ignore his attraction to her. He'd been truthful about not asking her out again, but acting as if it wasn't an issue at all? That was the first lie he'd ever told her.

Still, the choice had been simple: either he could be her friend and get over this thing with her, or he couldn't put his feelings aside and he'd distance himself. Honestly? If the latter was true, he had a feeling she'd see through it quicker than he'd actually accept defeat. Then, as previous experience with her had proven, she'd do half the work for him. Walking away entirely would only be difficult because his heart wouldn't have wanted to.

It had been months since their conversation in Kristin's kitchen and her cute little comment about reigning in her side-eye skills. That last real conversation between them had been on his mind often. She'd stopped so abruptly in that moment, he'd almost run into her, almost reached out to stop them from colliding. He'd said he was going to let time show her she could trust him and he knew that began, for now, with keeping his hands to himself under all circumstances. It was a good thing he had quick reflexes. That unbendable will he'd been accused of having was coming in handy as well. Lately, he had been like still waters—calm, steadied, fixed.

Field training and range time had picked up again, creating a busy schedule that didn't allow time to leave or spend leisurely lunches working on any budding friendships. Some weeks they were at the field for days on end. He visited the food truck occasionally but had mostly gone back to bringing his lunch to work. His visits were usually for pickup orders, so any conversation he had with Adriana was short. Thanks to the easy friendship he'd developed with Thomas and Danielle, he knew when Adriana worked, and that the farm and time with Isaac were why she wasn't there as frequently during the past couple of months. It was nice to have their insight since there was no way he was getting it from Kristin.

Treating Adriana no differently than any of his other friends was a challenge he threw himself into. How well could he convince everyone, himself included, he wasn't emotionally involved? He'd boxed up his feelings entirely from Patrick as well, hoping to keep his best friend out of the troubling position of having to keep things from Kristin.

When Patrick and Kristin's celebratory engagement dinner came up, Nathan prepared himself to step into the role of best man opposite Adriana's position as maid of honor. Adjusting the blazer he'd put over the sweater and collared shirt he wore, Nathan made his way up the walk. He saw Adriana as he approached the door. She was standing in the little waiting area off the entrance. She was stunning in a lacy black dress, her hair gathered at the nape of her neck.

She turned toward him as he let the door shut behind him.

"Hi," she said, giving him a polite smile.

He came to stand beside her. "Hey. Are we the first ones here?"

"Yeah." She looked toward the hostess table. "I told Kristin I'd get here early to make sure they'd arranged the space we needed. It's just about ready. I think she'll be here soon."

"Patrick was on the phone with her when I left the apartment," Nathan said.

She was aware he and Patrick were roommates, so he didn't elaborate. Especially because she looked like she was on the verge of saying something. Then, seeming to second guess it, she simply nodded.

Nathan could feel her gaze on him as he let his eyes scan the lobby of the restaurant, but by the time he looked back toward her, she'd turned her head to look out the window, her fingers drumming a rhythm on her elbow.

"How have you been?" he asked.

She looked at him again, that polite expression fixed in place. "I've been good. Busy. How about you?"

"I've been busy too. Training has been demanding lately, just as I like it." He smirked.

"You really like your job, don't you?" She had looked at him with an almost practiced indifference, but the tone of her voice said otherwise.

He laughed a little, nodding. He liked that she noticed things about him even while pretending she didn't. "It's been a while since we've had a chance to talk."

"Yes, it has. The farm and Isaac keep me home more during the summer. I'm back at Sol de Montaña more now that school is in session again."

The hostess walked toward them before they could say any more.

"Miss Morales? Your table is ready. If you'll please follow me."

Adriana complied, and Nathan fell into step right behind her. He took in their surroundings as they walked, but his eyes kept sliding to Adriana and the wisps of hair escaping her bun. The hostess led them to a corner of the restaurant where a large table had been arranged for their party.

The young woman gestured for them to have a seat. "Your server will be with you momentarily."

Libby and Kristin approached the table as the hostess walked away and Patrick followed right behind them. The rest of the party, which included their parents and siblings, Walsh, Villalobos, and their wives, followed right behind them.

During dinner, there were many conversations going on around the table, along with short speeches of congratulations for the couple. Patrick and Kristin also spoke more about how they met. Even Adriana took a turn giving a short speech, joking it would be the only time she'd find the courage, while Libby immediately offered to do the toast on their wedding day. Nathan loved watching her. She lit up their corner of the restaurant without even trying.

It was well after dark by the time they made their way to the parking lot. The wind had picked up, and the temperature had dropped significantly.

"We should have worn coats, I guess," Kristin said to Adriana.

Adriana shivered between the two of them. "At least it's just a quick walk to our vehicles."

As they all walked further into the lot, he noticed they'd

all parked within spaces of one another, Adriana's older model sedan parked directly in front of his truck.

Kristin asked, "Hey, do you want to sit in Patrick's truck while you wait for your heater to get going?"

"No, no. I'll be fine. It'll just take a couple of minutes for my car to warm up, and I have gloves and a blanket in there I can use while I wait."

"Are you sure?" Kristin asked just as Patrick elbowed Nathan secretively.

Nathan gave him a knowing look. He was on it, no nudging necessary. His truck had already been running since he turned it on with his key fob just outside the doors of the restaurant.

"Come on. You can wait in mine. I'm just right here." He pointed ahead of them as they stood next to her driver's side door.

"Really, I'm fine," she said, unlocking her door.

"Oh, just go with him," Libby said, coming up behind them. She leaned over toward Adriana, whispering something Nathan couldn't hear.

"I guess it won't hurt. Just for a few minutes," she reluctantly agreed. "Let me just get this started." She got in far enough to turn the key, the engine humming to life, then adjusted her heater settings.

Nathan looked toward Libby. "Would you like to wait in my truck too?"

Libby shook her head, smiling flirtatiously. "No, I have this beast of a coat on." She gestured toward the big coat she was wearing. "I'll be fine, but you are so sweet."

Nathan opened his door for Adriana. Before he could offer his help, she grabbed the handle and lifted herself inside, settling into her seat. He watched her feet, hoping she wouldn't slip. She quickly maneuvered her heels without incident. As he shut the door, he turned to walk around, but Libby was waiting for him.

"Be good, though, Nathan." She spoke quietly, giving him a pointed look and a wink, then disappeared inside her car before he could respond. Once he was inside, Adriana tilted her head in his direction, watching him.

"Are you comfortable?" He went to adjust the vents.

"I'm great, really. It's nice and toasty. Thank you."

He left the heating alone and focused on her. After a beat of silence, he forced himself to do something besides just stare at her mutely.

"So, we never got around to talking about it earlier. You said you stayed busy on your farm?" he asked, hoping to get her to talk a little more openly about her life.

"I help a lot with my parent's farm."

"I've heard a little something about that."

"You have?"

"Thomas and Danielle have mentioned it."

Her eyes tightened as if she was taking in that information and uncertain of what to do with it.

He continued, "I don't know much though. What can you tell me about this farm of yours?" He adjusted his position so that he faced her more fully.

She shrugged shyly, looking out her window and back at him again. "It's just a farm. We have orchards and grow produce. We raise bees and livestock. It's been handed down in my family since my great-grandfathers were neighbors, though every generation has expanded it in some way."

Her gaze didn't linger on him long. She continued to find things to fidget with—the rings on her fingers, the hem of her dress. She'd smooth it over the tights on her thighs as if she could extend its length, though it already nearly reached her knees. His eyes followed the movement, then peeled away. Her habit was his distraction. He let out a quiet breath and focused on the window just past her.

"Is that your full-time job?" he asked.

"In some ways, yes. We run a 'you-pick' season during the summer for berries and plums. Then there are apples and pumpkins during fall. We also do a corn maze and hayride. It's all very family friendly. We sell honey, canned goods, and other things produced from our land."

"No kidding. I didn't realize you had all that out there."

She nodded. "Thomas and Danielle come out sometimes. On a few summer evenings, we'll host local talent and evening picking hours. Guests get live music, freshly picked fruit, and they can stay to picnic."

"I've never picked my own fruit before," Nathan mused.

"You should come out next season, on a night Thomas and Danielle make it out."

"Well, in that case." He laughed, making it seem completely believable that the food was what really attracted his attention.

She smiled, looking over at her car, then out the window again. "I should go. I hate to leave my car idling too long and it's probably at least half as warm as yours by now."

"Here, let me . . ." He turned to get out and open the door.

She put a hand out to stop him, the tips of her fingers brushing against his biceps. As if she hadn't anticipated actually making contact, she quickly removed them. "Please don't worry about it. I'm okay."

She hurriedly opened the door, then slowed down significantly as she twisted around, seemingly contemplating the best strategy to maneuver her heels down to the ground while supporting herself and holding her dress down. He shook his head, hurrying out and around to her side. He noticed that Libby was still sitting there in the parking lot. Ah. She'd waited for Adriana. She waved at him, and he waved back. No wonder Adriana eventually agreed.

Looking up at him as he came around, Adriana stepped one foot down, a small crease forming between her eyebrows. "I told you I was okay."

He gestured toward her. "I see that. Just wanted to make sure." He stepped close enough that he could reach out and support her if she'd ever let him. "Those heels look like they mean business."

She laughed, looking down at her heels then back at him again. "I've got my eye on them, don't you worry." The cheeky smile that followed reminded him of their bookstore coin toss, and his heart squeezed.

"Good night, Nathan." Then, not waiting for a reply, she shut the door, waved at both him and Libby before hurrying into her car.

He was a man of his word. He didn't flip-flop. Sometimes, though, he could admit he might overestimate his own strength of will and stubbornness. In this case, it might just be an underestimation of his feelings. Whichever way it leaned—if this was really what friendship with Adriana looked like, he was in more trouble than he'd anticipated.

Chapter Sixteen

Adriana watched as Isaac pulled a stick that sent the marbles diving through the cylindrical container. "Aw man!" he exclaimed, drawing out the *n*.

Elijah and Sofia erupted in giggles and exclamations.

Kristin and Adriana were in the dining room with Marissa, Isaac, and the twins, playing a rousing game of Kerplunk while her mom and grandmother prepared home-made tortillas, guacamole, and pico de gallo.

Her family was having one of their big family dinners to celebrate her dad's birthday. Adriana had asked Kristin to stay after she'd come by to work out some wedding details.

"Let's go again!" Sofia quickly began setting it up for another round.

That was the third time they'd played.

Marissa intervened, "Espera, sweetie." She patted Sofia's little hands. "Why don't you three go play for a bit while we help abuelita with the food?"

Half-hearted agreement erupted from all three children as they began putting the game up.

"That was fun. Believe it or not, I've never played that game before," Kristin said, beaming more than you'd imagine a twenty-something would after spending over half an hour engaged in a kids' game. Then again, she was a teacher.

She looked over at Adriana. "We always played a lot of games when you'd sleep over. Do you remember?"

Adriana nodded, the memory of many game nights coming to mind. The three of them made their way over to where Adriana's mom and grandmother were busy working. Marissa grabbed more utensils for them to use while Adriana began washing lemons and limes.

"Girls, zest a couple each of those before you start cutting, please," Adriana's mom said as soon as she'd finished.

As they worked, Kristin continued, "It's so much fun to have people who humor me by joining in on my game nights."

"Oh, I think they do more than humor you. You make anything you plan fun. They are there because they enjoy it just as much as you do. I'm certain of it," Adriana said fondly. "Are you still trying to get one planned for this month?"

"Yes. We have a lot to do for the wedding, but we may have at least one more before it's wedding stuff all the time." Kristin was zesting away as she talked.

"If I planned it for Saturday night, could you make it?" She stopped zesting and looked at Adriana point blank.

"I don't know . . . I'd have to work out something for Isaac," Adriana replied.

Marissa and her mom piped in at the same time. Marissa with, "He can stay at our place." And her mom with, "You know he's always welcome here."

Kristin gestured at each of Adriana's family members. "See? You could spare a few extra hours."

Adriana, still looking skeptical, picked up a lime and began cutting. "I don't like taking so much time from him. I'm helping Danielle with a catering order too . . ." She trailed off.

Marissa had this ability to look simultaneously empathetic and exasperated. Then their mom spoke up again.

"Mija, there's nothing wrong with having some time for yourself and for Isaac to see you spending time with friends. The way you foster relationships will set more of an example than you might think."

"Mom is right," Marissa said, looking like she was about to jump up on her soapbox. "It's all about balance."

"I have plenty of balance."

When everyone looked at her skeptically, she sighed. "Okay, don't I get any credit?" she insisted.

Kristin came to her defense. "You do. You did sort of disappear for a bit there, though I know you were very busy. Hey! We could even do a more kid-centered thing! Daniel and Cassie bring their girls, Jacob and Mya can bring their three kids."

"If you ever do that, I'm sure Isaac would love it. As for this game night that you've got in the works now . . . I'll think about it."

Before Kristin had returned, it had been rare for her not to take Isaac with her everywhere she went. Kristin's mouth quirked. She didn't want her friend to feel bad or think she wasn't grateful for the moments they'd had together, but honestly, it was the most she'd ever been away from Isaac. And with all the wedding planning and events getting ready to slam into them, she'd prefer to be pickier with the invitations she agreed to.

Her abuela tsked under her breath but offered nothing

else to the conversation. Her grandmother's role had always been to listen and observe. She was a woman of few words.

Adriana's mom spoke again. "Don't overthink it. It's important to remind yourself you are more than a mother—you are a woman with friends and interests outside of that role. Trust me, you don't want to get to a place where you look over your life and don't know who you are without that title when Isaac is grown."

Marissa nodded firmly and lifted her glass of water. "Well said, Mama."

It was the most her mom had spoken about Adriana's parenting since before Brett's decision to terminate his parental rights. Back then, it had been a diatribe of Brett's faults and failures as a father and why Adriana should stop waiting around for him to change. But she couldn't even contemplate what life would be like when Isaac was grown. One day at a time. That was all she could focus on. She was doing just fine as far as she could tell. Having Kristin close again had been wonderful—a nice balance had been established in her life. It seemed some people didn't think it was quite enough of one. She pressed her lips together.

Kristin leaned toward Adriana, a pleading look on her face. "I'd sure love it if you'd come. We could work on some more wedding stuff if you wanted to come a little early."

"She'll be there," Marissa chimed in, giving her trademark eldest sibling look of authority.

Adriana shrugged and grinned at her best friend. Even with the annoyance of her family's insistence, it wasn't like spending time with Kristin was ever an inconvenience.

A few days later, Adriana pulled into Kristin's driveway two hours before game night. She zipped up her winter coat, then grabbed the bag of stuff she'd brought to make cheese dip. In the other hand, she picked up the plate full of homemade chocolate chip cookies she and Isaac had made the evening before.

Kristin was waiting for her with the door held open.

Once they were in the kitchen, Kristin clapped her hands together. "So. I have meatballs in one Crock-Pot and sliders cooking in the oven. Libby invited someone she's been talking to from work."

"A work date? I thought she was strictly against that?" Adriana asked, raising her eyebrows.

"I know!" Kristin said. "I have not met him yet, but she's talking about this one more than usual."

"Hmm. Well, I'm interested to meet him. Are all the usual people coming?"

"Yes. Although, I'm not sure about Nathan. He went home to see his family for the long weekend and I'm not sure when he was making it back. Patrick invited him. That's all I know."

"Oh? Where does his family live?"

"A couple of hours north of here."

Adriana began shredding the cheese.

"He rarely misses," Adriana said.

Kristin gave her a mischievous smile. "Disappointed?"

"Uh. No. He's just always here."

Kristin laughed. "He does have a life."

Adriana smirked. "I have to admit I wondered a little."

"You seem concerned for him." Now Kristin was just being a brat. She wiggled her eyebrows mischievously as she came out from behind the fridge door.

Adriana threw a piece of shredded cheese in Kristin's direction, causing her to erupt in laughter.

"In all seriousness, though. I'm glad to see the two of you have become friends."

Since Adriana had to ditch her plan to avoid him in the name of wedding preparations, the increase of time together had slowly and steadily broken a barrier between them. She didn't feel threatened anymore by whatever feelings he might have for her. It was easier to be around him, laugh with him, without wondering if she was giving him the wrong impression. There was a playfulness in him she hadn't expected. He laughed easily and teased her gently. Even with her reserved nature, it was hard to remain indifferent toward him.

"I guess we have, haven't we?"

"I'd say so. You're comfortable with him now. I mean, the two of you helped me and Patrick make some crucial wedding decisions here. That's bonding if anything is." Kristin laughed.

Adriana did too. She realized Nathan was a good friend, just as he'd said he could be. The first time she'd ever been alone with him in his truck after the engagement dinner, he probably hadn't realized Libby had stayed behind. Not until he'd gotten out to help her. Yet he hadn't flirted with her or made any moves at all. He'd done exactly what she'd imagined a good guy friend should do, just kept her company.

It was most of their usual crowd tonight with the addition of a three new people—a soldier Patrick had invited, Libby's date Chris, and Kristin's co-worker, Morgan. Morgan had apparently been coming throughout the summer, though this was the first time Adriana had met her.

They began the evening with the game Code Names. Patrick oversaw splitting them into teams. He put Adriana on Nathan's team. She pretended not to notice the immediate pleasure that soared through her at that simple decision.

Before long, everyone was teasing one another and laughing, the game going strong. An atmosphere had been created between those that were usually present, but the best thing about Kristin's parties was that even those who didn't always attend or who were new seemed to find their stride as well. Adriana noticed those things, as someone frequently on the outside of crowds. She found herself looking toward Nathan throughout the game—saw how he had such a similar personality to Kristin's. How that personality seemed to link Patrick to both, and in turn, link Adriana. The realization stuttered inside of her.

Was that why, despite herself, it was so easy to like him? Her heart's panicked need to push away was still there, nagging in the background. There was always this question of what to do about Nathan. As time passed, every answer she'd easily held tangled with these changing feelings that startled her. He made her unsteady. She couldn't seem to tear herself away long enough to shut him out and silence the curiosity that nudged against apathy, demanding space.

Chapter Seventeen

Nathan stood next to Walsh and Cassie among a large group gathered in the backyard that belonged to Adriana's parents. In lieu of a dinner after the rehearsal, Adriana's family had offered their home for an outdoor potluck and cookout the weekend before the wedding. He looked around the expansive space, trying to find Adriana.

Finally, he spotted her. She was standing with a group of women in the opposite corner of the yard, Elena Villalobos among them. She had a drink in her hand and was animatedly gesturing with the other as she spoke. The group burst into replies, smiles, and nods. Adriana laughed. There was no hint of that careful reservation he was used to seeing in her. He took a step forward, mesmerized.

"Hey!" Danielle blocked his view, greeting the three of them with a wide smile.

"Hey, Danielle," Nathan replied at the same time Walsh did.

Danielle introduced herself to Cassie then added, "Let

me show you around, and we'll look for Kristin and Patrick while we're at it."

The three of them followed her as she guided them further into the yard. Nathan looked toward Adriana again as they walked the opposite way. Danielle gave them the rundown of where to find things, pointed out different activities set up, and gathered them for introductions with everyone she knew along the way. Eventually, they came across Kristin and Patrick.

"You guys made it!" Kristin exclaimed.

"Would you mind taking over? I need to go check on some things in the kitchen." Danielle addressed Kristin.

"Of course! Patrick and I will get them settled."

Kristin and Patrick introduced them to more family and friends, specifically their own. Some people Nathan already knew. By the time they reached the back patio, Adriana and the gathering of women had been replaced with Danielle, Thomas, and another couple. Danielle waved them over.

"Come grab something to drink." She gestured toward the ice chests behind her.

Walsh and Cassie walked over to grab something.

Before Nathan could follow, the man standing next to Thomas asked him conversationally, "How do you know the bride and groom?"

Patrick spoke up. "This is my best man, Nathan Prescott."

Nathan noticed the woman's eyebrows shoot up as she looked toward Danielle.

The man held out his hand. "Nice to meet you, Nathan. I'm Logan and"—he gestured toward the woman—"this is my wife, Marissa. Our family has been friends with Kristin's for years."

Kristin added, "This is Adriana's sister and brother-in-law."

Ah. That explained a lot.

Nathan shook Logan's hand, then reached out to shake Marissa's. "Nice to meet you both," he replied.

Marissa scrutinized him, then smiled. "Great to meet you too, Nathan."

The group exchanged small talk before Patrick asked if they all wanted to get in on one of the corn hole games. Which is how Nathan found himself in the company of friends and strangers before once again spotting Adriana.

She was walking across the yard toward the fire pit, a few folded chairs in her arms, and a young man next to her carrying a handful of wood. They were talking as they walked, completely unaware of Nathan. Nathan abandoned his position and walked over as they passed him. Adriana started at his sudden appearance.

"Nathan." She glanced down, turning her head slightly before looking back up at him. "Hey. Glad you made it."

Her demeanor had changed since he'd seen her moments ago. There was a distracted hesitance to her body language.

Ignoring his own agitation, he smiled at her, "Hey. Can I help you with those?" he asked, pointing toward the chairs.

"Uh . . . sure." She held them out toward him.

He grabbed all the chairs and cradled them in one arm.

"Thanks." Adriana said, then turned to the young man. "Gabe, this is Nathan, Patrick's best man. Nathan, this is my younger brother, Gabe."

Nathan nodded, "Hey. Great to meet you, Gabe."

Gabe nodded back, looking at Nathan with open curiosity. "Nice to meet you."

They walked to the firepit and deposited the chairs

while Gabe began organizing the firewood. Adriana looked around, as if uncertain what to do next. Nathan didn't know what to say. He thought about catching her laughing earlier and wanted to tell her she looked beautiful and that he loved her smile, but that wasn't exactly something she'd want to hear. The more he looked at her, the more at risk he was of reaching out and taking her hands in his and pulling her closer. He wanted her attention, not her avoidance.

"Should we rejoin the group?" Adriana finally asked, gesturing toward where he'd come from.

Before he could reply, a little boy came to a running stop at their side. Adriana's fidgeting ticked up and suddenly that flightiness made perfect sense. He was a dunce.

"Hi, Mom!" Then he turned an inquisitive stare up at Nathan. "Hi. I'm Isaac. Who are you?"

Adriana put her hand on the boy's shoulders, "Isaac, this is my friend Nathan. He's Patrick's best friend."

Nathan masked his surprise over her introduction, then bent down a little and reached out his hand.

"Hello, Isaac. It's nice to meet you."

Isaac shook it like a little gentleman, though his smile was full of boyish mischief. "Nice to meet you. Patrick is really cool."

Nathan glanced at Adriana quickly. "I hope that means I'm really cool too."

Isaac examined him. "We'll have to see."

Nathan laughed at his honesty.

"Did you need something?" Adrianna asked Isaac.

"No," Isaac said. His eyes didn't move away from Nathan.

It made Nathan want to chuckle. He was being scrutinized by a kindergartener.

Two children called after Isaac, diverting his attention.

"I'm going to go play, Mom." He gave her a quick hug, then took off.

"Hey, it'll be time to eat soon!" Adriana called after him.

Isaac glanced back their way as he did. "Okay! See you later, Nathan!"

Nathan waved. He looked at Adriana who was still watching Isaac.

"Hey, you guys! Come over here!" Kristin's voice rang out in their direction.

NATHAN HAD EXPECTED Adriana to find ways to escape or avoid him as the night progressed. Instead, through games, conversation, and dinner, she wasn't far. He kept catching her giving him long, inquisitive looks. To be fair, he only caught it because he was frequently looking her way as well. He couldn't get a read on her tonight. Those loaded expressions made him wish he could, made him want to ask her. He wouldn't, because he knew how that would go. If she wanted him to know what was on her mind, she'd . . . well, she'd really shock him, that was for sure. She barely opened up enough to satisfy his curiosity most of the time. Their friendship hadn't changed much in that regard.

"I didn't expect there to be so many people tonight." Nathan observed, trying to draw her into conversation as usual.

"My family used to be close to Kristin's. Even though a lot has changed over the years, everyone has been genuinely looking forward to celebrating together." Adriana looked fondly toward the crowd mingling in her parents' backyard.

"Your parents know Patrick, right?" she asked.

"Yeah."

Patrick and Nathan had known one another long enough that they'd spent some of their holiday leave at one another's respective family homes a couple of times.

"Will they make the wedding?"

"No—"

Before he could elaborate, Nathan felt a light tap on his wrist. He looked down to see Isaac standing beside him.

"Nathan, do you want to help us make a hopscotch?" Isaac asked.

"Uh . . ." Nathan was completely caught off guard as he watched Isaac reach for his hand.

"Come on! Patrick and the uncles are helping!"

He looked to where Isaac was pointing. Patrick, Gabe, Thomas, and Marissa's husband, Logan, were standing with a handful of children at the side gate. Before agreeing, he looked toward Adriana. Her blessing seemed important. If Isaac's request was unexpected, Adriana's calm demeanor was even more so. He hadn't forgotten her initial refusal to share any part of her life with him, and as she waved them on, he couldn't help but wonder at the difference.

"Guess I'm off to play hopscotch," he said to her as he turned to follow Isaac.

Adriana's eyebrows were raised in amusement, but her smile was pensive. Just another thing to add to all the questions he had where she was concerned. As he followed Isaac, he passed Kristin making her way over to Adriana. The grin she gave him was far easier to decipher.

Chapter Eighteen

Adriana stood at the end of the aisle, fiddling with the paper towel tube in her hands, and refrained from sighing out loud. Adjusting her posture, she looked up in time to see Nathan walking toward her from the opposite side of the sanctuary. In twenty-four hours, they'd all watch Kristin and Patrick exchange vows, but first, they had to get through the rehearsal.

Kristin had decided everyone would use the tubes as their makeshift bouquets to preserve the real ones from being lost or ruined before their big moment. While it made sense, Adriana felt ridiculous. She couldn't wait to get home. All she wanted to do right now was relax and prepare for tomorrow in her own way.

Kristin's stepmom, Sandy, bustled over to her and Libby. "Okay, ladies, stand up straight."

This was a reminder she'd given on repeat. As wedding coordinator, she was taking her position of authority very seriously. Adriana was trying to avoid her critique, but Sandy couldn't be tamed. Adriana didn't know her well, so she wasn't sure anything she did would matter either way.

As maid of honor, she was to link arms with Nathan and walk beside him toward the altar, where they'd stand up beside their best friends. Though their friendship was now a familiar one, as a rule she kept a healthy physical distance from Nathan. Seeing him on a nearly daily basis the past month, as the wedding plans were finalized, had hindered her ability to ignore the growing familiarity. Lately, her body responded in ways her mind was not on board with—something she'd have controlled quite thoroughly otherwise, thank you very much. Last weekend had worsened whatever ailed her. It was the only explanation she could offer herself for the impatience pinching at her now.

"Okay, perfect." Sandy's voice brought her back to the task at hand. "Now. You are going to take steps at the same time toward one another, turning and joining arms. Adriana, you will link yours inside his, then rest your hand in the crook of his elbow. Step forward. Let's practice."

She guided them forward. As if walking arm in arm with someone was an entirely new concept. They both did as they were told. She intended to send them through this rehearsal breakdown twice. Adriana stamped down the impatience she felt at Sandy's exuberance.

"Good, good." She stepped in front of them, arranging them so they were a little closer to one another. "Let's act like we like each other though. Hmm?"

Adriana pursed her lips, glancing up quickly at Nathan. He cringed playfully, and the rest of the wedding party laughed. Sandy narrowed her eyes at him then sent them on their way up the aisle, instructions on pacing and next steps continuing as they went.

Nathan tucked Adriana's arm in tighter and she caught a whiff of him—it was something cool and woodsy. Instinctively, she leaned toward him, breathing in deeper. They passed Isaac where he sat in the front row. Focusing on him immediately grounded her, and she adjusted her posture. Ugh. She needed distance from this man.

When they reached the altar, Nathan looked at her, an intensity burning in his eyes. Her breath stuttered as he smiled tenderly. She felt off balance. He gave Isaac an air fist bump. One that Isaac matched enthusiastically, and her heart twinged.

"No fist bumps during the ceremony, best man," Sandy scolded.

In just a short week, it seemed he'd won over her entire family—Isaac included. Coupled with her own complicated emotions about Nathan, she'd been unprepared for this development.

She couldn't get the picture of Isaac playing with Nathan at the rehearsal dinner out of her head. It had been as if they'd known one another for years. To her son, who probably saw Nathan as an extension of Patrick and Kristin, this was not a big deal. In fact, he'd announced to all who cared to listen that Nathan was, in fact, just as cool as Patrick.

A confusing ache had settled in her heart. Spending time with Nathan, seeing him with Isaac, was no good. Once this wedding was over, some hard boundaries needed to be reestablished.

THE CEREMONY WENT off without a hitch, and after what felt like hours of wedding pictures, the reception was in full swing. Adriana stood talking to her mom and Marissa while placing some finger food on a plate for Isaac. The first dances were over, the dance floor filling up. She noticed Morgan talking to Nathan on the edge of the dance floor. Marissa did not miss her attention snag.

"He's way cuter than you gave him credit for when I

asked about him. It's no wonder you can't stop looking at him." Her eyebrows wiggled.

"Marissa," her mother scolded.

"What? I'm just making an innocent observation."

Adriana gave her sister an impatient look. "I thought I described him well. You just wanted me to gush over him."

"Well." Marissa gestured toward him.

Their mother tsked and smacked gently at her hand. Adriana grabbed tongs from a board of cheeses, keeping her expression neutral. She was not going to let Marissa's fussing add to her mess of emotions. As she worked her way down the table, Isaac continually reached out to grab at the food while laughing mischievously as if it was a game they were playing every time she waved away his attempts. Finally, she put the plate down and held firmly to his hand. Squatting down carefully in her dress, she leveled him with a strict look.

"Isaac. Ya basta. Knock it off. I want you to put your hands in your pockets until you sit down."

Isaac pouted and she let go of his hand, waiting for him to either comply or have a meltdown. The expression on his face told her it could go either way.

"We're going to go sit down," her mom said suddenly. "Marissa."

"Wha—Mom . . ." her sister protested.

Adriana raised her eyebrows at Isaac, still waiting for him to follow her instructions. Glancing up quickly, she was just in time to see her mom grab Isaac's plate, then nudge Marissa away, muttering urgently at her under her breath in Spanish. Maybe she thought Isaac would obey quicker without an audience.

She stood, looking down at Isaac, hands on her hips. He slowly tucked his hands out of sight, looking all the while like he was tempted not to. He looked up and away from her, his pout transforming into a smile.

"Looking sharp little man." Nathan's voice came from behind her. Isaac beamed.

"Thanks! I'm going to go eat," he said, jetting off in the same direction as her mom and sister.

What was with everyone ditching her? She avoided Nathan's gaze, instead focusing on adjusting the folds of fabric falling from her waist, then the delicate gold bracelet on her wrist, though she knew neither needed adjusting. Their rehearsed and memorized roles had been filled. Now all that was left was the two of them and she was certain he was coming over here for a specific reason. She scolded herself. They were friends. This shouldn't be complicated. Finally, she looked at him.

"Hey," he said, his mouth tipping up on one side.

"Hey yourself." She looked him over. "You look great."

The compliment felt strange on her tongue. It was the first time she'd acknowledged an attraction to his appearance. At least to him.

He laughed appreciatively. "You just stole my line. I was coming over here to tell you the same thing." Rubbing at the back of his head, "Actually, I came over for more than one reason."

"Oh?" She scrutinized him. He looked a little nervous, more so than she'd seen in a while and she knew she'd been right about what he was about to ask.

"Do you dance?" His mouth lifted a little on one side again in an almost shy, boyish half-smile.

She noticed a slow song beginning softly around them. "Um, not really." Shrugging, she added, "I haven't danced much."

"You can follow my lead. I'm pretty good at it." His expression and tone had that playful, persuasive quality of his. She wanted to resent it but instead had grown fond of his well-intentioned attempts to draw her out.

She crossed her arms and studied him. "Oh, are you?"

He nodded. "I can two-step and waltz. I know a few line dances and even some swing dance moves."

"Well, this is a fascinating development," she said. It seemed he was still surprising her. "How did that happen?"

He held his hand out, nodding toward the dance floor. "Come dance with me, and I'll tell you all about it."

She looked at his hand, feeling a little unsure. A dozen excuses skittered across her mind. She could complain about a sudden onset of stomach issues or blame some random maid of honor chore. The temptation to run and hide warred with an opposite desire. A desire to lean into him again, to breathe in his scent and feel his warmth. Shutting out the scolding she'd been giving herself since last week, she took a deep breath and placed her hand in his.

She was rewarded with a bigger smile—one not at all nervous and entirely too charming. Nathan clasped her hand in his and guided her to the dance floor. He wasted no time gently tugging her closer and placing her arm on his shoulder. The commanding movement stole her breath.

He took her other hand and lifted it with his, then placed his other hand on her back. She resisted the pull to step closer, grateful for the space he kept between them as they began moving in time to the music.

"Remember, just follow my lead," he said quietly.

She looked down, watching their feet move. She had to escape those eyes of his. They saw too much and being like this with him was doing funny things to her stomach, and it still felt like she was catching her breath.

"Adriana?"

"Hmm?" She didn't look at him.

He brought their hands in, tucking his index finger

under her chin, nudging it up. "It's easier if you just trust me to lead."

She rolled her lips in and nodded. Taking a slow, deep breath, she met his gaze again.

"Tell me about this dancing knowledge of yours," she said, desperate for a distraction. The trembling of her voice made her cringe a little.

"The short answer? I took lessons for a few months."

"And the long answer?"

"Well." He took a deep breath and looked away before meeting her eyes again. "My ex, Lindsey, enjoyed dancing. She asked me to take lessons with her."

In the mutual company they shared, Lindsey had come up before. Adriana still didn't know many details about their relationship, only the length of it and the unfortunate way she'd ended things. Talking about her now brought on compassion and something new, something suspiciously like protectiveness. Or jealousy? She couldn't keep her emotions straight.

"Did you enjoy learning?"

"Yeah. It took me a while. Some of the moves were difficult. I didn't exactly grow up around that sort of thing, so it opened a whole new world. Dancing like this is easy though. There's nothing to it. You don't have to know anything special. It's the simple language of movement."

"Not a language I speak." She laughed at her own self-deprecating joke.

"You are doing great."

"Maybe that's just because I have a good leader." The instant it came out of her mouth, she worried she came off flirtatious. It had sounded complimentary in an intimate way that was unfamiliar.

"A leader needs a good follower as much as a follower needs a good leader." His eyes roamed over her face. "I'm really good at leading." Then, fluidly, in his next step, he tucked her in a little closer as if to demonstrate, though their bodies still didn't touch.

The space between them buzzed with energy. The smallest of adjustments could change that. One little tug, one natural step forward. It would be so easy. An unwelcome longing simmered, taking up space her nerves didn't have room for. She wasn't sure how he kept time. She'd long ago tuned out the music, every movement only a response to his.

"May I cut in?" A familiar little boy's voice interrupted.

Looking down, she saw Isaac smiling up at them impishly.

She hadn't noticed his approach. The music was changing. The new song was still slow but more upbeat. Smiling down at her son, she stepped away from Nathan.

"Absolutely, young sir." He looked back toward Adriana like he didn't want to give up his position at all.

"Thanks for the dance." His voice was quiet and deep.

He walked away, and she followed his progress off the dance floor. She'd better keep in mind that there were watchful eyes anxious to read more into every move she made where Nathan was concerned. All she had to do was spend even a few seconds too long focused on him, and her whole family would speculate on a future she wasn't asking for.

"Ready, Mom?"

She bowed her head to him in a nod. "Of course."

He motioned for her to come closer and whispered, not quietly, in Spanish that his abuelo had told him she needed rescuing. He looked at her quizzically. "Did you, Mom?"

Laughing affectionately, she shook her head. "No, no, mijo. Solo está bromeando," she whispered back at him.

"He's only teasing." The song picked up, and she spun him out and in again, laughing with him.

It was her dad who requested the next dance. She was spending more time on the dance floor than she'd anticipated. Amid lighthearted conversation, he caught her off guard.

"Will we be dancing together at your wedding next?"

"I think Gabe will get married long before I do." Gabe didn't have a serious girlfriend, but the chance seemed just as likely.

"Ah, carino." Was she imagining his melancholy tone? "Perhaps." His expression was contemplative. "These things have a tendency to sneak up on us."

Chapter Nineteen

Adriana had promised Patrick and Kristin dinner from Sol de Montaña the night before they were due to leave for their honeymoon. Nearly a month had passed since the wedding. Their work schedules hadn't allowed them to take time off any earlier, so they were taking a delayed honeymoon. As expected, she went up to the patio to find the front door open. She knocked on the screen door before opening it.

"Hello?"

Kristin peeked around the corner. "Hey! Come on in."

Adrian walked into the living room to find Kristin stretching, her hand holding a foot behind her.

She blew a messy strand of blonde hair out of her face. "I just got back from my run."

"Where's Patrick?" Adriana asked, walking over to the counter and putting down the bags of food.

"He's still at work. He should be getting off any minute now."

"Are you all packed and ready?" Adriana looked around. Everything looked neat and clean, none of the usual light clutter that marred Kristin's livable spaces. She noticed two suitcases next to the doorway of the master bedroom.

"Yep. Not much left to do now. Our flight leaves at seven tomorrow morning. Thank you again for bringing us dinner. It makes everything that much easier, with the bonus of seeing you." She beamed at her.

"I'm happy to help."

Kristin finished stretching, then walked over to the counter, peeking in the bags.

"Mmm, smells amazing." She placed them in a stay-hot bag on her counter. "Do you want to sit out on the porch with me for a few minutes? It would be great to visit for a little bit."

"Sure."

They settled into the cushioned outdoor chairs on her patio, and both propped their feet on the ottoman.

"How's married life treating you so far?" Adriana asked, peering over at her friend. She looked even more content and at peace than she had in the days leading up to the wedding itself.

"Wonderful," Kristin replied breathily. She leaned her head back on the chair and turned to look at Adriana. "I don't know if it gets better than this."

Adriana smiled. "I'm so happy to hear that."

"How are you?"

"I'm great. Life is good," Adriana said, not lying but still feeling as if she was holding something back.

Kristin sat up, tilting her head. "Are you sure? I can't quite put my finger on it, but you've seemed different lately. Almost restless?"

She said the last word like a question, as if hoping Adriana would clarify. Kristin's line of questioning was putting her on edge. Adriana thought she'd done a good job of hiding the unsettled state of her mind and emotions.

She'd also counted on the wedding being the perfect distraction to keep Kristin from noticing.

Adriana shook her head and shrugged. "There's nothing different. I'm perfectly content. Maybe just contemplative. There have been some big changes lately."

Kristin studied her, her expression thoughtful.

Adriana hurriedly added, "Good changes, though! I'm truly so thrilled for you."

"Can I ask you a question?" Kristin finally requested, almost impatiently.

Adriana leaned toward her, wondering at this mood she was in. She rested her forearm on the arm of the chair. "Of course."

"Promise my question won't upset you, okay?"

Adriana felt her eyebrows twitch inward. What was this all about? Worrying for her friend, she nodded. "We've always been able to talk about anything, you know that."

Kristin took a deep breath. "Well. I know you were very clear that this was not on the table for discussion, and you mentioned in the past you didn't even want to consider the possibilities until Isaac's much older . . ."

Adriana's mouth tightened. She hadn't been lying about them being able to talk about anything, but this subject wasn't up for debate. Why was her life causing Kristin concern? It was the last thing she should be worrying about, with all the excitement going on in her own.

"Well, none of that was really a question."

Kristin nudged her arm. "Oh, stop. I'm getting there. Do you truly never intend to change your mind about relationships? No matter what?"

Adriana looked down, fiddling with the rings on her fingers. "Why are you worrying about me right now? You have just started the beginning of this exciting new chapter in your life."

"That's exactly why! I didn't even realize it could be this good, Adriana! Patrick is remarkable, and he loves me, of all people."

"You of all people? Ay. Stop right this instant with that nonsense. I'd be sorely disappointed in him if he didn't."

Kristin's eyes glistened. Her best friend's emotional state was throwing Adriana off a little.

"Kristin? Are you sure *you're* okay?"

Kristin both nodded and shook her head. "I am. Truly. I've just been wondering. You and Nathan get along well. You are comfortable with him. If you'd let that wall of yours down and actually consider it, couldn't you see yourself with him?"

Adriana sighed, trying to tamp down her exasperation. "We get along and are comfortable with one another precisely because we don't have our friends asking these sorts of questions. We can just exist together as we are. Where is all of this coming from?"

Kristin swung her legs and pounded her feet down on the cement, sitting up in a state of agitation. "He's one of the good ones. Like Patrick. Guys like them don't come around all the time, you know."

Kristin's liveliness finally had an explanation. She'd always seemed somewhat attached to Nathan, a symptom of her relationship with Patrick. It was apparent she looked up to him, much like she might a brother. That still didn't change anything for Adriana.

"Kristin . . ." She sighed, trying to form a clear rebuttal.

"I know, I know," Kristin interrupted. "I gave you my word that I would never try to set you up with anyone. It's just . . ." She locked her in with an almost pleading stare. "Would it really be the worst thing in the world if either of you saw the other as more than a friend?"

Adriana did not hesitate. "Yes."

Shock and surprise shaded Kristin's expression. "What? Why?"

How could she honestly expect Adriana to give her any other answer? Adriana sighed. "Well, first of all, I told you, I didn't want this to be a topic of discussion. More importantly, nothing has changed."

As soon as the words left her mouth, she felt the weight of the lie. It sank deep in her gut, leaving a sour guilt behind. She hated it but she didn't want to pursue the way she felt either. Admitting to anything was one step away from giving Kristin permission to interfere, or giving her hope for something Adriana wasn't going to let happen anyway.

There was a part of her that would be hard-pressed not to acknowledge there had been a time she wanted a lot more out of life than what she was settling for. Not that settling was quite what she ever felt she was doing. Life really was good. Even in difficulties, joy and contentment filled much of her days. She had so much, and she had no business demanding or expecting more. Except for this nagging sensation that wouldn't leave her alone any time she was around Nathan. As she'd decided at the wedding, she just needed to get more distance from him again, then the world would right itself once more, and she could go on following the same path she'd been taking for years now. Happily. This, right here? An unacceptable distraction from her plans.

Kristin gave her a look that told her she wasn't fooled. "Adriana."

"Okay." Adriana shifted restlessly. "So, things aren't exactly the same." She hesitated, not sure how to express all she was feeling carefully.

Kristin cut in where her own muddled thoughts twisted her tongue, preventing her from speaking. "Don't make light of things. Plenty has changed. You've gained a collection of new acquaintances, opened yourself up to new experiences. You've let Nathan in! I mean, you started an honest to goodness friendship with the guy! I never thought I'd see that blossom the way it has. These aren't small things. Seeing you dancing with him at the wedding made me realize the ease of your friendship with him. I had sort of failed to grasp what a big deal it was until then."

Adriana hadn't expected Kristin to jump to this conclusion over it. She'd been too worried about what assumptions her family would make and mistakenly assumed Kristin saw them together often enough not to put too much weight on her accepting Nathan's invitation to dance.

"Fine. I get what you're saying, but don't read too much into it. None of this is leading anywhere further."

"Really?" Kristin's disbelief and disappointment was obvious. "Nothing is going to change your mind?"

Adriana was trying hard not to let this get under her skin, to give her best friend grace. It was this very thing that had been her deal breaker all those months ago. The condition that hinged upon her being where she was right now had always been that no one would try to force something further on her.

"The bottom line is I don't see how any good can come out of it."

"Out of what? Dating? Considering the possibilities?"

"Out of changing my mind about Nathan." Adriana stopped her before she kept going, knowing this admittance could potentially strengthen Kristin's argument—if she really considered what Adriana wasn't saying.

Kristin leaned in, as if Adriana was about to divulge a secret. "Why?"

"Because. Isn't it obvious? I can't give him what he deserves."

Kristin narrowed her eyes at Adriana as if in confusion. "What do you mean by that?"

She sat back, leaning her head over the top of the chairback. She wanted to be angry right now for a few reasons, but she hadn't come here to fight. Leaving with a disagreement simmering between them was unacceptable. Staring at the blue sky above them, she blew out a breath and spoke out loud the problem Nathan always presented. Despite her long-held rules and whatever she might feel.

"His career. The truth is, I admire his passion and his drive. And you know I've always fully supported our service members. But the upheaval of such a life? All that moving and the constant unknowns? That's unthinkable to me. I cannot imagine a life like that for myself and Isaac. Just thinking about what it means for you makes my throat tight and my chest ache."

Kristin deflated, then quietly responded, "I understand."

Adriana reached over, squeezing her arm affectionately. "I don't begrudge you for choosing Patrick and signing up for what his life will mean. I wasn't expressing empty platitudes when I said how excited I am for you guys, but when the day comes that you have to move away, or I have to stand by and watch you send him off on another deployment . . ." She sighed, and feeling the depths of the certain loneliness and fear either of those things would bring made her next words shake with emotion. "It's going to be crazy hard."

Kristin frowned. "Oh, Adriana." She leaned over, gesturing for Adriana to do the same. "Come here, come here."

Adriana did, and Kristin grabbed her up in a tight, though awkward, hug, what with them both still seated. The moment only succeeded in sending them both over the edge in tears. The back patio door opened, and Patrick stuck his head out.

"Hey—" He stopped short upon seeing the two of them, then rushed out, squatting down beside Kristin. "What's wrong?"

His voice was tinged with worry and a strong urge to fix whatever needed fixing. Adriana let go and stood up, wiping her eyes. Kristin stood too, putting an arm around Patrick, then wiping her face with the opposite hand.

"We're just getting ourselves all worked up."

Patrick looked on, his concern unsatisfied by the vague explanation.

"I should go." Adriana composed herself and reached out, placing a hand on each of their shoulders. "I'm praying for safe travels. I hope you have the best honeymoon possible." She looked at Kristin specifically. "Don't worry about anything here. We've all got you covered."

While her words spoke of the things Kristin and Patrick needed done while they were gone—all of which were being handled by their friends and family—it was also meant to encompass everything they'd just discussed. Kristin's somber nod let her know she fully understood.

Chapter Twenty

Adriana walked up to the axe throwing trailer with Kristin, Libby, Morgan, and Elena. Nathan and Seth were taking their turns in each of the two lanes, throwing like pros. As if maybe this wasn't the twenty-first century and axe wielding was still an actual thing, not just a fun group activity. Watching as the momentum of Nathan's swing caused his muscles to flex, Adriana was transfixed.

"Well. Hello," Morgan said, appreciation thick in her tone.

Libby giggled and agreed enthusiastically.

As Nathan turned, a satisfied grin took over his face. She'd meant to look away before he could catch her blatant staring. Taking a deep breath, she looked down and adjusted the knot of the flannel she'd wrapped around her waist.

The rodeo was in town, and Kristin had gathered a large group to enjoy it together. Most of whom had arrived with plenty of time to enjoy the shops' activities set up on the outside of the arena before the rodeo was set to begin. With

Kristin's gentle encouragement, Adriana had agreed to participate in the axe throwing, despite feeling intimidated by the mere thought of it. If an activity required putting herself in front of a large group of watching eyes, her typical response had always been to pass. When her turn arrived shortly after, she swallowed her renewed misgivings and stepped forward. The older gentleman manning the station asked if she'd ever thrown before.

She cringed. "No."

"Okay, that's not a problem. If you'd like, I can run through some instructions and let you have a couple practice throws."

She looked around the station. There weren't many people around. Maybe this wouldn't be as painful as she'd expected. "Sure. That would be great, thanks."

The attendant came parallel to her, then demonstrated, instructing her in each step as he went through it.

Grabbing an axe from the table, he handed it to her. "Ready to give it a try?"

"As ready as I'll ever be," Adriana said with trepidation. She didn't see this going well but was willing to give it her best effort anyway.

He moved aside and told her to go whenever she was ready. She swung that first axe. It missed the target entirely. Laughing with embarrassment, she asked for a moment.

"No problem. Take your time, then grab another and try again. It takes some getting used to," he said with casual encouragement.

She began wrapping her hair in a twist at the nape of her neck, securing it with the tie she had around her wrist. She was stalling, not quite ready for her next round of fresh embarrassment.

"May I?" a familiar voice came from behind. Her senses went on high alert as Nathan stepped into sight.

"You want my turns?" She was only half kidding.

He shook his head, an amused half-smile turning up his mouth. "No, I was offering to help."

"That guy already tried to help me." Her tone was bordering on bratty, so she took a breath and worked on softening the impatience she felt. It was more about being embarrassed than actually annoyed. "I'm not sure more advice will help. I probably just need more practice."

"We can arrange that, but until then"—he stepped closer —"I can help you work on the stance he showed you and teach you some throwing tricks. If you'd let me?"

He was all polite helpfulness and spoke to her as if he was afraid she might bite. That had probably been true when he'd first approached. She wasn't entirely sorry for it —putting emotional space between each other would serve them well. They were getting way too comfortable and being around him was still causing undeniable havoc to her senses. The barrier they had been behind last year was long gone. For better or for worse, Nathan's place in her life would not easily fizzle back to what it had been.

"Okay. Show me," she said, ignoring the thoughts screaming at her to manage on her own, come what may.

He grabbed an axe. "First, make sure your grip is good. You want to hold it firmly but not too tight. No death grips, okay?" He smiled playfully, and she found herself smiling back.

Looking down at the axe he held, he continued, "Put your hands like this." Demonstrating, he explained the positioning and which hand went where, just as the attendant had, then he held the axe out to her.

She took it from him, her fingers brushing against his. Breathing out slowly, she kept her gaze focused on the handle of the axe and worked on mimicking his positioning. He came closer and maneuvered her hands a bit.

"Put your hands closer together."

His touches were deliberate, purposeful. A tingle went down her spine, and her heart felt jumpy. She could not look at him.

"Okay. Perfect." He stepped back. "Now remember what he said about aiming the axe before you pull back?"

She nodded.

"Get in that position."

She did as he said, trying to be loose and relaxed. Awareness sparked through her nerves. She could feel his eyes take in her form. Maybe it was just for teaching purposes in his mind, but not for her. His gaze was like the heat of a bonfire settling over her entire body. He stepped closer again, and in the next breath, used the toe of his boot to nudge hers.

Near her ear, his low, instructive tone continued. "Widen your stance a little."

It was so unexpected, she forgot where she was. The sounds around them fell away. What was her deal? It's not like she couldn't be close to this man without holding herself together. The toe of his boot nudged her again. Realizing she hadn't moved, she adjusted as he had asked.

"Exactly like that. Remember, when you go to throw, you'll step forward with your non-dominant foot as you swing. Maintain fluid movements when releasing—no flicking, no jerking." They nodded to one another, and he continued, "Pull back and swing like you are going to throw, but don't let go."

She looked at him skeptically, not sure what direction this was going, but she did as he asked. As she stopped, he came back into her field of vision and demonstrated again. "When it reaches here, release. Okay?"

"Yes," she said, also nodding. She looked from him to the target, then back to him.

"Pull back again," he instructed, as he took a wide step behind and beside her.

"Like this?" she asked, barely turning her head to glance in his direction.

She heard him step closer again. Then his fingers were resting lightly on the back of her forearms, warm against her skin. She was going to need him to try a hands-off approach if they had any chance of seeing this make a difference in her throwing skills.

"Pull back further."

She adjusted a little, but her mind was focused on his touch and not at all on what she was supposed to be doing. Her movement must not have been enough, because his fingers wrapped around her wrists, gentle but firm. Every move he made seemed designed to unravel control of her senses. She imagined him taking his palms and running them up the bend of her elbows and down across her triceps. Her poor heart was in serious danger.

"Does this feel okay? I didn't pull too far, did I?" he asked.

He was all business, his demeanor calm and collected. While she was a chaotic mess. It seemed vitally important she not have a weapon in her hands under these conditions. She forced herself to focus on the target in front of her and the feel of the axe instead of the warmth of his hands. She swallowed.

"No, it feels fine." Her voice was annoyingly squeaky.

He let go.

"Good." His voice was gentle, still instructive. "Now swing forward without throwing again. Remember your feet."

She did as he asked, then looked at him. He nodded, his expression revealing nothing but pleasure at how well she was taking his instruction, while she felt as if hers exposed everything she was feeling.

"Now what?" Her voice still felt strained.

"Take your aiming position, and you are ready to go. Just work on relaxing your shoulders. You're a little stiff."

Nodding, she looked at the attendant, who gave her a thumbs up, then she focused on the target again. Practicing an aim and swing one more time, she took a couple of breaths, then let the axe loose. It bounced off the board.

Nathan brought her another axe. "You did great. Try again."

"It didn't even hit the target." This was ridiculously embarrassing.

"You've got this. Just remember to relax." He gestured toward the target and moved out of her way.

She took her time setting up. This was not going well. She was too aware of Nathan—of his closeness and his gaze. It made her jittery. Despite her misgivings, she aimed and went for it. This time the axe stuck with a loud thunk, just outside the innermost ring.

Her mouth fell open, and she jumped up and down, too excited to care how silly it might look. "I got it!"

"That was awesome!" Nathan exclaimed. His smile only made hers wider as he handed her another axe. "You've got one more."

This time, the axe hit near the outermost ring. Nathan went for a high five. The rest of their group stepped up, congratulating her with high fives as well. She felt her cheeks warm with the awareness that they'd had a captive audience throughout that entire encounter.

Adriana turned back to Nathan. "Thanks to you, that was more fun than I expected it to be."

"It was my pleasure." He put his hands in his pockets.

"Maybe we can get the group together for an axe throwing night sometime."

Adriana laughed. "A few minutes ago, I would have told you that was a crazy idea, but I actually like the sound of that."

As the group separated once again, she felt able to catch her breath. The low hum of her constant awareness of Nathan had both energized and frazzled her. And the night had only begun.

AFTER SOME MORE SHOPPING AT the vendors around the arena, Adriana was getting her face painted with Kristin and Libby. The crowds had picked up, the main event was about to begin. She was waiting patiently for the last swirls of the design she'd chosen to be painted when Nathan came up to join the group gathered in front of them. He'd been talking to Daniel and Cassie as he walked their way until he noticed her watching his approach. She'd always been quick to look away in moments like these. This time, she didn't.

Letting her eyes roam, she took in everything she could about him. His broad shoulders, the way his clothes fit, and the shadow of his ball cap over his eyes. The strong line of his stubbled jaw, the muscles in his arms and legs, the strength of his hands. How those hands had felt touching her.

When their eyes met again, her stomach flopped, and her already elevated pulse jumped. Was it her own changing feelings making everything so intense lately? Finally, she broke eye contact, careful not to move her head and disrupt the artist's work, and she trained her eyes on the ground in front of her. All this back and forth going on in her mind—it was like fighting against the tension of a stretched rubber band. Her body seemed intent on pulling toward him, her heart more and more willing to follow. Every reason protested on a loop, telling her how foolish she was, because she knew deep down it could never work.

NATHAN COULDN'T STOP LOOKING in Adriana's direction. God knows he tried. His eyes slid back toward her as the artist handed her a mirror. She turned her face, admiring the work the woman had done, then smiled and spoke. Nathan rubbed the back of his head and turned back toward Walsh, who was still talking. What was it he'd been saying?

As Adriana rejoined the group, Nathan stepped closer to her. "Nice flower," he said, winking. His fingers itched to trace the lines that swirled around her left brow and down her cheek bone. He shoved his hands in his pockets.

"Thanks." She looked away from him, a shy smile tipping her lips up. When she looked back toward him again, it was as if she was trying to hide, but Nathan didn't miss her searching gaze.

As they made their way toward their seats, Nathan hung back from Adriana when Elena and Cassie pulled her into conversation. This placed Nathan between Seth Fontana and Brock Muna once they got seated, with Morgan on the opposite side of Seth. Morgan engaged the three of them in conversation as the rodeo began. It didn't help keep his attention from wandering to the row in front of him where Adriana was sitting. He knew it was best they hadn't ended up next to one another. He valued her friendship and needed to renew his efforts at remembering that's all they shared.

"I'm going to grab a drink. Does anyone else want something?" Adriana stood, pulling on the flannel she'd had tied around her waist.

A few of them spoke up, so Nathan stood as well. "I can go with you."

"I don't mind grabbing something for you," Adriana protested.

"I mind," he said, his tone leaving no room for more argument. "It sounds like you'll have your hands full."

"Okay." She shrugged, her face impassive.

A couple more requests and they had made their way out of the rows of seats, weaving toward the concessions.

"Kristin mentioned you were taking a vacation soon. I think she called it something else . . ." Adriana asked, uncertainly.

"Yeah, I am. Leave is the military version of vacation."

"Are you going anywhere fun?" Adriana asked, looking toward him, then away as she stepped around a couple standing in the middle of the walkway.

"To the Pacific Coast, but I also plan to visit my family for part of it. They live a couple hours north of here."

"It must be nice to have family close while being stationed here." Adriana stopped at the end of the line, then turned toward him.

"It is. I can visit them more frequently than I've been able to in the past."

"Do you travel often when you get time off?"

"Occasionally. I enjoy getting away. Sometimes a change of scenery is necessary."

"I guess I can see that." She paused, considering. "Your scenery changes so often compared to most people."

He nodded, agreeing, then turned the conversation on her. "Do you get much of a chance to take trips or get away?"

"Not really. It can be challenging since I help with the

farm. I don't mind though. Maybe it's boring, but I like staying close to home."

He didn't find her boring. Not by a long shot. Spending time with her had become one of his favorite things to do lately.

She looked as if her thoughts had taken her far away, and she played with a strand of her hair that had come loose. He wanted to reach out and brush that hair behind her shoulder, still her movements with a gentle caress, distract her from her nerves with a kiss. Knowing what it was like to have her in his arms and touching her earlier had fed a spark he could no longer ignore. If he had never touched her at all, he might not be in this predicament. It was too late for what-ifs now.

He realized she'd been saying something. He blinked, reigning in his errant thoughts. Their number was called out, interrupting any effort he could make to ask her what she'd been saying. The crowds had grown thicker, so they walked single file back to their seats, their hands full. Adriana walked in front of him. His full attention narrowed on her and their immediate surroundings, like a vigilant bodyguard.

Once back in their seats, his mind was reeling. Nathan wondered what he was going to do. This wasn't working. When he first told her it wouldn't get complicated, he had believed it. But awareness hit him like a punch to the gut. How had he not seen this coming from a mile away? He was going to break his word. He'd fallen in love with her.

Chapter Twenty-One

"I have it on good authority that Morgan thinks you're hot," Libby spoke up, excitedly.

Nathan, chewing his food and temporarily unable to respond, looked around at the three people sitting at the table with him. He was having dinner with Kristin, Patrick, and Libby—who had joined at the last minute after showing up earlier than planned for the upcoming game night. He didn't miss Kristin's immediate look of annoyance at her sister's outburst.

Patrick, who hadn't yet noticed his wife's displeasure due to his attention wrapped up in the pork chop he was slicing, nodded. "Morgan might be interested. She's a flirt, though. Maybe if you just wanted to go on a few dates or take someone to the ball, you could ask her."

He looked up from his meal to witness Kristin's expression turned toward him. "What?"

He met her stare, and they did that thing where an entire conversation seemed to pass between them without a spoken word. It drove Nathan a little crazy to sit there and try to act unaffected by it.

Kristin sighed and looked at Nathan. "If you want to go to the ball and need a date, they aren't wrong. Morgan would happily go with you. I don't think she'd care that I said so. Not that we should be saying so." She pierced her sister and husband each with another look while adding that last part.

Nathan didn't have to see Kristin's expression to know she did not care to share this news. It could be her lack of interest in playing matchmaker extended beyond Adriana or another reason entirely, Nathan wasn't sure. He had assumed Morgan's flirting was more a personality trait than directed interest, and he said as much.

"It appeared like any of us," he said, referring to himself and the other single soldiers that came around, "were just fun to flirt with."

Kristin shrugged. "You didn't read her entirely wrong. However, I'm certain she'd accept an invitation from you most of all. Let's leave it at that. We all agree she's great and a lot of fun, but . . ." She sat up straighter. "You could always ask Adriana? You'd have fun with her, too."

It was Patrick's turn to look at Kristin with annoyance. Libby had been swirling a carrot stick in the hummus bowl, appearing to have tuned out the conversation entirely. Until she spoke up.

"Good luck with that. If she says she's *intentionally single* one more time, I'm going to strangle her."

The looks going around the table were intense. The last thing Nathan wanted to do was cause an argument over anyone's idea of what he should do when he was more inclined to go alone or skip it altogether.

"What?" Libby was staring at Kristin. "It's true. A little spice in her life would be a good thing, but she won't get there on her own, as stubborn as she is."

She turned toward Nathan. "Asking Adriana is a good

way to get absolutely nowhere, with the added bonus of rejection."

"Hey. Don't be unfair." Kristin huffed.

Libby put her hands up in surrender. "Look, you know I love Adriana. But let's be honest, she isn't going to start dating. Even though she should. I'm fully on board with trying to make that happen, though I know it will inevitably make her mad." She stood and left the dining room.

Patrick reached out and grabbed Kristin's hand, then looked at Nathan. "Start moving on, man. It's the best thing for both of you."

Kristin looked both angry and deflated. She sighed heavily. Nathan, as usual, had more questions than answers when it came to Adriana.

"You don't expect him not to move on, do you? She's been clear about how she feels. You should know that better than anyone, babe."

Patrick had spoken like the realist he was. Nathan couldn't ignore the stab those words caused or the suspicion this was not the first time the two of them had discussed this recently. Kristin shook her head, swirling her fork through what was left of her macaroni and cheese.

"Maybe I have started moving on," Nathan considered out loud. He'd thought about it, at least. They were supposed to think he had moved on a long time ago.

Patrick gave him an incredulous look. "We saw you two at the rodeo. That was some serious flirting."

"That's what I'm trying to say! Maybe Adriana isn't such a gamble," Kristin piped up, reanimating.

Patrick looked over at her. Nathan could tell they were having another of their silent conversations. Concentrating on his plate and the little food he had left, Nathan tried to ignore them.

"We should just stay out of this." Kristin stood abruptly.

"Nathan. If you don't want to take anyone or go at all, you should just stick to your guns." Then she stomped out.

Nathan's eyebrows shot up. He looked over at Patrick.

"Don't fight with your wife over this," Nathan said.

"We aren't fighting," Patrick assured him.

"If you say so," Nathan said, taking a drink of his water.

Patrick pinched the bridge of his nose. "We're not. She just . . ." He seemed to choose his words carefully. "Hates being in the middle of this. And she's right. We don't need to interfere."

"I'm not upset about it," Nathan assured him.

"I know. Just like I hope you know I've got your back. Which is why I need to say one last thing."

"You know you always can."

"Once again, let things with Adriana be." Patrick frowned, looking sorry he'd said it.

The thing was, Nathan knew Patrick meant well. The man wasn't wrong—letting things be would be the best course. He'd been trying to tell him that since the beginning. Hadn't Nathan decided for himself that distance was necessary? Yet here he was, not following through. That was all on him.

Libby came back into the room, placing a stack of games she'd brought in on the buffet table. "I hope whatever this weird tension is takes a hike, because everyone should be here for game night in less than an hour." She looked around. "Where's Kristin?"

Patrick got up. "Probably out back. I'll go check on her."

Libby started collecting the dinner dishes, so Nathan stood to help.

"That got stupid fast." She paused, looking at Nathan with unusual seriousness. "Take note, Nathan. Be careful with Adriana, because Kristin will not see her get hurt if she can help it."

She shuffled toward the kitchen, and Nathan followed silently. Nathan never had any intention of hurting Adriana, and he'd never intended to involve his friends so thoroughly in any turbulence surrounding his feelings.

A few minutes later, Kristin shooed them out of the kitchen while Patrick started a pot of coffee, and she finished cleaning up. Libby and Nathan sat in the attached living room. They all moved on from the mood that had threatened to ruin a night with friends before it even began, avoiding any touchy subject altogether.

DURING THEIR THIRD round of the dominos they'd been playing, Brock brought up that his long-distance girlfriend was flying in to attend the ball. He was excited about her plans to stay in town for the week leading up to it. Naturally, the discussion of the ball continued, with everyone talking over their plans for the event. Nathan wondered how they were going to escape another potential tension-filled conversation about this insignificant subject.

"Are you going to the ball, Nathan? Who are you taking?" Elena asked with curiosity.

All the guys had spoken up by this point, so of course someone would think to ask him about his plans. Kristin had been talking quietly to Adriana on the opposite side of the table as they flipped dominos over. She looked up and exchanged a glance with Patrick and Nathan.

"You should ask Morgan," Seth Fontana said, scooping a large glob of guacamole onto a chip, oblivious to the looks being exchanged around the table.

Libby immediately began chiming in. "That's what we tried to tell him." Too late, she remembered herself, and clearing her throat, fell silent.

Adriana seemed to be deliberately avoiding the conversation. He'd never seen anyone so fully absorbed in slowly removing a dark chocolate truffle from its foil wrapper.

Kristin stood. "I'm going to grab the rest of the snacks and drinks before the next round."

Adriana's expression was full of turmoil and determination, though if Nathan was guessing right, she was doing her best to hide her true feelings. She stood, offered Kristin help, then popped the chocolate in her mouth. They both walked out without another word.

Hoping to avoid further tension building around this table for the second time tonight, Nathan spoke up as they walked out. "Let's get these dominos ready so we can start when they get back."

THE NIGHT WOUND DOWN with everyone on the front patio as they slowly made their way to leave. The chirping of crickets along with the gentle gong of Kristin's large-barreled wind chime created a peaceful atmosphere. Nathan could almost pretend it was as low-key as it appeared.

But as he leaned against the railing between Patrick and Adriana, he could sense the tension still emanating from her. She had been friendly enough, yet also stealthily avoided much contact or conversation with him.

Everyone began saying goodbye, and Patrick offered to walk Cassie and Daniel down as Kristin headed inside after saying good night.

Once everyone was out of sight, Nathan turned toward Adriana, leaning his hip against the railing next to her. She looked toward him, her silence stretching on.

"You've been quiet tonight," Nathan observed.

"I'm always quiet," she said, stubbornly disagreeable.

"You can be, but not usually during game night."

He couldn't always read her, but he knew she didn't want to talk to him right now. He thought back through more of their night together. After showing up late without explanation, she had been a little more reserved even upon arrival. He was certain it wasn't his imagination that the true change in her demeanor had occurred after the conversation about the ball. So, as he'd been apt to do in those early days, he decided to push a little anyway.

Before he could say another word, she straightened and squinted her eyes as she looked toward the street. "I need to go."

Nathan nodded. "Okay. I'll walk you to your car."

Chapter Twenty-Two

Adriana had arrived later than everyone else, forcing her to park down the street from the cul-de-sac. They passed Patrick as he made his way up the drive, and she said another farewell while Nathan let him know he'd be back up in a bit. They walked in silence. Her mind was incapable of making polite conversation, and he seemed content to let her have the moment.

Trying for weeks now to not only accept her feelings but move on from them, she attempted to take this opportunity for what it was. If Nathan and Morgan ended up dating, getting over this little crush could be easier. She wouldn't want to have feelings for a friend's potential boyfriend. She and Morgan weren't close, but they got along, and she was around often. Which was another thing to consider. She would have to come around even less under those circumstances. At least until she was over whatever this was. Kristin would understand.

As they reached the driver's side of her car, she turned to face him. Searching his eyes, a book of things left unsaid swirled in those hazel depths. She'd felt like she was the only one struggling with these feelings. Now she was sure of nothing. The friendship was genuine. Safe. But things between them felt different, and she was struggling to pretend otherwise. He'd winked at her for heavens' sake. He hadn't flirted with her like that since the day she'd told him she wasn't interested.

Maybe she hadn't been wrong, and time had simply rekindled his feelings? What about Morgan? She'd prefer not to need answers to these questions. Even better, not to feel this way at all and continue life as she always had. Why was he always in her way?

Reaching up, he lightly tapped a finger against her temple, temporarily shocking her enough that she held her breath.

"I'd love to have even a hint of the thoughts spinning wild circles around that head of yours."

His eyes searched hers as he took that same finger and tucked a strand of hair away from her face, almost as if he hadn't meant to touch her at all, his finger barely tracing against her skin as he did it. Without a thought, she leaned toward his touch, unable to look away.

"Can you do me a favor?" he asked quietly.

"What?" she asked, jittery and afraid to pursue the direction of this conversation.

"Tell me what is bothering you."

She shook her head. "Nothing is bothering me."

He ran his hands through his hair and looked away from her. There was a restlessness to his movements. "This is a long shot, but here goes. Does it bother you that everyone was suggesting I take Morgan to the ball?"

The question jolted her, and immediately her defenses were up. "No. You can take whomever you want. It doesn't matter to me."

His eyebrows lifted in clear disbelief. "It doesn't matter to you?"

Lifting her chin indignantly, she crossed her arms. "Not at all."

Her heart stuttered at the words. She was such a liar, and the way he was looking at her convinced her he knew it. It would do neither of them any good for her to voice the way she felt, so lie she must. Even better, she should put an end to this. She turned to open her door.

Nathan moved, resting his hand against the top of the door before she could get the handle lifted.

"Nathan." Her pulse quickened from his closeness and her agitation. She would shove him out of her path if she had to.

Leaning toward her, his voice still quiet, he called her out. "It seemed like it mattered to you back there."

Stepping closer so that now she stood blocking her door, she looked at him with frustration. "Are you calling me a liar?"

She hated that he knew it, hated that it was true at all. Nathan's gaze softened as his eyes roamed over her face. As if he could peel away every layer and expose all her secrets. It was both unsettling and invigorating.

"No. I just want you to stop hiding from me and tell me how you really feel."

It was all she could do not to melt in absolute surrender. He desired a depth she didn't feel capable of giving, and he deserved far more than she could offer. As much as she didn't want to, being mean was her next recourse.

"How I really feel. Hmm." Forcing her voice to stop being shaky, she took a breath and continued. "I feel that you should make a decision. If you don't want to go to the ball, don't go. If you do, then go. Take a date or don't. Ask

Morgan like everyone suggested." Her throat tightened. "Or don't. It doesn't concern me."

He looked at her impatiently. "I never planned on asking Morgan to go with me. As a friend or otherwise." He looked down and shook his head. "I couldn't care less about what those guys suggested."

"Why not? She's great, and you'd be lucky to have her with you." Honestly, Morgan would be lucky to have Nathan, but she was trying to be gracious because both were true.

"Come on, Adriana. Do I have to spell it out for you?"

"Well, maybe you do. Since clearly I'm missing something you think I should understand." She knew she was being a brat, but she couldn't help herself.

"Okay, fine." He stood straight, crossing his arms. "Go with me."

"What? That's not . . ."

"Adriana," Nathan interrupted. "If I'm going to take anyone as a friend, I want it to be you."

"Why?"

His expression was affectionate, all impatience wiped away. He took her hands in his. "Stop asking questions with obvious answers and just go with me."

There were plenty of reasons why she should firmly tell him no. Going with him was the last thing she should do—it wouldn't be a good idea for either of them. Tired of fighting against everything she felt and all the back and forth raging in her mind, she ignored all of that.

"Okay. I'll go with you." She breathed out the words like a sigh of relief.

Nathan squeezed her hands before releasing them. "I would have just asked you days ago if I'd known."

"Known what?"

"That you cared so much."

His playful smirk made her shake her head. "You're impossible."

He laughed. "Wait." He looked around. "Is there a mirror somewhere? Are you talking to yourself right now?"

With that, she shoved him playfully. He didn't budge, just laughed more, then moved away from the door of his own volition, opening it for her.

She got inside, looking back up at him before he could shut the door.

"How is this going to work, exactly?"

"I'll be in touch and see you plenty before then. Good night, Adriana. Drive safe." He offered her one last smile before shutting the door.

She watched him from her side mirror as he walked back toward Kristin and Patrick's house. This inability to walk away from one another was going to cost them both, but all she could think about was how she couldn't wait to see him again. Groaning, she dropped her forehead onto the steering wheel.

Chapter Twenty-Three

Nathan walked back toward the house in a haze, flipping his favorite quarter back and forth between his fingers. He'd made a bold move. One he hadn't planned on—it had been an uncharacteristic impulse driven by her tense mood, their friends attempting to set him up with Morgan, and the insistence of his feelings for Adriana.

When he walked back in the house, Patrick was vacuuming and Kristin was wiping down the counters, recently washed dishes on a drying rack near the sink. He'd planned only to go in, grab his keys off the hanger by the door, and say good night. But he was too keyed up to leave without telling them.

"I asked Adriana to go to the ball with me."

Patrick had shut the vacuum off as soon as he'd come through the door. Kristin forgot her chore and looked at him. Kristin's expression was elated. Patrick's was not.

"What did she say?" Patrick asked.

Nathan couldn't keep from smiling. "She said she'd go."

Kristin immediately grew animated, her face lit with excitement. "She did?" She was nearly squealing.

"I did ask her to go with me as only a friend. Nothing more," Nathan clarified.

"That is so great! So, so great." Kristin's tone was higher pitched than normal. He half expected her to start skipping around the room, raising her hands in praise.

Patrick shook his head infinitesimally. He'd been adamant that Nathan should work harder at creating more space between Adriana and himself. Nathan had always intended to go along as he'd promised, only changing course if that's what Adriana wanted. Ignoring how much he wanted to reach out for her was a battle every time they were together. For all he knew, she just felt comfortable with him because he kept his word, or because they were friends. He had been overconfident in his ability to keep his feelings in check, that was for sure. He had never planned on letting her know it, though.

When Adriana had initially captured his attention, he'd seen a gorgeous woman. He'd been fascinated by her—that unexpected playfulness and witty sarcasm. Leaving it at that could have been simple. That is, until they'd been gloriously destined to be in one another's lives—because how else could he see it with Kristin and Patrick involved? Nathan's heart hadn't stood a chance.

Adriana was unselfish, kind, determined. She embraced simplicity and valued things that were important to him as well. Her warmth and loyalty toward those she cared for was a driving force in her life, impossible not to appreciate.

Yes, she was also defensive when she felt challenged; stubborn, closed off, and untrusting. He loved all of her—the easy and the challenging. The belief that he could separate his feelings from their relationship had been honorable but thickheaded. Strong will and determination aside, he'd set himself up for this exact outcome. And he'd still been blindsided by realizing the strength and permanence of his feelings. He really was a fool.

This ball would test his ability to keep their boundaries and his promises in place. Though, asking her at all teetered a line they had always avoided. Could he succeed at sticking to his word and not blurring those lines to the point of no return? His own stubbornness was convinced he absolutely could. However, their conversation at her car was a prime example of how tremendous the pull of his feelings were. He wanted with everything he was to love and cherish her, to protect and support her, and it reached a fever pitch any time they were near one another now.

ON SUNDAY, Nathan went for an early morning run with Patrick before church. It was something they'd done since they moved to this duty station. Kristin, who did not have any inclination to add a run to her Sunday routine slept in while Patrick was gone.

"I've gotta say, asking Adriana to the ball was a mistake," Patrick said as they hydrated and stretched by their vehicles. Worry etched across his face.

"Eh, yeah. I know it wasn't my brightest hour. What's your deal, anyway? You've been brooding over this. I thought you liked Adriana."

"This isn't about what I think of Adriana. This is about what *you* think of Adriana. We both know it is not just friendship for you. How everyone isn't clued in by this point is lost on me."

"Am I that obvious?" Nathan asked.

Patrick raised his eyebrows, then shook his head. "What do I know?"

"If I was that obvious, Adriana would avoid me. Of course, I think she was nearly convinced I was on the verge of being involved with someone else."

"Are you talking about Morgan?"

"Yeah. You know I don't think of Morgan as more than a friend, right?" Nathan had to make sure there weren't any assumptions floating around their friend group. For all their sakes.

Patrick rolled his eyes. "Dumb question."

Nathan nodded, lifting his hands in mock surrender. "Hey, I had to make sure."

"Morgan flirts with others, but she flirts with you the most."

"I don't flirt back."

"No. I'm sure she's noticed that. As for Adriana possibly convinced there was something there?" Patrick considered quietly for a moment. "Maybe that's wishful thinking on her part."

Nathan squeezed his water bottle, and a stream of water showered across the top of his head. He slicked it through the rest of his hair then down his face with one hand.

"You think Adriana wants me to date Morgan?" He couldn't hide the disbelief in his tone.

Patrick finished stretching and took a long drink of water before replying. "If she thought you needed a little redirection, it's possible."

Nathan looked at him with doubt and maybe a little agitation. Patrick wasn't usually this prickly.

Patrick shrugged again. "Adriana isn't going to change her mind."

"That's fine," Nathan said, knowing he came off more dismissive than he'd intended.

"Is it?"

Nathan let out a breath in annoyance. "I've been her friend this long. I think I can manage to continue as such."

"I believe you think you can."

"I'm not going to hurt her or make things weird—if that's what you are worried about."

"Once again, I'm not worried about Adriana or anyone else. I'm worried about you." He shook his head and laughed without humor. "You know, Kristin has this starry-eyed hope that the two of you will work out your hang-ups and end up together. I'm not convinced."

"I don't know, man. I'm kind of on Kristin's side here."

Patrick pointed at him. "And that, right there, is the problem." He looked up at the sky. "You really plan to go down this road again? After everything Lindsey put you through when she didn't want a part of you or this life anymore? It messed you up, and don't say it didn't. You want another woman putting you through that?"

Nathan considered that. "Are you suggesting Adriana would make me choose?"

"No. Hypothetically, though. Which are you more willing to give up if you had to choose? Loving Adriana or being a soldier?"

"If that choice was presented to me . . ."

He thought about it seriously. He knew what he felt for Adriana. His feelings for her solidified the suspicion that he had never been in love with Lindsey. Which is why they'd been together nearly three years without a proposal.

There was a time he believed he was headed there with her, but there were things that held him back. On bad days, he would pin all those things on Lindsey. On good days, he accepted his part as much as he recognized hers. Sometimes he still wondered why she'd done any of it, especially moved closer to him, only to break up with him. There were never any forthcoming answers.

Nathan couldn't imagine Adriana giving ultimatums the way Lindsey had. She never seemed put out by his career—only uncomfortable by what it meant. It seemed to him there was a vast difference there. Adriana wasn't in a relationship with him—but if she were and she had the same problems as Lindsey? Well. He wasn't giving up who he was and what he'd worked so hard for.

"I'm where I am supposed to be, Patrick. You know how I feel about that. Besides, comparing Adriana to Lindsey seems unfair. They are nothing alike."

"That's not what I'm trying to do. Adriana is great. You'll remember, I wasn't convinced Lindsey was going to stick it out."

Patrick had never been hostile toward Lindsey, but he'd shared some concerns. In fact, his parents had been much the same way.

"Yet you believe as great as Adriana is, she isn't right for me either?"

Patrick put up his hands in surrender. "Hey, if I thought it would work out, I'd be all for seeing you two together, but she can't be what you need. Trust me on this."

"What aren't you telling me?" Nathan asked, not missing how specific Patrick's wording was. Nathan knew that was deliberate because he knew Patrick.

Patrick sighed. "Bring it up. Give her the opportunity to know once more how you really feel, then give her a chance to answer that same question without the pretense of friendship. She'll back out."

Nathan was not going to do that. It could give the impression he wanted to back out and was too cowardly to just do so himself. Even if it was a bad idea, he didn't want to lose this chance to be with her. Conditions and all.

"What if I don't need to? What if I know the answer and I'm choosing to go forward anyway? I've thought a lot about this. I'm leaving for Ranger School soon. I'll have distance and get over her then."

Patrick's concern overrode his annoyance once more. "I think you're better off getting your mind right before then. I'm just trying to look out for you."

Nathan slapped his hand on Patrick's shoulder and jostled him around, light-heartedly. "And I appreciate that."

"But you aren't going to change your mind, are you?"

"I'm not taking back my invitation, no." Nathan knew he'd have to face his feelings soon. Prolonging the inevitable wouldn't ease the ache he knew was coming.

Patrick nodded as if resigned to leave Nathan to his own devices. "Well, whatever happens, I've got your back."

"Never doubted that for a second."

Chapter Twenty-Four

"Mom, can we see Nathan again sometime? He could come over for dinner! I think everyone likes him."

Isaac's question pierced her heart. Nathan hadn't been around Isaac much, yet he had made an impression quickly. And not only with Isaac. Her family had pulled her aside at different times during the rehearsal dinner to confirm Isaac's own observation. They thought he was great. Based on some of her female relatives' comments, she hadn't been wrong in the assumption that his attractiveness was rather universal. How he hadn't been snatched up for good was beyond her. Though she'd never say so out loud.

Some of her cousins had assumed they were dating. Her tíos and tías were probably gossiping to her parents about how it was time she'd brought someone home. She wasn't sure how he'd so quickly become attached to her in their minds. What did they see that made them speculate so much? It was worrisome. For the first time in a long time, she didn't feel fixed on a particular path toward her future. If she could snap her fingers and go back in time, she'd have kindly refused Kristin's invitations. Wouldn't she? Even that declaration felt wobbly at best.

Isaac was getting older. He was noticing things and asking more questions. The type of questions that deserved gentle but truthful answers, and those answers were stirring up memories and old emotions. She'd gotten it so wrong before. Allowing Nathan further into her life, into Isaac's life, wasn't something she could afford to get wrong. She kept telling herself it was better to maintain the distance she'd established long ago. So why did the idea of burning that bridge feel so painful? The two of them being the topic of conversation around her family gatherings only served to further put her on edge.

"Maybe. Nathan is very busy. He works a lot."

"Do all shoulders work a lot?"

"Soldiers," she corrected gently, "and I'm not sure."

"I could ask him next time I see him," he said, still contemplating.

"You could," she agreed.

Did she want him holding conversations with Nathan? The simple answer was, despite everything, it didn't fill her with trepidation. During the wedding activities, the two of them had frequent interactions. Nathan seemed to carefully consider the attention he showed Isaac. It wasn't forced or staged. She trusted that Nathan didn't have ulterior motives where her son was concerned, and that made a big difference in her level of comfort.

If only she could relax. She took a deep breath and held it for a few beats before releasing it. Then shakily stretched out her hands, only now realizing how tightly she'd been clenching them in her lap.

"Mom, are you okay?" Isaac was peering at her with all the concern he could muster.

"Oh, mijo. Sí. Yes. I'm more than okay." She smiled at him and reached out to pat his hand.

ADRIANA SAT by the window of the shoe store while Isaac hopped around, alternating feet like he was playing invisible hopscotch. They were waiting for the clerk to come back with shoes for Isaac to try on.

Suddenly, he exclaimed, "Nathan!"

She jerked her head up. Sure enough, Nathan was striding down the walkway. He surveyed his surroundings as he approached the store they were in. Isaac began waving exuberantly and bouncing as he poked his head out of the store. It didn't take Nathan long to notice him and wave back. As he approached the store's doorway, he looked around. For her.

He followed Isaac into the store as Isaac talked with him about what they'd done so far today. His gaze slid to her more than once.

"Hey," he said after responding to Isaac.

"Hi," she said, smiling at him.

How did he always show up like this? On days when her need for distance felt desperate. It was no wonder she couldn't pull herself away. Indecision was often met with the best things about him, and even her strongest aversions silenced under that weight.

"Would you like to sit?" she asked, gesturing toward the seat next to her.

He looked caught off guard. He glanced at the chair she'd offered, at Isaac and the clerk who had just approached with three boxes of shoes stacked in his arms, then back at her. "Sure."

The clerk worked with Isaac, making conversation as he did. Isaac included Nathan in every step of the process. It didn't leave much room for Adriana and Nathan to talk, but it was ideal for observing Nathan. Somehow, that had become her new favorite pastime when he was around. After they'd settled on two new pairs, they headed out of the store.

"What brings you to the mall?" Adriana asked Nathan as they walked out.

"Oh, I was just shopping for new running shoes." He held up the bag he'd been carrying.

"Nathan, we're going skating! Do you want to go with us?" Isaac asked. He let go of Adriana's hand and jumped just ahead of them, his body turning to face them as he did. He was a ball of energy today, and Nathan's presence had exasperated that.

"Skating, huh?" Nathan asked, avoiding an answer.

She had had no plans of inviting him, but now it seemed awkward if she said nothing.

"I'm sure Nathan has other things he needs to do," she said to Isaac gently before looking at Nathan apologetically. "You're free to join us, but please don't feel obligated to say yes to him," she offered quietly, shocking herself with the invite she'd just extended.

Nathan looked between the two of them, slow to respond. Finally, he shrugged. "Well, I didn't have anything else going on today," he said, mostly just to her. "Skating sounds like fun," he smiled at Isaac.

"Yes!" Isaac pumped his fist and made whooping noises.

Chapter Twenty-Five

As Nathan double knotted the laces on his own skates, he watched Adriana help Isaac tie his securely. Watching them together invoked a fierce protectiveness and longing in him. It wasn't the first time the feeling had rushed through him, but it still caught him off guard. She was good at that—and he wasn't used to anyone easily catching him off guard.

As they made their way onto the scratched but gleaming surface, he wobbled a little.

Beside him, Adriana reached out reflexively. "Oh, be careful!" She laughed like she was embarrassed at her outburst. Isaac had turned to watch them, completely at ease in his skates.

"Have you skated much?" she asked, as they slowly made progress onto the rink.

"It's been a long time," Nathan said, feeling more confident with each stride.

"You're doing great, Nathan!" Isaac came beside him, cheering him on.

"Isaac and I like to come here. When we first started, I

was nearly as wobbly as he was. It's a lot like what they say about riding a bike, though." She smiled encouragingly at him.

"If I fall, just make sure no one runs me over," Nathan joked.

She laughed. "Deal."

After a couple times around the rink, Isaac squeezed slowly between them. He reached out a hand to each of them.

"Let's skate together."

Nathan took Isaac's little hand into his without hesitation, looking up at Adriana as he did. Her eyes, focused on him, quickly darted away. He searched her profile for signs that she was about to freak out. Seeing none, he looked at Isaac again. He was smiling with abandon at Nathan, his happiness contagious, and Nathan found himself smiling right back before looking toward Adriana again. She was watching him and grew suddenly unsteady on her feet. Righting herself before she took the three of them down, she didn't look his way again.

They gained a little more speed, skating in sync, with Isaac leading their pace. Laughter bounced between the three of them as they went. It was a moment he wouldn't forget.

After another circle around the rink, Isaac let go, getting ahead of them. Adriana pulled out her phone, slowing down and aiming to get a picture of Isaac as he turned to look back at them, laughter and joy lighting up his features.

Nathan reached out. "Here, let me see that. Go up there. I'll get one of both of you."

She handed him her phone, the camera mode open. She skated to Isaac, picking him up in a fluid rotation and tucking her face into his neck as she said something to him. Isaac looked up at the camera and they both smiled, waiting. The vision in front of him was distracting, and he momentarily forgot the task at hand. He smiled. Then, quickly remembering himself, he focused them within the frame and pressed the button. He looked at the picture he'd captured, wanting it for himself. There was a lot of that going on these days.

Adriana was still ahead of him, Isaac's hand in hers as they skated a wide circle around and back toward him. He held her phone out to her once she was beside him again, the picture bright on the screen.

"That's a great picture of the two of you," Nathan said.

Adriana looked from him to the picture and came to a stop. "Aw. It really is." She looked up at him, smiling happily. "Thank you."

Nathan nodded. "Sure. Could you send it to me?"

She looked back up at him, her eyes searching his. He wondered if this would be the misstep he kept thinking he was on the verge of making. But before he could take the request back, she looked down and tapped at the screen. After a moment, she handed it over to him again.

She leaned in, pointing at the screen. "The photo is there. Just add your number and hit send."

He quickly typed his number in, then handed it back after hitting send. "Are you going to save my number?"

She shrugged shyly. "I thought it might be a good idea with the ball coming up. Unless you don't want me to?"

He laughed a little then glided closer to her, leaning in. "You don't really need a reply to that, do you?"

She shook her head, her expression unreadable. He looked away from her and began to skate forward, trying to shake off the desperate desire to kiss her.

Adriana came beside him, skating slowly, meandering in a path behind Isaac. Nathan kept stealing glances at her and caught her doing the same. Finally, he waited for her to look again and gave her a wide smile. She smiled as if chagrined she'd been caught. Isaac saw a classmate and asked if he could take a break from skating and go to the play area with his friend. Nathan had noticed the play area when they'd walked in. It looked much like one you'd see at a fast-food joint.

"Sure. We'll just come over to the tables. You can leave your skates with us." Adriana looked over at Nathan. "You don't mind hanging out, do you?"

"Not at all. I'll grab some water. Do you want anything else?"

She shook her head, focusing on Isaac as he made his way off the rink. Adriana found a table tucked between the play area and the rink. By the time Nathan made it back from the concessions, she'd settled in, Isaac's skates on the floor under her bench.

Nathan handed her two bottles of water. "Here. For you and Isaac."

"Thank you. What do I owe you?"

He waved her off as he sat down across from her. "It's on me." She'd already insisted on paying for his entrance and skate rental. He was going to make sure she didn't pay for anything else while they were here.

She looked up toward the play area, seeking out Isaac. When she caught sight of him, she smiled and turned back toward Nathan. "Why don't you tell me all about this ball while we wait for Isaac."

Nathan looked at her, a little surprised she'd asked. "Yeah?"

She nodded. "Yeah. Kristin has shared things, but I like to be over-prepared for what I'm getting myself into."

She was making fun of herself a little. It was cute. He could spend a lifetime with her across from him, smiling like that. Well, he'd prefer a lifetime of her much closer, but this was its own kind of wonderful. He started telling her about the traditions around the ball and how the night typically went. She asked a few questions, but mostly listened.

Finally, he brought up the one aspect they'd yet to discuss. "I'd like to pick you up and take you home at the end of the night. Would that be okay?"

She looked at him, that familiar uncertainty of hers clear on her face. After a moment of consideration, she replied, "Okay. We can do that."

He'd expected her to try to convince him otherwise. Taking a chance on her agreeable mood, he decided to broach another topic he'd been mulling over.

"Do you remember the night I asked you to go to the ball?"

"Of course."

"Something else was bothering you, wasn't it?"

She took a long, slow sip of water. Then, keeping her eyes down as she fidgeted with her bottle, she answered, "My day hadn't been the best."

"Do you want to talk about it?" Nathan asked, hoping she would open up to him. Despite how closed off she was, they'd had enough conversations that it wasn't out of pocket to assume she might finally do so on a deeper level.

"Not particularly." She waited a beat, then screwing her lid back on the bottle, added, "It's hard for me to let people in or to even talk about my problems with anyone outside my family, if at all."

He knew that and wished he could reassure her, but there were certain things she'd have to come to on her own. Trusting him was her choice. "It can be challenging to put yourself in unfamiliar territory."

"It's just easier not to. Though I suppose that's unrealistic." She mumbled that last part before continuing in a clear and curious tone, "How do you confront a new unknown?"

Her eyes searched his face, as if every answer she sought awaited her there.

He considered his answer, not sure if it was what she was looking for. "Some situations require immediate action. I must lean on everything I already know, experience and training. When that doesn't apply, I pray, then I move."

She looked a little surprised but leaned in, propping up her chin on her hand as he continued.

"We don't have a choice, do we? Life can't remain unchanged. Too much is outside of our control. Our only choice is what we do with what we're given. So with that in mind, when something new comes or I reach a fork in the road . . . that's what I do. Pray, then move."

"No coin tosses?" she teased, leaning back.

"Well," he played along, "one can never discount the opportunity for that."

She laughed a little, grabbing the bottle again to fidget with. "You haven't been by the food truck in a long while."

He let her change the subject. It didn't surprise him, though it wasn't the subject change he'd been expecting. "My workload has been extensive lately."

That would not slow down, but he wasn't ready or sure at all about sharing with her that he was leaving before the end of the summer. He'd finally received the orders he'd been waiting on and hoping for—acceptance to Ranger School.

"Oh," she said, looking down at the table.

"Did you have a good vacation?" She slid into another topic of conversation before he could explore her statement further.

"I did. I tried to surf."

"Oh? How did that go?"

"Not great, but not terrible. I might try again one day." Nathan smirked. "I ate a lot of fresh seafood, but I still preferred my mom's cooking to anything I had in California."

Adriana smiled warmly. "You're close to your family, aren't you?"

"I am," Nathan said, thinking of how often they stayed in touch.

"Is it hard to be far away from them so much? Or to feel like any one place is home?" she asked, concern etched in her features.

He wondered what made her ask these questions. She seemed antsy. He measured his answer before responding, hoping to express meaningfully the life he'd made himself.

"I've learned to make wherever I am home. It's a state of mind for me, not a place. But yes, it can be hard if I'm too far to visit them. I try my best to make the important stuff at least."

"I can't imagine not having family dinners and things like that. Seems lonely."

"It's an adjustment. You make friends that become family."

She studied him. "Making friends like that can't happen everywhere."

"No, not necessarily. It's different everywhere I go."

She played with a strand of hair that hung over her shoulder. Her focus again went to the play area, and he watched as she twisted and curled that strand around her finger. He wanted to entangle his own fingers in her hair, feel the smooth thickness of it sifting through them.

Nathan looked around. The bench they sat in was about as secluded as two people could get in such a public, open space.

He decided to take a chance. "I'm curious about Isaac's father. Is he around?"

"No," she said it simply. He could see an inner struggle behind her expression.

He decided to nudge her a bit, as he often needed to do, caution and care in his tone. "And . . . how do you feel about him not being around?"

He could see how the set of her shoulders tensed, and he hoped he hadn't pushed too hard. Somehow he'd always believed that if he understood her history, he'd more accurately understand her tendency to retreat.

She looked up toward the play area, appearing to consider something, then turned back toward Nathan. "He wasn't a good guy, and our relationship wasn't good either. That's the super short version, but of course it's more complicated than that. I don't know why I stayed with him as long as I did."

"Will you share the less short story with me?" Nathan asked cautiously.

She clutched her hands on the table in front of her. "We'll have to save most of that for another time."

She nodded her head in the direction of the play area. "I'll just say that he did not want to be a father. He saw my pregnancy as a problem, which made me realize it was the same way he often treated me. Before my pregnancy, I never faced the painful truth. Suddenly, I had someone else to think about. That's all it took to get out from under whatever hold Brett had over me."

Nathan wasn't sure how he felt about this revelation. He supposed he had always suspected that whoever Isaac's dad was must have meant a lot to Adriana at one time. Maybe still did to some degree, despite clearly being undeserving of such devotion. It poked at Nathan. He was furious with the guy for treating her and Isaac like they were disposable.

"I'm sorry you went through that. Many women in that situation may have chosen differently."

She lifted one shoulder in a half-hearted shrug. "Maybe. I told him from the start that I was doing it with or without him. He didn't like that."

She'd made a principled decision despite pushback from the one person who should have stood by her side, supporting her. He admired her for it, and he said so.

"For me there was never another option. And as I've told you, my family was there for me every step of the way. We all help each other. I was never alone, despite his absence."

He nodded. "It's a blessing to have family like that surrounding you."

"Yes." She nodded solemnly. "They make a lot possible for me. Still," she continued, "it's been this goal in my life to get to a point where I can do it on my own. I want them to see I'm capable and that their efforts were not taken for granted. Especially now that I'm trying to finish school again."

"I have a feeling they do see those things," Nathan replied, gently. He wondered why she would want to do something alone that she didn't have to. What pushed her to think she needed to prove any such thing, or that anyone saw her as a burden?

She sighed, leaning back, and pierced him with a scrutinizing stare. "It just got really deep. Ready to bolt out of here yet?"

He met her stare with matched intensity. "I'm not easily scared off."

Chapter Twenty-Six

Adriana watched Isaac run up to their table, his hair near his forehead damp with sweat and cheeks slightly flushed.

"That was fun!" he said, a giant smile on his face as he bounced in the space next to the table.

She handed him a bottle of water and asked if he was ready to rest. The deejay announced they were starting games and Isaac's attention wavered.

"No, I want to skate some more. Can you skate with me again?" He looked between her and Nathan expectantly.

Adriana agreed to play the dice game but bowed out for red light, green light. She watched Isaac and Nathan from the table, laughing and cheering them on. Once limbo was called out, Nathan took his turn to bow out, and Isaac went to stand in line with his friend, Chloe, and her siblings.

"He's a great kid," Nathan said as he sat back down.

Adriana smiled. His presence today was unexpected, though she'd swallowed her misgivings and thrown herself into enjoying the moments as they came. She wasn't sorry for a minute of it. There was something about him—he made her feel looked after. And like Isaac was, too. How could she not come to care for Nathan as she had under these circumstances?

"Can I ask you something?" Adriana inquired as she folded her napkin into squares, smaller and smaller.

"Of course," he said without hesitation.

"Why did you come here with us?" She looked up at him.

"I'm trying to build something worthwhile."

"What are you trying to build?"

"One of those obvious questions again," he said affectionately. "Let's start with the beginning, when we agreed to be friends. Trust. Relationship." He paused. "Things that last and are built on time and effort."

She wasn't sure what she'd expected. Probably she should have been prepared for exactly what he said, but as always, he was unexpected in a most intriguing way. It seemed there was a lot unsaid in the words he chose. Still, despite whatever he wasn't saying, she knew Nathan was reliable, honest, and caring. Knowing him as she did, it seemed inevitable for her to be in this predicament. Her heart demanded a resolution that her mind was still resisting vehemently, and her mind was what she trusted most.

As they walked to her car, Nathan's attention was fully on Isaac, who was telling him a detailed story about helping Chloe conquer her fear to go to the top of the play area. Adriana was able to walk slightly behind them, slowing down to watch as Nathan reached out to stop Isaac and remind him to look before crossing the parking lot.

Longing coursed through her unhindered. She wanted

to grab him up in a hug, feel his arms surround her. Somehow, she knew she'd feel a security that she ached for more than she cared to admit. Revealing so much about herself and her past hadn't been the plan, and part of her had expected him to recoil at her story. After all, she'd been way too young, an unmarried girl making foolish decisions. Instead, she received compassion, and a strange sense of freedom had washed over her. The freedom that comes only from being authentically yourself. Her heart felt exposed and raw, and uncomfortably needy.

They reached her car, parked on the far side of the lot, and she unlocked the doors. Isaac, who was still focused on Nathan, asked if he'd help him with the belt as he climbed into his booster seat. Nathan looked toward her as if he wasn't sure. She only nodded, then watched as he did so.

"Today was the best day. Thanks for coming with us, Nathan," Isaac said, a tired but content smile on his little face. He yawned as Nathan patted the top of his head.

"Thanks for inviting me. I had a lot of fun."

He stepped back, and Adriana double checked the belt, a habit she didn't think she'd ever break. Isaac grabbed the book that had been propped up on the seat next to him. Adriana rolled all the windows down halfway and shut both hers and Isaac's doors, then stepped back, placing herself in front of Nathan. He was leaning against her car, one leg propped and crossed over the other. He'd been looking around the parking lot and now focused on her.

One more step and she could do what she'd imagined doing—wrap her arms around Nathan's broad, muscular torso. Her body yearned to comply with her heart's desire, but she held herself back, her unbroken rules the steadiness she needed to keep her in check. The late afternoon sun caused her to squint as she looked up at Nathan.

"I'm glad you came with us today. You made Isaac's day. Thanks for that," she said with gratitude.

"What about you? Did I make your day?"

His question and the intensity behind it reignited the urge to lean against him and tell him how wonderful he made her feel, how much she appreciated his caring attention of her son. She watched as he adjusted his position, his height blocking the immediateness of the sun's rays. Her eyes felt instant relief, and she was able to look at him more clearly. He was always doing things that made her feel noticed and valued.

She rolled her lips in, trying to hold back the smile that wanted to burst through. Looking down, she gave in to that smile as she spoke the truth. "I agree with Isaac's sentiments."

Nathan's abrupt movement caused her to look back up at him. He'd straightened, and one arm had reached out in front of him. As quickly as she could look up at him, his arm went back to his side, and both hands flexed into fists.

"Best day ever," he echoed, looking away from her again. His smile spoke of contentment, but his eyes were full of turbulence.

Adriana stepped back, needing more distance before she did something rash. Nathan peeked in at Isaac, who was leaning his head back, the book nearly up to his nose, his eyes heavy.

"I better let you two get going." He took a couple slow steps backward away from the car. She watched his progress, not ready for the day to end yet, knowing she should have been gone already.

"See you soon?" Nathan asked.

She nodded. The ball was next weekend.

"You have my number now if you have any more questions about the ball." He raised his eyebrows. "Or ever just feel like talking." Nathan smirked and her heart twinged.

She nodded again, smiling. "Bye, Nathan."

That smirk widened and took her heart right with it. He turned, releasing her from the weight of his attention. That attention was like stepping up to a precipice. She was looking over the edge. She was scared to face it, but at the same time, the pull toward it strengthened. This is why she knew distance had always been what she needed with Nathan. Lines were blurred now. She didn't know how to gain the traction of those earliest days back. He'd found his way into her heart and turning against that felt more unbearable by the day.

Chapter Twenty-Seven

Adriana had attended very few formals between her middle and high school years. Those events were the only thing she had to remotely compare the ball to in her mind. Even with helpful advice from Nathan, Kristin, and Patrick, it was hard to visualize something she'd never experienced before.

The day of the ball, she took Isaac next door to visit and have lunch with her parents. Gabe and their part-time farmhands trailed in behind them, taking a break from their work. Marissa and Logan showed up with the twins shortly after. It wasn't an unusual occurrence during this time of year, with so much work being done on their family's land. Marissa had agreed to help Adriana with her hair and makeup once lunch was over.

Her family history and her upbringing shaped her ideas of the life she wanted. Her desire to stay close and live within the shelter of her large family was the way of many who had come before—working the farm, connected and close together.

Adriana had once desired distance from that for reasons

she barely understood then and certainly had trouble coming to terms with now. Isaac's birth had drawn her back to her roots. Agreeing to go to the ball with Nathan was a decision she was not fully able to separate from her changing feelings for him. It complicated things.

They were friends, that was true. However, Nathan mattered to her far more than she let on. And those feelings felt like a turning away from the second chance she'd been given to make right all the mistakes she had made in the past. Not because, as it had been with Brett, she'd have to be someone she was not. But because he was a soldier with no permanence here. It was a life she didn't know how to reconcile with her own.

She would do this—as his friend. Then she'd step back, and she would commit to letting go of everything else she felt for him. However hard this proved to be, she knew her strength. She was no stranger to difficult decisions.

ADRIANA WAS SITTING in one of her dining chairs next to the living room window, her eyes closed while Marissa slowly drew eyeliner across her lash line. The sunshine had been intermittently peeking out from behind the clouds, providing additional light to the otherwise well-lit room. Marissa had already brushed out and rolled Adriana's wavy hair. The rollers, still warm, sat atop her head and made it feel heavy.

Marissa seemed just as keyed up over the event as Adriana, her incessant chatter a sign she had a lot of nerves wrapped up in it. It was one of the few things they had in common personality-wise. Between her heartfelt compliments of Adriana's so-called natural beauty, Marissa was trying to encourage Adriana to admit that her feelings leaned into something more than friendship.

Adriana had not told anyone her feelings where Nathan was concerned, outside of the little she'd admitted to Kristin.

She'd instead continued to maintain her original insistence that Nathan was a friend who had been little more than a nuisance only a short time ago. Knowing she'd probably never hear the end of it, Adriana decided to share her thoughts with her big sister.

"What does admitting I might have feelings for him matter if I don't have any intention to act on it?" Adriana asked, her exasperation hard to disguise.

Marissa stopped digging through her collection of eye makeup. She looked at her younger sister with searching eyes and a failed attempt to hold in one of those *I knew it* smiles of hers. "Okay . . . now that you've finally admitted it, can you help me understand why you won't act on it?"

Adriana sighed. "He's . . ." She paused, guilt gnawing at her for the way she felt.

"Kind? Good looking? Clearly interested and probably perfect for you?" Marissa chimed in, filling the silent space of Adriana's struggle.

"Kind and good looking, yes. Also not perfect, and most importantly, not sticking around. I should have kept my distance."

"But you agreed to go tonight?" Marissa looked confused, something that happened so rarely. She always appeared to have everything figured out for herself and everyone else. Adriana knew, despite appearances, Marissa didn't really think she knew everything. Her sister cared about her and had always mothered, sometimes to the point of annoyance, but she meant well.

Adriana looked toward the open window, cringing at the truth. "I had a moment of weakness."

It was Marissa's turn to sigh, though it was not full of judgment or disappointment but of empathy and even uncertainty.

"Look up," she said kindly, getting back to the business of finishing Adriana's eye makeup.

She'd opened a brand-new mascara and swiped methodically at Adriana's long lashes. Marissa wasn't going to argue with her about this? That was a surprise. Adriana relaxed.

Once Adriana's hair was rolled out and arranged with most of the front pieces secured at her crown in decorative pins, Marissa came back around, the subject of Nathan seeming to have taken a backseat to the task at hand. "Now all you have to do is get that gorgeous dress on."

Adriana's dress was a shade like champagne, with a tulle skirt that flared gently, and a tight, modestly cut corset top with a ribboned back reaching down to the natural waistline. The dress had been one of Libby's many formal gowns. It still had the tags on it. She'd called it an impulse buy. Adriana could see the appeal, it had drawn her attention immediately, and when she'd put it on, it fit almost perfectly. The length was a little longer than she'd hoped for, but the three-inch heels she'd borrowed from Danielle added enough height to prevent tripping over it.

"Try not to overthink tonight, okay?" Marissa said as she made sure the dress was properly fastened and securely in place. "He asked you to go with him as his friend. Enjoy it, have fun together, and let all those hard decisions you need to make wait until tomorrow morning."

Adriana nodded, surprised at how long Marissa had stewed over this quietly. Marissa enveloped her in a long, comforting hug. She had never been good at shutting off her mind. Still, she understood what her sister was suggesting. The invitation had been accepted. She was seeing this through. The only thing to do now was walk into it with a smile and enjoy it for what her and Nathan's spoken intentions were. She didn't have to let the maybes of how either of them were feeling toward one another drown out the simplicity of having fun together with their friends—something they'd done plenty of times before. It was different and very hard to pretend otherwise, but she could attempt an honest effort for a few hours.

The kids came up with their abuelos just as Adriana strapped her shoes in place.

"We're all cleaned and ready to send you off with abrazos y besos," her mom said as they all reached the top of the stairs.

"Mom! You look pretty!" Isaac said, running up to give her a hug.

"You look like a princess!" Sofia gasped, looking up at Adriana with stars in her eyes.

"We picked these for you." Elijah handed Adriana and Marissa a few dandelions each.

Adriana carefully knelt down to hug them and kiss their cheeks. Marissa helped her up, giving her another hug before her parents took their turn to give those promised hugs and kisses. Nathan was probably already on his way.

For the dozenth time since her family left, Adriana stood in front of the mirror, both checking on and second-guessing the effort her sister had made with her hair and makeup. It wasn't like Nathan hadn't seen her with this amount of time spent on appearance. For Kristin and Patrick's wedding, she'd had an even more elaborate hairdo.

Though, her eyes had been far less dramatic. He'd looked at her then with an undeniable appreciation. If she was being honest, he looked at her like that a lot.

Her stomach flipped at the sound of tires coming up the drive. Using a light touch, she pulled the curtain back just enough for a sliver of the window to be exposed. She watched as Nathan got out of his truck. Knowing she was going to see him in that uniform again had been an undeniable benefit of attending this ball. He was attractive in everything she'd ever seen him wear, but there was something spectacularly enticing about that dress uniform. Looking at him without his watchful gaze on her caused a thrill to shoot through her. When he disappeared underneath the covered porch, she hurried and grabbed her things.

She took the stairs down to the door as soon as she heard the doorbell and opened it wide. He was there, patiently waiting, an expectant look on his face.

"Wow," Nathan said, looking at her like she was the best thing he'd ever seen. The warmth in those hazel depths captured her.

She breathed out a bashful laugh. She wanted to tell him how handsome she always found him, yet forming words was impossible.

They made their way to the passenger side of Nathan's truck, Nathan walking beside her. He paused before he opened the door.

"When I said wow back there, that wasn't . . ." He took a deep breath in and let it out slowly.

Watching him was like putting a visual to the tension she'd begun to feel inside any time he was near.

"What I wanted to say was that you are beautiful. You're always beautiful. That dress is stunning because it's on you."

She looked down, avoiding the gaze that revealed truths she couldn't face. Goodness. He made her all too aware of herself. It was a strange feeling for that to be accompanied by such acceptance. No man had ever called her *always beautiful*. Except maybe her dad. And that was very different.

Nathan finally opened the door and offered his hand to help her up. When she placed her hand in his, she felt his fingers tighten securely around her own. Looking down at their hands pressed together, then up at him, her heart stuttered. He was standing so close to her, unmasked emotion on his face. If friendship was what they were aiming for tonight, they were on the brink of failing. Everything in his eyes and the fluttering inside of her said so.

She took in her surroundings, once again being afforded a glimpse into a space that was all Nathan. There were no spots of dust on the dash or tiny fingerprints on the windows. That same warm cinnamon vanilla smell she'd remembered last time, wafting like a whisper in the air. Everything about the interior of his truck was as meticulous in nature as she believed Nathan to be.

When they arrived at the venue and he shut off the engine, she began reaching for the door.

"Hey, now," Nathan said, his voice warm.

She acquiesced, placing her hands in her lap without protest. When he opened the door, he reached out to take her hand so she could brace herself once more against his grip as she maneuvered out of the vehicle. Warmth spread through her as their hands touched again. Amidst her heart's fluttering, she reminded herself this was not a date for what felt like the hundredth time. These feelings of hers were not to be entertained.

Making sure her dress wasn't caught on anything, she came around to the outside of the door so he could close it, and as she did, she chanced a quick glance at him. Noticing for the first time how the heels—the tallest she'd worn, maybe ever—afforded her an increase in height that put her at eye level with his mouth. A distracting and fascinating advantage, to be sure. She looked away quickly, taking in their surroundings before he turned back toward her and offered her his arm. She hesitated before taking it, over-thinking as her sister had said she shouldn't do.

He was so polite. It made her wonder—who taught him to be such a gentleman? Was it his father? His mother? Neither? What made a man not only a good man, but a chivalrous one? Was there motivation behind his decision or simply a natural inclination to his behavior? When he was in a relationship, did those things fade away with time and familiarity? And how could she foster those same traits in her son? How much was in her power to make sure Isaac grew into a good man?

She pondered these things as they made their way to the building. They met up with their group at the immediate exterior before going indoors. The women gushed over one another's dresses, and greetings were exchanged before they headed indoors.

Inside, people mingled everywhere. They were sepa-rated from their friends and surrounded by rambunctious laughter and the low, heavy thrum of conversation. The desire to reach out and grasp hold of Nathan again washed through her. Before she could think too hard on that, she felt him loosely wrap an arm around her back, his left hand coming to rest on her waist. Her heart jumped. The move was protective, possessive even. It both centered and unsteadied her. She looked over at him, and he smiled that little sideways grin he gave her sometimes, his eyes searching her face before he leaned in to speak to her.

"It's a little crowded as everyone arrives and mingles. Would you like anything to drink?"

She shook her head. While water would probably be nice, she didn't want him to move away from her quite yet.

He gently led her to an area on the edge of the crowd where the rest of their friends had gathered. How had she lost track of everyone so quickly? It was as if she'd blinked and lost track of more than the briefest of seconds. One in the group happened to be Connors, the flirty guy from so long ago. He smirked at her sheepishly.

"Hey, Adriana. Nice to see you again." He reached out to shake her hand. She took it politely with little hesitation.

Introductions were made among their crowd for those who'd brought dates. Nathan had let her go when they'd come to a stop there among friends, so she made her way to talk with Kristin, Elena, and Cassie. More than one conversation bounced between their group, with breaks to take a few pictures. More people she didn't know came around, prompting more introductions and changes in conversation. She watched Nathan as covertly as possible, her insatiable curiosity elated at this glimpse of him among those who he spent so much time with. She observed those around them, watched interactions, and admired dresses.

When the call for the formal receiving line was announced, Nathan tucked her close again. "Just watch Kristin. I'll introduce you as we move forward. You're going to do great," he reassured her with gentle instruction and his calm smile.

Before she knew it, she was being presented to the guests of honor, and Nathan, voice formal and professional, introduced her by her first and last name. She shook hands and shared brief greetings. It was just as simple as Nathan had promised, and she relaxed a little as the monotony quickly eased her fears of messing up.

That is, until she was introduced to his first sergeant. The gentleman spoke accolades over Nathan. She could only stand there smiling, uncertain of what she should say in reply. She was such a small part in the grand scheme of

Nathan's life, and she knew little of what that entailed most of the time. Nathan was stoic through it all, professionalism tempered with that ever-present humility that was entirely him.

As they made their way to their table, following the two couples in front of them, Nathan leaned down and whispered, "Sorry about that."

She looked over at him. "Don't apologize."

"It's more than a little awkward to have someone talk about you like that in any setting, but especially in front of you." He laughed nervously, and seeing her expression, he continued, "I don't want you thinking I have some sort of Captain America complex. I'm just a regular guy trying to do my job the best I can."

She smiled reassuringly at him, her heart soaring at the pleasure she felt being here with him. "I don't doubt that you do."

They'd reached the table, and he'd pulled out a chair for her. She sat and he leaned down behind her, his mouth close to her ear. "Careful. You might have me believing I am, in fact, capable of being a super soldier."

His teasing and closeness made her cheeks flush. As he sat next to her, his cheeky grin made her shake her head and widened her smile. He was a handful. The more they got to know one another, the harder he was to ignore, and the more convinced she was she had no idea what to do with or about him.

He sat close to her, and that alone was its own sort of distraction but when his knee continued to brush against hers, it was like the pop of a sparkler igniting every time. They'd touched so much off and on tonight, in innocent and minute ways. Each time leaving a shadow of tingles. Going backward, placing him at a distance was going to make her heart ache.

Everyone was quickly finding their places in the large space. Though she was prepared for the continued traditions and formalities, she breathed a quiet sigh of relief, the pressure in her chest relaxing now that they were once again among people she'd grown comfortable with. Their table full of familiar faces, she no longer worried if every single movement she made was possibly being critiqued.

Chapter Twenty-Eight

Nathan had a perfect view of Adriana as the night continued. Through the speeches, toasts, the grog, and every other moment steeped in tradition, he tried to see it through her eyes. It appeared she was fully engrossed, her eyes only leaving the front of the room to steal sporadic glances his way. As always, he wanted to know what she was thinking. Her draping earrings caught the light with any movement. They'd brush up against the side of her neck when she flicked her head his way, and he was mesmerized. It was all he could do not to reach out and trace where they'd touched. When he let his mind go there, he forgot everything else. He'd think about how he'd like to lean into her, breathe her in, and gently press his lips against her skin.

No matter how involved he was in everything going on around them, his attention was a disaster right now. Whether she was doing it intentionally, he couldn't be sure, but her awareness of him was tripping him up. She leaned toward him, lingered close, and watched him often. He was always aware of her, always noticing. This was probably the first time he'd ever believed she was drawn to him, instead of simply paying attention to maintain physical distance.

Her hands kept moving toward the curled strands of her hair that surrounded her face, as if she meant to brush them behind her ears before thinking better of it. She was the most beautiful woman in any setting, always. Tonight, she was radiant. Sparkling and more impossible to ignore than ever.

Everything about her tested his resolve to walk away. Because that was what he had to do. He was done trying to convince himself he could just be her friend. His feelings were going to get in the way. They were already getting in the way. She just hadn't realized it yet. Once she did, this would be over anyway.

Maybe the timing of ranger school was even more perfect than he'd realized. The time and distance, the challenge and the focus required, would finally get him to a place where every action wasn't colored with this selfish hope that she'd change her mind.

Later, as the room dimmed and dancing began, Adriana slowly approached their table after excusing herself to the restroom. Nathan watched her approach as he talked to Villalobos and Fontana. He met her halfway and held his hand out.

"Shall we?" He nodded toward the dance floor.

She smiled, her hand reaching out to take his without hesitation. They danced in a group with their friends to a couple faster paced songs. She let him show her some of the dance moves he knew, let him spin her out and close again. She was beautifully unrestrained. As he watched her laugh after another spin, he realized he'd gained exactly what he'd hoped—for her to trust him, feel safe with him. She had let him in, and it pierced his heart anew with how much he loved her. He'd never desire to attend this or any other moment of his life with anyone but her.

When a slow song began, he drew her in, much like he had at the wedding. He looked at her, tried to memorize her face and the delicate citrusy floral scent of her. The makeup on her cheeks and eyes sparkled under the light.

"Here we are again," he said, his voice rough.

She looked up at him under her eyelashes, a pleased little smile turning up her mouth. He swallowed. What he wouldn't give to kiss those lips right now.

"Let's try something . . ." he whispered.

Pulling gently on the hand he held, he guided her arm to his shoulder, letting his fingers trace down her hand and wrist before falling to her waist. He saw her mouth drop imperceptibly and heard her quiet gasp. He tensed and breathed slowly in and out, waiting for her to pull back.

After a moment, he asked quietly, "How are you doing?"

"I'm doing great, how about you?" she said quietly.

"Great."

That one word hardly covered what he felt right now.

"I know all of this probably hasn't been nearly as exciting as you may have anticipated."

"It's been wonderful. Truly." She pulled back and looked at him, a softness in her expression. "All of this ceremony and tradition is so much more meaningful than I realized. When we raised our glasses in a moment of silence for the fallen . . ." She took a moment, contemplative. "That was a really beautiful moment."

He nodded slightly, appreciating that she recognized the significance. Reflecting that way honored those they'd lost, and it could be a powerful thing. He didn't need time purposely set aside to think of those he knew that had lost their lives. He sighed.

She leaned in closer, her temple near his jaw. That strand of hair he'd watched her fight against all night brushed against his skin. All he wanted was her, yet he knew all she wanted was something much different. That she was letting him stay this close to her was more than what he'd hoped for tonight. It didn't feel like they were here as friends, and that was a dangerous place to sit, because nothing had changed while everything had.

"Have you been to a lot of these balls?" she asked, her voice still quiet and thoughtful.

"Quite a few, yes," he admitted.

"It feels a little like a secret society, all this pomp and circumstance."

He laughed quietly. She wasn't far off. "Military life is heavily steeped in tradition and ceremony, but it is full of the same type of normality you're familiar with too. It just might look a little different, is all."

She grew quiet after that, and he let her, his every sense on high alert. He wanted to soak in everything. The way her voice sounded near his ear, the warmth of her radiating against him. He felt her chest rise with a breath, then the breeze of it tickled his neck. Maybe perfection didn't exist anywhere in this life, but he'd found something close to it in his arms. The temporary pleasure was glorious torture. It wrecked his resolve. It made him want to cling to her and plead for a chance.

∿

THE BALL ENDED LATE, and as they made their way back to her place, he could tell she was distracted despite their easy conversation.

"You have a lot on your mind." He couldn't ignore it anymore, stating it as fact and not a question.

She looked at him briefly. "Yes. Probably accurate to say I always do."

"I'm convinced of that. Tell me something that's got that mind of yours going."

"There's so much I could say. My train of thought can be hard to follow."

Her tone had an odd quality to it. He could tell she was holding back.

"Come on, tell me one thing."

"There was a moment during the grog ceremony that I wondered what exactly that awful concoction might do to a person's stomach later."

Nathan shook his head, laughing. "Well, that's not quite what I had in mind, but a valid thing to wonder, nonetheless."

They pulled into her drive, and he put his truck in park. Looking out the windshield at the dark windows above the garage, he wondered about her home. Was it neat or cluttered? Did she sleep with a fan on? If he walked up there and saw that space, would he immediately think of her? Her movement pulled him out of his thoughts. She was unbuckling and turning to face him.

"How long have you been in the army?"

Her question was a swift subject change. Settling into his seat, he answered, "Almost ten years. I enlisted while I was a senior in high school but didn't leave for boot camp until a few months after I graduated."

"What did you do in the meantime? Between graduation and leaving?"

"I went on a week-long mission trip to Mexico. Camped and hiked a couple national parks, visited New York City and Washington, DC."

"You did a lot before you left. So, since I know now that

you really enjoy traveling and sightseeing, do you get much opportunity to do so?"

"Not much. I get time off, sure. It often comes with contingencies though. I've had a rigorous training schedule most of the time. Everything I might want to get away to do takes planning around that training."

"You really enjoy it, don't you? Life in the military?" Her eyes fixed on him. She looked certain of his answer, despite asking.

He leaned back, his body half against the edge of his seat, the other against his door. "Mostly, yes. I always knew I'd enlist."

"What made you so sure about it?"

He liked her interest, though it surprised him. Maybe tonight made her wonder about these things. He'd always thought he'd tell her anything she wanted to know, but he had refrained from sharing something important. Tonight was not a good time to bring up the fact that he was leaving. There'd been many times he wanted to tell her. The fact that the subject hadn't come up around her with everyone else had seemed an unusual lack of opportunity, and instead of remedying that, the not telling just stretched on until he wasn't sure how to bring it up anymore.

"I grew up in it. My parents were both in the military. It's a life I felt familiar with. As long as I can remember, I wanted it for myself. I know it is hard to understand for someone on the outside of it, but it is fulfilling."

She was contemplative again and nodded slowly. "So, you'll stay in as long as you are able?"

He nodded, trying to read her expression and body language. "That was always my plan."

Even as she looked away from him and out the windshield, he didn't think she really saw what was right in front of her. Her mind was lost in thought. He itched to tug her into his side, hold her, and tell her he loved her and wanted a life with her as part of that plan.

He sighed. "I should get you inside."

Chapter Twenty-Nine

—————

Adriana tried to empty her mind while she waited for Nathan to come around. It was always an unsuccessful task. She'd never possess the ability to shut off her thoughts.

The late-night summer air had a slight chill to it, and she shivered a little when he opened the door. Nathan offered his hand once more. When she stepped down, they stood there, not moving. She had nowhere to go to create space between them. Between the opened door and Nathan, there wasn't a path to step around him without being obvious. There was also the tiny matter of discovering how much she liked him in her space. He was looking at her again, but looked away quickly as their eyes met, his gaze searching the darkness beyond her driveway. He looked like he had so much he wanted to say.

She watched his jaw clench, and her eyes trailed to his lips. Breathing in deep, noting the shape of them, she was lost in how they might feel against her own. Her pulse sped up, the vision in her mind shoving away all her normal practicality. His mouth twitched. Her eyes flicked quickly back up to his and her stomach dropped. She'd been caught, and he was watching her again. How long had he been looking back at her face? She could feel her cheeks grow hot. His eyes grazed down from hers to her mouth, lingering there for a moment. Unbridled emotions stirred between them. All she had to do was lift her face to his and lean in. She looked down and licked her lips before taking in another deep breath and closing her eyes.

His fingers grazed her own, the lightest of touches. She opened her eyes and watched as they entwined with hers. His thumbs rubbed across her knuckles, and he sighed. She was a fluttery mess of indecision, wondering if he was going to kiss her and if she'd let him. In that moment, his lips pressed against her forehead, lingering there. Her insides turned molten. It was the sweetest kiss she'd ever received, and once again he made her feel cherished by such a seemingly small gesture. After a breath, he slowly stepped back. Still holding onto her hands, he gently drew her away from the truck.

He let go and turned away from her, not meeting her eyes as he closed the door. "Come on. I'll walk you to the porch."

She tingled with expectation and desire. What was she doing? This was the opposite set of emotions she'd resolved to feel by the end of the night. She pulled her keys out of her purse, then turned to face him as they stepped onto the small porch. His expression was unreadable as he looked her over.

"You should go inside. You have chill bumps." He reached out and touched her arm.

Her eyes followed his fingers' short caress before landing on his again. Something intense passed so quickly over his face that she almost missed it.

"Good night, Adriana." Her name was quiet on his lips.

She let out a shaky breath. Not so much from the chill as the sparks igniting her nerves. "Good night, Nathan."

He moved away from her and down the step. She waited, watching him. Nathan looked back at her before he rounded the front of his truck. His steps hesitated, and she almost called him back. What would that stand to accomplish, though? She wasn't going to invite him up. She couldn't change her mind, so she shouldn't be disappointed in his resolve. Lifting her hand in a little wave, she turned to unlock her door.

She stole another glance as she stepped inside. He was getting into his truck now, his eyes still fixed on her. It was his turn to wave. She turned and closed the door, leaning against it she tried to calm her heart. He'd always kept his word.

Tonight had felt so different, allowing her imagination to run amuck. If she was being honest, things had been intensifying between them since the wedding. Instead of backing off like she should have, she'd leaned in, still in denial. She'd thought about it on the way home, and he'd known there was something serious on her mind. She'd avoided him, like she was so apt to do, because it was easier to continue to lighten the moment with something trivial, prolong the inevitable, and deny the truth. But it was beating around inside of her, desperate to be acknowledged. She had fallen in love with him against all reason and sense.

NATHAN BARELY REMEMBERED the drive back to his own apartment. His mind was consumed with Adriana and all he hoped they could find in one another. There were too many moments tonight when his strength had broken, and every time it did he had expected her resistance. Instead, it was as if she was inviting him to give in, and he hadn't known what to do with that. Had he acted on it, would his regret be deeper than it was now?

Walking away from her had been difficult. There was an urge radiating between them that he didn't think he was imagining. When he'd caught her looking at his mouth, it had almost ruined his willpower. It took all he had not to forcefully guide her to her door then run away from her. He was that convinced he was not going to make it through the night without grabbing hold of her and kissing her until they both forgot any determination they had to continue as merely friends.

He was done lying to her and to himself. He couldn't do this for one more day. He might not know how to let her go, but he had to do just that. Maybe by the time he came back, he'd be able to say he was over her and simply be her friend.

He was going to have to tell her he was leaving first.

Chapter Thirty

The section of Adriana's family's farm that was open to the public was enjoying a comfortable crowd for this evening's Pick & Picnic event, the first of the season. Thomas and Danielle had pulled in and set up as the four o'clock hour began. Adriana had just come over to relieve Gabe from manning the basket station.

She'd been keeping an eye on the twins and Isaac while sitting in the backyard, trying to study for an exam she had for one of her summer courses. Instead, she found her mind wandering to Nathan. He'd been on her mind the last week and a half—not like that was anything new these days.

Gabe was filling her in on their sales so far that day when she looked up and saw Nathan walking their way. Her eyes followed his progress. Gabe's voice faded into the background as his approach finally brought him to the window of their little building.

"Hi," she said simply.

"Hey." He smiled at her, then turned to greet Gabe.

"What are you doing here?" she asked with curiosity.

She hoped he caught the pleasant surprise in her voice and didn't take her to mean that she didn't want him there.

"Thought I'd take you up on the offer you made me a while back. Kristin and Patrick may have told me tonight was the first of the music and picnics."

She nodded. "It is. I'm glad you came. Would you like to pick some berries before you settle in to picnic?"

"Nathan!" Isaac came around the back side of the building, empty but recently used baskets stacked in his hands. "Hi!"

"Hey, little dude."

Isaac placed the baskets down. "There's the last of what we collected."

"Wait for Tío Gabe to take you back to the house, okay?"

Gabe spoke up. "Why don't you go ahead and show Nathan around? Isaac and I will hold down the fort a little longer."

She looked over at her brother. "Are you sure? Aren't you ready to eat?"

"Nah. I'll wave someone down and have them bring us some food."

She considered a little longer before finally agreeing hesitantly. "I'll see if I can get Danielle or Thomas over here to bring you something."

He waved her away then helped Isaac climb onto the stool.

She grabbed a basket and handed it to Nathan. "Have you done this before?"

"Never," he replied.

She walked the path toward the blackberry bushes, and he followed. "Come on. I'll show you."

She began demonstrating while talking through the intricacies of harvesting berries off the vines. "It's not really picking so much as it is coaxing them with your fingers. If they are ready, they'll easily fall right into your hands."

He looked up at her, his gaze intense. Feeling tingly all over, she looked down, gently plopping most of what she'd harvested into his little basket, then she held out the one hand she hadn't fully emptied.

"Hold out your hand," she instructed without demand.

He did as she asked, barely glancing down as she released all but one of the berries into his palm, then plopped the other into her mouth with a smile.

"One of the benefits of picking your own berries is eating them right off the plant," she said, ignoring the way her pulse had sped up. The temperature felt like it had been turned up exponentially.

They worked together picking berries until Nathan said he probably shouldn't take home too many more. Adriana transferred the blackberries from the basket to a bag.

"Do you want to see the property? We can talk a walk? Or would you rather eat?"

"A walk sounds great."

She pointed out and named lines of produce, vines, and trees as they walked. Trying to explain how much of the land was theirs, she pointed out the direction of the creek, the ranch land, and where the corn maze was set up in the fall.

"It sort of seems like you've disappeared since the ball." She finally blurted out the thing she'd been thinking since she saw him.

His forehead creased in a frown before he looked away. By the time he looked at her again, his expression was closed off, but his tone wasn't agitated. "I apologize if it seemed that way."

She frowned and looked out in front of them.

"Adriana."

He said her name like a gentle request. She looked over at him, hoping her face didn't give away the mess of her emotions.

"There's something I need to tell you."

There was a hesitance in his voice she may have missed if she hadn't been so tuned in. Was he going to tell her he still had feelings for her? And if he did, would she be brave enough to admit her own? No, she had to stay strong. Because she didn't know how to give up the life she had. Not even for the way she felt, not even for him.

Maybe it was something else—he was moving away or had started seeing someone. Her mind didn't seem able to decide which was worse, having to tell him goodbye or congratulations.

She stopped and turned toward him, waiting.

"In a couple of days, I'm leaving for Ranger School. I'll be gone for a while." He ran a hand through his hair.

Everything seemed to freeze. He was leaving? Her heart screamed to tell him not to go. Except she knew that wasn't how any of this worked. This was his career, his life. And more importantly, he was not hers to cling to.

"What's 'a while'?" she asked, trying to keep her emotions in check.

"The course is sixty-two days, but it's common for it to take much longer due to the challenging nature. Many soldiers end up essentially starting over."

"That sounds really intense and . . . uncertain." Worry and longing settled in her gut. She did not want him to leave.

He nodded. "I've wanted to do this for a long time. Due to the deployment rotations I've been on, I had to wait."

This news should be the very kick in the head she needed. It proved what a bad idea it was to get so emotionally involved with him. Despite all that, the curiosity that had awakened was not so easily squashed.

"Can you tell me more as we walk?"

"Of course."

They started walking again, following a path she frequented along the berries and into the orchards. She listened as he talked. She could tell this was something he wanted very much. It made her happy for him despite the ache over such an extended absence.

"I'm sorry if it seems like I'm springing it on you."

"Do you think making it through this school will make moving on sooner more likely?"

He studied her and she was certain he could see right through her. Sighing, he shrugged slowly. "Maybe. Maybe not. I don't know. I go where I'm called, so it's always a waiting game."

There it was again, that inconvenient truth. How did anyone live that way? Certainly, there were people in the military with strong ties to home, and they managed. Nathan was an example of that, wasn't he? As were Cassie and Daniel, Marcos and Elena. Even Patrick and Kristin, since she had no doubt they were going to make it work. Her situation was different, though. It wasn't only her feelings and circumstances on the line.

She looked down. "Oh. I know you are used to it, but do you ever struggle to accept when orders come? Is leaving hard?"

"I've always appreciated the experience of moving around and going new places. There have been times when leaving has come with more reluctance . . ." He paused, kicking at a small rock in their path. "I make the best out of whatever comes. If I don't, it's that much harder to step into it when I have no choice."

He stopped and stared at her. There was a crease

between his brows, something pent up swimming in his eyes. She felt as if he was waiting for something from her. As she had many times before, she felt exposed under his scrutiny.

"It makes you uncomfortable, doesn't it? The shadow of the unknown that I live in?"

He deserved the truth, and it was as close as she could get without also giving word to her deepest feelings. Her heart was heavy, and the ache she'd been desperate to avoid burned in her gut. She didn't have to worry about Nathan breaking her heart. She was doing a fine job of that herself.

"Yes. Very." She breathed out the words. They'd made a loop and were on their way back toward the picnic area.

He nodded, a resigned look in his eyes. "I thought as much."

A solemnness hung between them. They walked along in silence until they were near the parking area. A slight breeze cooled the warmth of the early evening sun. The sounds from the picnic gathering grew louder as they walked closer.

"Do you want to stay awhile longer?" she asked, hopeful.

Nathan seemed to consider a decision he'd already made, then he shook his head. "No, I should go. Thanks for the berries. You guys have a great place out here."

She forced herself to smile, trying not to let her struggling emotions warp her expression.

"Take care, okay? I'll see you sometime after I get back."

She nodded, unable to find her voice. His farewell was sounding a lot more final than any had before, and the knot in her stomach squeezed tighter. He turned to go. Ugh, what was her problem? He was leaving and that was it? Was she going to let him go with little more than a nod?

"Nathan!" she called after him.

He turned. "Yeah?"

She took a few steps toward him. "I know you're going to be amazing at whatever they throw at you over there."

Holding her breath, she quickly took another wide step right into him. He'd raised his arms to adjust his hat, and she took that moment to wrap her arms around him.

He slowly and gently wrapped his arms around her. His hesitance and recent distance chafed a little. Still, hugging him felt as wonderful as she expected it would. She didn't want to let go. Adriana forced herself to pull away first, taking that same wide step, only this time backward. She smiled up at him, feeling the wobbly unsteadiness of it. Her breathing was quick and shallow, unshed tears burning behind her eyes.

"I know you've got this. We'll all be praying for you." She hoped he could see her determined belief in him.

His face had registered shock, then lit up in a smile. "Thanks. That means a lot."

They were better off this way. It might take some time, after all these months together, to come to accept that, but they would. She had wanted separation, distance, time to regain her balance and get over these feelings that were only risking harm to both of them.

Well. She was about to get it.

Chapter Thirty-One

Nathan drove straight to his parents after leaving Adriana's. He had walked away and left her standing alone to stare after him. That was twice now. It made his insides twist. He never wanted to walk away from her like that, with things feeling more like goodbye and not just a "see you later."

He had created a mess. It had never been possible that he could control his feelings and be everything she needed without his own conditions. Turns out he wasn't that self-sacrificing after all.

The whole drive he'd struggled with the choice he'd made not to tell Adriana one more time how he felt about her. It had to be up to her. If she wanted him, she would have to say it. Because he had made a promise. He kept saying that to himself again and again. Telling her he was madly in love with her had been on the tip of his tongue too many times already.

He was sure he was as transparent as glass. He couldn't make her love him back, and he didn't want to. He wanted her heart, freely given. Yet he was also painfully aware of the way she reacted any time he shared the way his life revolved around the military. This was everything Patrick had warned him about.

By the time he'd arrived at his parents' house, he was in a state of agitation. His dad had commented on it, thinking it revolved around training. They sat together, talking about the baseball game on TV, the training he had coming up, and the neighbor's new puppy digging holes in his mom's flower garden. It was comfortable—normal. Far removed from the problems he'd just left. Nathan felt the tension twisting him in knots loosen.

Before he headed to bed for the night, he asked his dad a question from a story he already knew, hoping for some new insight. "Dad, how did you convince mom to give you a chance?"

His parents had met while both were stationed in Hawaii. His dad had been goofing off and ended up running into her on the beach while he was showing off for another woman. It was months later before they shared an actual conversation and built an uneasy friendship. They had many differing views and challenged one another regularly.

"I kissed her," his dad said, half kidding, a twinkle in his eyes.

Nathan remembered that part of the story. As his dad would tell it, their fate changed during a heated argument when he ended up kissing her passionately and she'd returned that kiss.

"What if that method wouldn't work?"

His dad chuckled. "Well, son. If that method is unsuccessful, she's probably not the one you should be trying to convince."

Nathan choked on a humorless laugh. His dad wasn't wrong.

"Sometimes you just have a good feeling about these

things, like I did with your mom. I took a chance, sure. But I was pretty certain it would work in my favor."

Nathan pursed his lips together. This situation with Adriana wouldn't work out quite that simply.

He looked back at Nathan. "In all seriousness, son, just be honest about who you are and what you want. That's the best advice I can give. Your mom and I were very different, but we were also the same—we both loved and lived passionately and with conviction, we believed in communication and forgiveness. We were there for each other, we supported one another, and stood firmly together even when we didn't always agree. That's how I knew I had found the one. Sure, I fell hard and fast for her beauty, but it was her heart that won me over and knotted us together with permanence."

NATHAN SAT ON HIS PARENTS' patio, enjoying the coolness of the early morning air. His dad's words had been playing on a loop in his head since last night. He'd gone on a run when the deep black of the night sky was barely giving way to the inky blue of an approaching dawn. Now he sat watching the sun rise over the horizon.

He grabbed his phone from the side table, setting the earphones he'd laid on top of them to the side. Opening his photos file, he chose the album with a coin emoji as the title. Inside that album were a handful of pictures—all of them of Adriana.

There were a few from the wedding and a couple from the ball. One that Kristin had insisted on taking as a large group. There'd been these silly props at a photo booth in the main hall. Adriana and Nathan had masquerade masks on sticks against their faces and everyone had a silly expression. And another of the two of them standing near their table together. Cassie had been snapping pictures all night and had sent him and Adriana that one. He wondered if she'd saved it.

Then there was his favorite picture. It wasn't the best in quality due to the lighting at the skating rink. Still, Adriana looked radiant, a smile full of joy on her face. Her hair was pulled back and Isaac snuggled close in her arms, a big smile on his face. It was the one he paused at.

He heard a noise behind him and quickly clicked his phone screen dark.

"Who is that?" Heather asked as she came around from behind him, two glasses of iced coffee in hand.

Clearly not quickly enough.

"Just a friend," he replied, accepting a glass from her.

She sat down, fixing him with her raised eyebrows and *mmhmm* look. "Pretty sure you don't go mooning over pictures of your friends."

"Who said I was mooning?" Nathan asked, attempting to avoid his sister's curiosity.

"Okay, fine. Keep your secrets." Heather crossed one leg over the other and took a long, slow sip of her coffee.

"She really is just a friend," he said after sipping his own drink.

"That's a shame. She's beautiful."

"She is. Inside and out."

"So, what's the problem, then?"

"It's complicated."

"It always is." Heather sighed. "Love sucks. How'd Mom and Dad make it work so well?"

Nathan breathed out a laugh. "I wish I knew." He looked her over. "What's got you so bent over it?"

"Trevor and I broke up."

"What happened?"

Last Nathan knew, they were celebrating their eight-month anniversary.

"Apparently, he was seeing me and another girl at the same time. A mutual friend caught him, and he didn't deny it." Heather grumbled under her breath. "Anyway, I dropped him like rotten apples. Obviously."

"I'm sorry. Want me to exact vengeance for you?" Nathan was only half-teasing.

Heather laughed, her mood lightening. Mission accomplished.

"No, I'll be fine. It gets old putting time into a relationship only to have it not work out, that's all. Thanks though, big brother."

Nathan knew exactly what she meant.

Their mom stepped out onto the patio. "Good morning," she said, deep affection in her tone and expression. "It is so wonderful to see the two of you sitting together. I love so much when I have you both home." She came over to embrace and kiss each of them on the head.

"Mom. I live here," Heather said, in mock testiness.

"Oh . . ." Their mom waved her off and went to sit on a chair across from them. "So, Nathan, we didn't get much of a chance to talk by the time I got in last night. How are you? Are you ready to go?"

Before Nathan could reply, Heather jumped and scooted to the edge of her seat. "Nathan has a friend." She emphasized *friend* conspiratorially.

"Oh?" his mom asked.

Nathan shook his head. "Not quite the way Heather put it."

He could tell his mom was patiently waiting for more information. Nathan had refrained from saying much about Adriana to his family. They knew just enough that his talking about her wasn't cause for further inspection.

"Nathan was totally mooning over her picture just now."

"I wasn't mooning," he insisted again without much exuberance. "It was only Adriana, Kristin's best friend. The maid of honor I helped for Patrick's wedding."

"Ohhh. She's *the* friend," Heather said with a loaded expression, as if she was connecting the dots. Maybe Nathan had talked about her more than he thought. "I think I need to come down and visit my big brother. I need to meet this girl."

His mom was studying him. "She is not just Kristin's best friend, is she?"

"No," Nathan admitted. He didn't know why he'd bothered trying to deny his feelings.

Heather looked at her watch. "Dang. I've got to get ready for work. I want to know everything that's said when I get back home!" She stood in a rush, leaning in for a quick hug before setting off into the house.

"Do you want to talk about it?" his mom asked.

He nodded. Once he started sharing how they'd met, he seemed unable to stop. His mom listened quietly as he told her how they'd become friends and how his feelings for her had grown and why he had to walk away.

Finally, his mom spoke up. "She has made it clear she isn't interested in a relationship because of wanting to focus on her son, but you think it also has something to do with your being a soldier?"

"It's crossed my mind. I think my life makes her uncomfortable. She doesn't want a relationship, and I'm definitely the last guy she'd change her mind for." Nathan sighed.

His mom nodded, taking her time to respond. "Military life is full of many uncertainties and sacrifices. Being a single mother surely intensifies her longing for stability."

"I wish I could make her see, despite my life being what it is, I could be that for her. Even if a life with me wasn't exactly always certain. I'm good for her, and she's good for me. I could take care of her, stand by her."

"Oh, Nathan." His mom leaned over, squeezing his hand. "I wish she would see that, too."

She moved away, scrutinizing him. "I know it is difficult to do, but try to see it from the perspective of those constantly left behind. A military spouse or child must come second to the job, no matter how much the service member tries not to let that be the case. In these times, we live daily knowing you will leave, and do so often. You will march directly into danger as immediately as you are called. That is terrifying to be left behind with. Even for strong and independent partners."

Nathan knew his mom was right. Though he also knew that plenty of couples managed, he didn't pretend to believe it was easy. He knew better. Knowing better about a lot of things should have kept him from this moment altogether.

Nathan sighed.

"Adriana seems like a good woman. Yet even a good woman capable of deep love may shrink away from a romantic relationship with a soldier. Add a child and her history into the mix? It's a wonder you've formed a friendship at all."

Nathan let his mom's words sink in. Despite everything, Adriana had let him into her life. Not only hers, but she'd allowed him to be around Isaac. That was no small thing. How could he ever forget it?

"I love her, Mom. You know, there have been these moments between us . . . I could almost convince myself she has feelings for me too. Wishful thinking, probably. I don't know how to walk away, but I'm going to try."

Even if his being in the military was a big point against him, not trusting anyone to abandon her and Isaac was an even bigger one. Neither were fears he could fully alleviate. No matter how much he wanted to.

"I am sorry things aren't working out with this young lady. I only pray someone else comes along that is right for you," his mom said, squeezing his hand again. "You deserve so much."

Leaning back, he looked out toward the horizon. After a few moments of companionable silence, he looked back over at her. "Dad told me how all he had to do was kiss you and you fell for him."

She let out a hearty laugh. "Oh, that man. He's such a romantic. You'll find your great love, Nathan. I know you will. Be patient, don't lose hold of that dream."

"I don't think I'm going to be out there trying to meet someone, Mom."

"Well, why would you, when your heart isn't yours to give?" She gave him that knowing look of hers.

She stood, resting a hand on his shoulder. "If it's time to let her go, then take care of your heart, and do what needs to be done. God will see you through it."

He spent the rest of the day with his parents, fishing and hanging out near the lake not far from their home. Sunday after church, he went on a bike ride with Heather on one of the greenways nearby before eating lunch with her, their parents, and his grandfather.

Before he left his parents' house that Sunday afternoon, they embraced him and prayed with him. The time they'd spent together settled him, and the drive back to his apartment was met with peace rather than agitation.

Loving Adriana had come easily. Getting over her would not. But nothing about what was coming was meant to be easy. Nathan visualized it as another task on the horizon. And just like the rest, it was one he planned on mastering.

Chapter Thirty-Two

Adriana worked beside Danielle, scooping homemade frosting into piping bags. The action of baking and detail in decorating relaxed her as the low hum of their voices and the quiet background noise of Danielle's favorite playlist carried them through each task.

They were working on another wedding order. Danielle had secured quite a few jobs since Kristin and Patrick's wedding. Adriana finished the mini cupcakes and began piping small mounds of frosting in a row, beginning around the edges of the regular sized cupcakes.

"This is the most composed I've seen you in days," Danielle observed.

Adriana bit her lip, not looking up or responding.

Danielle continued, "You've been so restless lately. Scatterbrained—which is very unlike you, by the way."

Adriana wanted to insist she was fine. She'd been insisting that anytime her mom or dad or Kristin brought it up. When the pretending all was well and good and normal slipped, she shut down any conversation regarding her mood with practiced evasion.

"Does this have to do with Nathan?" Danielle asked.

Adriana piped out a lopsided glob. Cringing, she took the scraper and removed it, then sighed. She could feel Danielle watching her work, waiting for an answer.

She was so tired of pretending.

"I take that as a yes," Danielle said compassionately.

Adriana began reworking the frosting and tried again to pipe out the perfect mound to add to the row. Once she finished, the only reply she could manage slipped free with a sigh.

"I should be relieved he's not around making a nuisance of himself," Adriana said.

"But that's not what you feel at all."

Adriana shook her head, and she was sure she looked as gloomy as she felt. "No."

"This is about more than him being gone."

"Yes, it is."

"You've grown to care about him, and it wasn't part of the plan."

Adriana nodded. "Choosing him would mean letting go of everything else. I can't imagine leaving my family to follow some guy. Regardless of how I feel about him. And trust me, I've thought about this way more than I ever thought I would."

It was true. She had thought a lot about it. The thing was, she could see Nathan tucked into their lives. In different circumstances, he could have been everything she wanted or needed in a partner.

None of that mattered against the stronger urge to tether herself to what she'd always known.

Danielle put her arm around Adriana. "First of all, I don't think even *you* believe he's just 'some guy.' Second, sometimes things are not meant to work out the way we determine they're supposed to. Decisions like this? They don't have easy answers. They aren't meant to."

"I don't want Isaac getting hurt. There's been far too much of that on my hands to last him a lifetime."

"Because Brett left you guys? That's on Brett."

"Yes, and not only do I have to live with that, but I have to watch Isaac learn to live with knowing his father didn't want him."

Danielle sighed and shook her head. "I know Isaac will face challenges because of it, but he has you. You'll always make sure he feels wanted—we all will. He's got a whole lot of somebodies standing in his corner for keeps."

"But one day, he might not think it's enough. Then what?"

Danielle's expression fell. "I don't know. One day at a time . . . that's all there is. But why do you assume your feelings will lead there?"

Cupcakes done, they started collecting the remaining frosting and decorating tools. They made their way further into the kitchen and began working through memorized cleanup.

"Because what comes of choosing to pursue my feelings or make them known? He eventually leaves and we're left behind to deal with that, or what . . . he asks me to go with him? Either seems like a path that will inevitably lead to pain for Isaac."

Danielle looked at her with such concern and love. "Oh, Adriana." She sighed. "Say he asks you to go with him. I assume you think that's painful because Isaac would have to leave us. But we'll always be here, and you could visit us as often as time and money allowed."

She came over to Adriana, placed one of her hands in Adriana's, and squeezed. "Any decision you make has the potential to cause more pain for either of you. Remember, the best you can do is the best you can do."

Gratitude and frustration mingled with uncertainty. She didn't want to feel this way. She sometimes wished her path had never crossed with Nathan's. Never mind some of her favorite memories the last couple of years were with him. Why did he have to be so absolutely, impossibly amazing?

"Do you really think that this is all God has for you for the rest of your life?"

"I don't know . . . I'm okay with it if it is. I wish things were as they'd always been. It feels easier. Safer. Predictable."

"Nothing about life is really all that safe or even predictable."

Deep down, she knew that was true. Of course she did.

"I just need a little more time. I'll get over it," she said, taking the piping bag back with a gentle hand.

Danielle looked like she didn't quite believe her.

This was only a grieving period. It would get easier. That's all she had to keep telling herself.

THE SUMMER DAYS PASSED. Slowly.

Berry season ended. School began, including her fall semester classes. She took on more hours at Sol de Montaña once again. Life was much as it had been before that day she'd first seen Nathan at the food truck. It was like God had given her exactly what she had asked for.

And Adriana was going out of her mind.

Nothing had gotten easier. Nothing was the same. This was where she found herself again on a night becoming like so many others before. Standing and pacing and pondering every possibility while Isaac was in bed, sound asleep.

She would wear a bare spot on her rug before the back and forth of possibilities would slam together and give her an answer. It was like Danielle had said, there were few simple choices. There was always this—the easy and the difficult blending together. Choosing Nathan would never not mean having to give something else up. Choosing not to let him any further in her life wouldn't either. She merely had to decide which direction she could tolerate living in. That was all. Just that small, little inconsequential decision. She slapped the heel of her palms onto her forehead. This was why it was easier to avoid change.

Moving forward into an unknown frightened her. It was like having to pry her own fingers loose from the control she wielded over everything. Control was an illusion. A comfortable lie. Danielle's words had been the nudging she'd needed to listen to that still, small whisper. The one that told her to trust, to open her palms, and let all the fear and worry go.

She knew exactly what she wanted, Isaac's well-being always at the forefront. She continued to wonder if it was really what they both needed. Memories of Nathan and Isaac flitted through her mind. They always made her smile, erasing doubt.

This whole thing mattered little if Nathan came back only to turn around and leave right away. Or worse—not care for her any longer the way she was so certain he did.

She gave up pacing. Walking into her room, she flopped face down on her bed and groaned loudly.

ANOTHER MONTH PASSED.

Adriana was at Kristin and Patrick's with Isaac. Patrick was still at work. They had cut up some construction paper for craft projects Kristin was preparing for her classroom, while Isaac was playing not far from them.

"Have you guys heard from Nathan?" Adriana asked as nonchalantly as she could muster, whispering when she got to his name so as not to alert Isaac.

Kristin glanced at Adriana without pausing her cutting. "Patrick hasn't heard anything in a while. He always says, 'No news is good news.'"

"Do you think he'll be home soon?"

Kristin put her scissors down and studied her. "Maybe? Hard to say until we hear something. What's going on?"

Adriana struggled. What to say?

I think I'm in love with him and I'm desperate to see him.

He ran off with my heart, and if he doesn't come back soon, I'm going to pull my hair out from the waiting.

Settling on something simpler, she took a deep breath and let it out, blowing her cheeks out as she did. "I guess I just miss him."

"Wait. What does this mean?" Kristin sat up on her knees, craft paper ignored. "Have you changed your mind?"

Adriana looked toward Isaac. "Don't say anything."

Kristin grasped her hand. "I think you have some explaining to do, my friend."

"Do you know if he might still . . . think of me that way?"

Kristin looked at her like she'd asked a stupid question, then stood up. "Come with me really quick."

She helped Adriana up and gestured for her to follow her to her bedroom. Adriana looked at Isaac. He was digging through the collection of blocks he'd brought.

As soon as she walked into the room, Kristin shut the door and turned to face Adriana.

"That man is crazy about you."

"He told you so?"

"Well, no. Not lately, but I'm not blind." Kristin was animated, as she usually was when making a point.

"I was getting some mixed signals there before he left."

"Adriana. Trust me. You matter to him. You told him adamantly, on more than one occasion, you weren't interested and only wanted to be friends. He honored that."

"That is all I wanted for a long time. Even after realizing how I felt about him. You know that."

"And now?"

"Now I don't." Adriana leaned against the door, like the weight of telling the truth was too heavy to stand straight against.

Kristin put her hands on Adriana's shoulders. "You're going to have to tell him how you feel. Point blank. No holding back."

Adriana frowned. "Well, maybe I don't have to be so candid."

Kristin raised her eyebrows. "Oh, yes you do." She broke out into a gleeful smile. "You love him, don't you?"

Adriana wasn't sure why this made her feel shy. It was Kristin, for goodness sake. She didn't need to give her an answer. Kristin knew her well enough to know this wouldn't be an issue if her feelings were anything less.

Adriana opened the door, gesturing toward Kristin, much like she'd done to her. She needed to get back out there before Isaac started asking questions. They went back to work, but the focused mood was broken. Kristin's gaze kept meeting Adriana's, her eyes twinkling.

Suddenly, she clasped her closed fists under her chin and raised her shoulders up, her face full of glee. "I can't believe I'm actually seeing the day!"

Adriana raised one eyebrow as she glanced at Kristin with a slight smile. "Remember. Not a word."

Kristin pretended to seal her lips, a grin breaking through.

Everyone always blamed these invisible rules. They were more like unspoken promises to herself and Isaac. Promises, rules, whatever. It was time to make some new ones.

Chapter Thirty-Three

Nathan had forgotten how long and hot southern summers were. He felt like he'd been bathing in sweat and grime every hour of every day for months now. The humidity constantly pressed into him, making any attempt at staying clean and dry frustratingly inadequate. That discomfort alone was enough to get in anyone's head. Not to mention that even this far in, the physical toll hadn't decreased even minutely. It both weighed him down and pushed him forward. It was a mental game. Always had been.

Sixty plus days had multiplied into many more. Going into this, he had prepared himself for that possibility. There were familiar faces among the guys here, connections reestablished, and new ones formed. They helped push each other onward. At the end of the day, it was always up to each of them on their own, but all these guys knew what it meant to be part of a team working toward a common goal. It was one reason military life had always been so appealing. He liked leading, felt strong in it and capable of doing so in a meaningful way. However, that strength magnified when surrounded by others striving as he did, and even by those who needed a hand to help them believe they could. He was made for this. It wasn't a necessary reminder but being here solidified that.

He let out a slow breath until his lungs felt empty then pulled the wrinkled MRE beverage bag from the chest pocket of his uniform. Inside he kept two things—a picture of his family they'd laminated and given him years ago and that ever-present quarter. He pulled the quarter out, flipping it between his fingers before closing his fist around it. He stared out in front of him but saw nothing. He should bury it right here in the dirt. Leave it behind. The movement around him pulled him to the present. It was about time for their next challenge, the short meal break coming to an end. Closing his eyes, he leaned his head back, then opened them and stared up at the endless blue sky.

Two more weeks and he'd graduate. Determination was as constant as his exhaustion. He stared at the coin in his palm before dropping it back into the plastic and tucking it securely into his pocket.

Two more weeks. Then he could go home and try not to forget he was letting Adriana go.

Chapter Thirty-Four

Adriana's phone dinged in a quick succession of message notifications. She was sitting out on her parents' back patio, watching Isaac play with his cousins while working on homework. Or at least trying to. Her mind was all scattered. As usual these days.

All the texts were from Kristin.

> Hey! Exciting news!

> Nathan made it! He's on his way home!

> I'll keep you updated.

> Have you decided? Please tell me you won't wait long.

> Ahh!

Adriana smiled. This was Kristin in a nutshell. She typed out a quick response.

> Yay! Yes. Calm down before you explode. It's a secret.

Kristin had replied before Adriana even put the phone down.

Duh.

~

SHE DIDN'T HEAR a word from Nathan. Kristin had kept her updated incessantly until his arrival home. Then even she had grown silent where he was concerned. It puzzled Adriana. She grew tired of waiting.

Isaac was sitting across from her, making swishing noises as he swirled fruit into his yogurt. Putting down her coffee cup, she opened her phone and pulled up Nathan's number. She took a breath and sent him a text.

Hi. It's Adriana. Welcome home. I heard you passed. Congratulations!

It was a simple message. One easily construed as friendly. Nothing more, nothing less. Yet, the butterflies in her stomach had erupted into a frenzy as soon as she started typing it. Tapping her fingers on the table, she tried to wait patiently. Tried and failed.

Finally her phone vibrated in her hand.

Thanks!

She stared at that one-word text until it went blurry. He was not going to make this easy on her, apparently.

Would you be able to come by Sol de Montaña this evening? I'm working until closing tonight.

She planned to take her break with him if he came.

Much like she had all those months ago. It wasn't the place for telling him how she felt, but it was a start. She didn't know how else to get him somewhere naturally. Contacting him at all was out of character enough that he must have been surprised.

> Maybe. I'll do my best. Might be a late night at work. I can explain later.

Well. She'd hope for maybe then.

ADRIANA WAS LOST in thought as she wiped tables at the end of the dinner rush. She reconsidered her decision to reach out to Nathan, playing made-up scenarios in her head of all the possible ways finally seeing him would go. Knowing he was busy at work didn't lessen her disappoint that he was a no-show tonight. Had he thought of her at all while he was gone?

Stepping back into the food truck, she placed the dirty rag with the other used ones.

"I guess I should head home," Adriana said to Thomas, untying her apron.

Thomas nodded while scooping rice into a to-go container.

"I don't mind staying longer." Adriana was stalling.

"Ay, hermana. Go. Get home to my nephew," he scolded good-naturedly.

Adriana said goodbye then walked over to Danielle's van to do the same. Slowly she walked to her car. Every movement was deliberately hopeful, waiting. Putting the key in the ignition, she turned it to start. The lights came on, but the engine didn't. She tried again. Nothing changed.

Mumbling to herself, she got out of the car and lifted the

hood. She knew basic stuff. How to jump a battery, how to check her oil, fluids, and tires. It probably wasn't the battery. She shut the hood again. Turning around, she stopped in her tracks. There was Nathan. Just a few steps away, walking toward her.

Seeing him for the first time since June brought a flood of emotions. She wanted to pull him close and hold tightly. His appearance was unexpected. He'd lost weight. His eyes looked tired. Weary, even. They scanned over the length of her, then the length of her car.

"Hi," she said, unable to take her eyes off him.

"Hey. Is something wrong?"

She glanced at her car, then back at him. "It won't start. I think it's the starter or alternator. Or something non-battery related."

He looked around. "Do you want a ride home?"

"Would you mind?"

"Not at all."

"Let me tell Thomas and Danielle. I'll call my dad too really quick." She turned to go then stopped. "Are you hungry?"

He shook his head.

She took in his appearance once more, tempted to argue or insist, but she left it alone and turned away. Once she'd done everything she needed to, she found herself back in his truck. He had the windows down, a classic rock song on low volume coming through the radio.

"Sorry I'm so late," he said as he put the truck in reverse.

"That's okay." She knew how demanding his job could be and hoped that was all that had kept him away.

"How have you been?" she asked, taking in every inch of him without trying to hide it.

He kept his eyes on the road. "I'm pretty good. Tired."

Adriana could barely keep her eyes off him. She tried to

focus elsewhere with no success. "You came back to a full workload, it seems."

"Tell me about it. Field training is coming up, and I had a lot to catch up on otherwise."

"I'm glad you're home." Adriana's voice came out almost in a whisper.

Nathan glanced at her, questions in his eyes. "I'm glad I'm home too."

"Was it very difficult?" Adriana asked, knowing it was a silly question. Of course it had been.

"More than I expected most of the time," Nathan admitted. "It's been a very long four months, if you couldn't tell." He looked down at himself quickly.

She was able to keep him talking about his experience, not giving him much opportunity to ask about how things here had been. Listening to him talk put her at ease. It was so much like times they'd shared before. It helped too. Because she needed some fortitude right now. There seemed to be a growing chasm between what she wanted and what she needed to do to possibly get it.

"Well. We're here," she said awkwardly as he pulled into her drive. She looked up at the dark windows of her apartment.

Isaac was probably fast asleep in his bedroom at her parents' house next door. Clearing her throat did nothing to ease the feeling that her heart was trapped there. The plan had been to spend some time together tonight. Then she would have asked him to go on a short hike with her so they could talk alone. That was how she planned to tell him how she felt. In a secluded and neutral space. Tonight had not worked out in her favor. As much as she was scared to move forward, she didn't think she could put it off another moment. It was time to improvise.

"Would you like to come up? Maybe talk some more for a little bit?"

His eyes were focused on her, his expression dubious. She wondered if she looked as pleading as she felt.

"Sure. I'll come up."

His hesitance and uncertainty made her want to take back her request. She was questioning herself all over again and tried to shove down her anxiety. Nathan was worth the risk of putting herself out there, even if it was unfamiliar territory.

She sent a quick text message to her mom as she waited for Nathan to come around as he always did. Before he could offer to help her, she braced her hand on the door frame and stepped down. It felt like it took forever to reach her door. She unlocked it, flipped the stairway light on, and led the way up to her living room.

"Would you like anything to drink?"

"I'm good." He was looking around, taking in her space.

She felt shy again. This was the first time he'd been up here. Thankfully, it wasn't too cluttered. She usually cleaned on weekends, decluttering every space she tended to let go during the week.

"What's with the sleeping bag on the lounge chair?" Nathan asked, looking out through the patio door onto the balcony.

"Oh, there's a meteor shower peaking tonight. I thought I might stay up late and try to catch some."

A smile tugged at Nathan's lips. "Is that something you do often?"

"When I can, yes." She nodded. "Do you want to go out there?"

A startled look passed over his face before he quickly recovered and cleared his throat. She inwardly cringed. A request like that right after he'd asked about a sleeping bag was poorly timed.

"We can just stand out there and try to spot some. The real show doesn't start until after midnight, but we might catch a few if we're lucky. That's all I meant," she quickly explained. She pulled the clip out of her hair, just to have something to do. Her nervousness was making her feel twitchy.

His mouth quirked, amusement in his eyes. "I'll hang out with you for a bit."

She looked around. It would need to be dark for this. "Okay, hang on."

Grabbing a flashlight from a kitchen drawer, she switched the lamps back off. "Darkness is crucial."

He stood where he'd been since they made it upstairs, watching her until she opened the balcony door and went through. She poked her head back in when he didn't follow.

"Are you coming?" She moved the light until it was on his chest, barely illuminating his face.

The question got him moving, but he didn't reply. Once they were both out on the balcony, they leaned against the railing and stared out across the great expanse of darkness around them. The moon was low on the eastern horizon, slowly rising.

She peeked at Nathan out of the corner of her eye. He wasn't as close to her as she'd hoped. He'd come to almost the complete opposite side of the rectangular space.

"I've always liked looking at a starry sky. This is a great view," he said, looking up.

She smiled at his profile, completely ignoring those stars. She knew exactly how it looked on a night like this.

"There's one!" He lifted a finger to the sky, and she caught it just in time. A particularly bright meteor flashed along the sky, giving them a glimpse of what was to come.

He turned and smiled at her before looking back toward the night. His excitement was delightful, and it bolstered her confidence a bit. She used that moment to step closer to him. If she reached out, she could lay her hand on his arm. It wasn't close enough. She studied the sky above her, clasping her hands tightly on the railing.

This shyness of hers was going to have to lose the battle tonight, because if she didn't get him to stay long enough for her to tell him how she felt, she wasn't sure she'd ever get it out.

All those months of nearly tripping over herself to avoid him any time he so much as shifted in her direction. Now all she wanted to do was grab him by the collar and hold him against her. She wanted to breathe in that familiar warm, woodsy scent until he surrounded her senses. Closing her eyes, she breathed deeply, the night air stinging her nostrils. The temperature was dropping fast, but she didn't feel the cold. When she opened her eyes, she looked over at him. He was watching her with that depth of emotion she'd seen so many times mixed with a new weariness.

He pushed off the balcony. "I should go."

She was taking too long. Letting go of the railing, she turned and stepped even closer to him. If she reached out now, she could almost put her arms around him. Her shoes didn't give her anywhere near the height of those heels Danielle had let her borrow. She was going to have to do a little leaning and reaching this time. He held his hands at his sides, working his fingers against his thumb almost as if he wanted to crack his knuckles, but there was no force behind the action. His nervous energy spurred her forward. She moved to take another step.

"Adriana."

There was a warning to the way he said her name. He put his hands on her forearms, gently but firmly pushing a touch more distance between them. Looking down at her, he searched her eyes. She wasn't sure what he saw there. She needed to say something, should have led with words over action.

"I made a promise to you that I intend to honor." He let his hands drop.

What he didn't say made her understand something very clearly. And some of that worried her a little. Did he think she would so heartlessly lead him on, only to shove him away and punish him for it? His carefulness, the trust she had in him, was part of the reason she loved him. How could those reasons not be?

Looking back on all the moments they had shared, she saw that he'd always cherished her, respected her. Even when he was questioning or challenging her. His determination not to let her make a move—well, she needed him to let go of some of that discipline right now.

If he wouldn't, she supposed she was going to have to guide him through it, as he'd done for her many times over the course of this friendship. Letting her eyes meet his, she settled her mind and her heart on what to do next. He was fixed and still from his brows to his toes.

Leaning in, she raised up on her tip toes, using the railing to brace her while resting the other arm lightly on his shoulder. Her mouth near his ear.

"Kiss me, Nathan. Break that promise."

That was all it took. She heard his intake of breath, the tension in his shoulders release. His hands found her hips and instead of pushing, he tugged her in toward him. He looked down at her, his eyes stormy. She felt the heat of his hands. Her pulse thrummed wildly. Their breaths mingled together as he brought his mouth close to hers, still watching her like she might turn and run.

"Close your eyes," he demanded in a whisper as he looked at her lips.

He removed his grip on her, as if he'd tamed whatever had been let loose only a moment ago. She did as he asked, sure her heart was going to jump right out of her chest. His breath brushed her lips again. The waiting and wondering were excruciating.

His fingers brushed her eyelashes, traced a barely there touch down her cheeks. Another finger tipped her chin even more as his thumb brushed lightly against her bottom lip, and his other hand moved to cup the back of her head. Then he finally kissed her, a soft whisper of their lips touching. Once, twice. So many sensations exploded through her.

She pushed herself closer, tried to stand taller on her tip toes. He met that demand by wrapping an arm around her and pulling her in until she was braced against him. His mouth claimed hers in a gentle dance of sweeping caresses. If this was what she'd been missing, she should've been kissing Nathan ages ago.

When he let her back down and pulled away, he leaned his forehead against hers.

"Does this mean you don't want to be friends?" he asked quietly.

She let out a breathy laugh. "Nathan. Stop asking questions with obvious answers. You should know I don't go around kissing my friends."

He kissed her again. It was meant to be a quick kiss, but she wrapped her arms around his neck and followed it with more of her own. When they pulled apart again, her eyes skimmed his face—his eyebrows, nose, and lips.

"What changed your mind?" Nathan was still checking on her, wondering.

She reached forward and smoothed her fingers over his chin and jawline, feeling the stubble barely peeking through. "I didn't want to waste another moment convincing myself I haven't fallen in love with you."

He brushed her hair back, trailing his fingers through the loose waves. Joy sparkled in his eyes.

"You have no idea how long I've wanted to tell you the same thing."

"You were taking too long," she teased.

He looked shocked, holding her away from him. "Oh, yeah?"

He twisted her around and tickled her a little. Laughter bounced between them.

"Adriana." He said her name like it was precious.

She came back around to face him.

"You know why I didn't. Right?"

"I think so," Adriana replied, almost like a question.

"I was going to walk away and give you space. It was killing me, but I didn't want to lose your trust or force my feelings on you. Not after you kept telling me you weren't interested in a relationship."

Adriana looked at him, so many feelings tumbling around inside of her. She shook her head and sighed deeply. "That's why you've been distant."

"Yes. I don't know if I would have lasted much longer." He tugged her closer. "Are you sure? I know my situation doesn't exactly mesh well with the life you have."

"Nathan, this is not a decision I've made lightly. I have wrestled with doubts and fear and my resistance to change. I know what I want, and I know what choosing it means. When the challenges come, we'll face them together. For as long as you'll have me." Adriana hoped the full sincerity of her emotions was evident.

"As long as I'll have you?" Nathan shook his head and smiled down at her like it was a ridiculous notion. "There's something I need you to understand. When I said I was building something this past summer? I was grateful to be in your life as your friend but you, this right here? This is what I longed for. That is not a changeable thing." He kissed her brow, then the tip of her nose. "And Isaac is included in that. Just so it's said."

His lips found hers again, a quick, gentle kiss. "I love you, Adriana."

Her heart couldn't possibly soar any higher than it was right now. He made her feel so loved and safe. Those feelings radiated warmly. There was so much she could say. Simply put, her heart belonged to him. She cradled his face in her hands, pouring all her love into her eyes and told him so.

"Tienes mi corazón mi amor," she whispered back, just before he captured her lips with his once more. The truth of those words settled over them. Every wall she'd believed impenetrable, he'd broken down. Her heart was his, and he'd always be her love, one of the most important people in her life.

Chapter Thirty-Five

Nathan was driving in a daze, wonderstruck over the night. It was as if he was in shock. His mind had not yet fully comprehended everything that transpired. It was real, though. The reality of kissing her and hearing her tell him she loved him was far better than anything his imagination had conjured up.

Adriana loved him. The woman that four months ago, he was certain was going to let him walk away, convinced she would never give in—he had been going to let her do it too.

Getting a read on her didn't seem so impossible lately, even doubting as he did. Probably due to the amount of time they spent together and how much attention he paid. Knowing the truth now, he recognized, at least in part, the battle he'd seen raging in her eyes both the night of the ball and the day he'd last seen her.

He pulled over to the side of the pitch-black country road and got out of his truck. Breathing in the crisp mid-autumn air, he jumped into the bed, raised his hands up and shouted, "She loves me!"

Laughing to himself, he stared up at the sky. He still didn't quite believe it. The stars twinkled above him in the darkness. Sitting down, he leaned his head back over the edge of the truck bed. It wasn't comfortable but he'd sat through worse. He waited, hoping for another meteor or two to shoot across the sky. Wondering if she was at home, snuggled in that sleeping bag doing the same thing.

Nights like these would always make him think of her now.

～

THE NEXT MORNING, he pulled into the parking area where he always met Patrick for their early Sunday morning run. He was going on very little sleep, though he hardly noticed.

He slowly paced the length of the greenway in front of the lot while he waited for his best friend to arrive. Patrick pulled in only minutes later.

"What's got you smiling to yourself over here? You're looking a little creepy, man," Patrick teased as he walked over to him.

"Adriana loves me," he blurted. There was no way he was holding this in a second longer.

Patrick's smile took over his face. He slapped Nathan's arm excitedly then laughed, nodding his head.

"I think we're going to have a long warm-up jog today," Patrick said. "Now tell me what happened."

Upon returning from Ranger School, Nathan had still been figuring out how to keep his feelings in check. Take away the grueling distraction of that training, and he was right back where he'd been—wanting nothing more than to see her and hoping she might feel the same way he did. He thought he was as far gone as he could be. Turns out, there was still further to fall. And it had been both a thrilling rush and as comfortable as coming home.

Chapter Thirty-Six

On their first date, Nathan drove Adriana south to a popular downtown river walk. They had lunch, then spent the afternoon hours walking around and visiting a museum. As daylight faded, they went to a scenic outlook near a cliff's edge off a large reservoir. There was a little trail nearby, and the location was perfect for watching the sunset.

She'd brought an ice chest when he told her they might take a short hike, and as he gathered blankets, she went to grab it.

"We aren't walking far, are we?" she asked, her hand clasped around the handle.

"No." He pointed in front and to the side of his truck. "Just down that way a few steps. What do you have in there?"

She smiled slyly. "You'll see."

As they settled in on the cushioned space he'd created, she put the ice chest in front of her.

"Are you ready?" she asked, looking at him expectantly.

She certainly had his attention. Of course, what was new? She always had his attention.

"Yes," he answered.

"Close your eyes."

He did as she asked and heard her open the zipper on the soft-covered cooler.

"Okay, open them."

Cradled in her palm was a churro cupcake. The dessert that had sort of started it all. Adriana's smile was wide as she held it out to him.

"I suspect you didn't exactly spend your birthday celebrating, and I know it's late, but happy birthday."

He took the cupcake carefully from her hands. The sweet, thoughtful gesture was the last thing he had expected.

He laughed, amazed at her. "Thank you."

She smiled then pulled out a cupcake for herself. While they ate their treats, they talked about the things going on and the upcoming holidays. Nathan's parents had invited Adriana and Isaac to visit with him during Thanksgiving weekend, just as Adriana's had invited him. His own family had always been flexible with their traditions, so their celebration this year would be Friday. Nathan anticipated things would go very well, though he knew Adriana was a more than a little nervous.

"I can't wait for my family to meet you."

"I'm looking forward to meeting them too," Adriana replied, looking as nervous as he'd expected but smiling happily anyway.

"It's going to be great," Nathan reassured her.

She nodded, smiling in agreement. She folded her cupcake liner and put it in the ice chest then wiped her hands. "Do you get used to your holidays looking so different all the time?"

"More like, we've learned how to deal with it. There's good that comes with it too. Like the opportunity to create new traditions and new experiences you wouldn't otherwise," Nathan said, not wanting her to focus on the negatives without hearing out the positives.

She moved the ice chest to her other side and stretched her legs out. "It's hard to imagine it all. Especially what starting over so often looks like."

"I've known it for so long, I can hardly imagine what not doing it looks like. Still, I realize it's the complete opposite of what you know, and that is scary," he said, his stomach dropping a bit.

Her eyes examined him. He must not have hidden his feelings too well, because she twisted to face him better. "I meant what I said, Nathan. I love you, and I want to be with you."

"So you aren't scared of the thought of constant changes anymore?"

She laughed without humor. "I'm terrified."

"Terrified? I don't want you to be . . . Is there anything I can do to help you not be so scared?"

Leaning toward him, she kissed him quickly before pulling back to lock eyes with him again. "It's okay. I'll get there. I've made my choice. I choose you, scary parts and all. It's been said that sometimes you have to do things scared. One day at a time, that's my new plan."

The sun was beginning its descent, slowly turning the sky a riot of colors. She glowed in the golden light. Her hair was pulled back in a braid she had resting over one shoulder. He reached out, skimming his fingertips along her braid until he reached the end, then pulled gently where the knot of her hairband was gathered until it came loose in his hand. The thick sections untwisted some on their own. He brushed his hand through her hair, further loosening the twists until her hair cascaded down past her shoulders. He could feel her watching him.

Tucking one leg in, so it was bent at the knee, he scooted closer. His shin rested against the side of her thigh, and he wrapped one arm behind her.

"I want you to know, I'm never going to abandon you or Isaac. I can't promise I'll never have to leave you, because we both know what my life holds, but as much as it is in my control, you'll never be alone. I'm coming right back to you every time." And he meant it, with everything in him.

She leaned into him, holding on to the arm he had wrapped around her and bringing the other hand up. Her fingers traced over his collar bone then behind his neck. She placed a gentle whisper of a kiss on his lips, and he took that moment to further explore hers. The kiss increased in intensity, as she tugged him even closer and used the movement to face him more. The kiss obliterated his equilibrium—all he could sense was her. He was just hanging on, hoping she wouldn't let him go.

When she pulled away, she kissed his jaw then tucked her face into his neck, holding him close. He felt wrapped in her love. And certain of one thing—he was hopelessly, head over heels devoted. He'd pledge forever to her right now if she'd let him. Knowing where her heart stood in all of this was the first step. Next was talking to her dad. He wanted Isaac to be part of the decision as well. He was so young. Could he truly understand the implications? Nathan wasn't sure. Maybe her parents could help him know how to proceed where Isaac was concerned.

All he wanted was for her to stand by his side for the rest of their lives. Maybe it was crazy, to feel so sure when they had just started. But it had been much longer for him. Regardless of the status of their relationship up until this point, they had spent the time getting to know one another in many of the ways that mattered. He was not willing to wait simply for the sake of worrying they were moving too fast. Nathan knew challenges would come. Some, perhaps, sooner rather than later. He was ready to face it all with her. He planned on doing this right.

"I swear I came up here to watch the sunset with you, not just kiss you senseless. Although, that's been wonderful." Nathan nuzzled his face into her hair, inhaling her familiar citrusy floral scent.

They stayed close together, as both braced back on their hands and looked out past the expanse of land and water in front of them. She sighed, a sound full of contentment, and let her head fall to his shoulder again. He leaned his head against hers and watched the sun slip over the jagged horizon.

Certainty burrowed deeper within him. He wanted every day to end feeling just like this, confident she'd be right there beside him.

Epilogue

Adriana and Isaac made their way toward the zoo entrance, remnants of a late winter snow dotted along the grass. Nathan was standing off to the side in the shade. As soon as he spotted them, he walked the length of space left between them.

Isaac let go of Adriana's hand, running to meet him.

"Hi, Nathan!"

They exchanged fist bumps before Nathan turned his attention to Adriana, wrapping his arms around her in a hug. She basked in the warmth and security of his arms as she did every time he'd held her in the few months they'd been together.

They began their slow trek through the zoo with the rest of the guests starting their late Saturday morning outdoors. The weather was perfect for it today.

Isaac was full of energy and conversation. He loved coming to the zoo and seeing the animals. Many were active today, allowing them to pause much longer than Isaac would have been willing to otherwise.

Eventually, with more than half of the zoo checked off

their map, they stopped to eat lunch and let Isaac burn off more energy on the playground.

"I'm surprised he's walked the entire time we've been here," Nathan observed.

"Now that he's eaten and we're about done, I suspect this thing will get some use besides hauling our stuff," Adriana said, nodding toward the wagon beside the picnic bench.

The thing came in handy now that Isaac's stroller days were long over because the stage of hauling a ton of stuff still wasn't. Adriana watched as Isaac climbed around. His boundless energy had not abated since their arrival, and she thought having Nathan here with them was part of the reason for that. The newness of Nathan's presence hadn't lost its sparkle for Isaac. Or for her. Nathan had become a fixed part of their lives overnight, and it was wonderful.

She slid her eyes over to Nathan, hoping to look at him without his noticing, but he was already staring at her. She did a slight double take, unable to hide her smile.

"What?" she asked.

He grinned, slowly perusing every inch of her face. "Nothing. I just like looking at you."

She smiled, shaking her head at him and looking away. Hearing him talk to her like that and seeing the way he always looked at her so freely was exhilarating. Not in a way she had ever experienced before. With Brett, it seemed she existed on the seesaw of someone else's ever-changing emotions. This time it was like free falling into a safety net, and that sense of security calmed her fears.

It wasn't anything she could explain, even to herself. Given what this choice would mean down the line—a future that could barrel into them at any time and one that she had no idea how she would navigate. The more rational response would be one of holding her breath, waiting for the bottom to drop out from underneath her. Sometimes, like now, she thought about it. That she should be anticipating something just around the corner. Wondering if that fear was on the verge of sinking its teeth into her again and dragging her into irrationality. It hadn't, though. The thought would pass with her still as sure as the night she'd stopped pacing in her living room.

"Mom! I'm ready to see the rest of the animals. Then the carousel!" He jumped up and down beside the bench.

"Can I ride in the wagon now?" he added, leaning into her for a quick hug.

Adriana looked knowingly at Nathan. "Of course."

Once they stepped on the carousel, Adriana let Isaac choose the animal he wanted to ride on, then lifted him up.

"Let's strap you in. Are you comfortable?"

"Yep." Isaac wiggled a little, then held on to the pole in front of him.

"Okay, stay still so I can get the belt secure."

Nathan stood on the other side. She could feel his eyes on her as she clipped the belt in place and tugged it a little tighter.

"Good?" She looked up at Isaac.

He nodded. "Mmhmm."

She let her eyes travel over to Nathan. He came to stand beside her, placing his hand not far from hers on the head of the horse Isaac had chosen.

"Ready for this wild ride?" Adriana teased.

"Mom. It's not wild," Isaac protested.

Nathan looked around. "I might be a little nervous."

Isaac looked at him incredulously, making them laugh.

After the carousel, Isaac insisted on walking, hand in Nathan's, as they made their way toward the exit. At one point, his shoe came untied, and Isaac stopped to tie it. Standing there, waiting for him as he slowly worked the laces like she'd taught him, she snuck another glance at Nathan.

He'd been holding her hand since they'd gotten off the carousel ride. As soon as she looked over at him, he kissed her cheek. A quick, light touch of his lips.

Isaac looked up at them at that moment, eyes first wide, then thoughtful.

"Are you going to be my dad, Nathan?"

Grabbing Isaac under his arms, Nathan spun him around before swinging him up on his shoulders. Isaac's laughter was full and boisterous. His question momentarily forgotten.

Then Nathan stepped purposefully back toward Adriana until the tips of their shoes touched. He looked down at her. His eyes were full of so much love and intention. He leaned closer to Adriana, his mouth near her temple as he held Isaac in place.

Isaac ruffled her hair, laughter still bubbling out of him.

Nathan spoke low, his words for Adriana alone. "That's my plan."

He walked backward slowly, eyes fixed on her. And as they smiled at one another, she finally understood what Nathan had said all those months ago. In this life, home wasn't a fixed place. She was looking at her home right now, because it would always be wherever Nathan and Isaac were.

Acknowledgments

It took a long time to make this dream a reality but finally it's happened—my first published novel! I think I'll be pinching myself for a little while longer. I have much to be grateful for. ☺

Thank you again to my husband, Aaron, and to my children, Lexi & Zach. For all the sunshine you add to my days and for cheering me on every step it's taken to get here. I am beyond blessed. Your determination and bravery have always been my inspiration.

Thank you to my family—yes, all of you. Your support and love will always mean the world and helped inspire some of the familial connections in this story. Family isn't perfect but its importance cannot be understated and I'm so grateful for mine.

Thank you to my Romance Writer's Group. Our Monday movie nights are often one of the highlights of my week. Special thanks to Dana who invited me to the group. I'm grateful for your friendship and all the conversations we've shared about writing, our stories, and life. Also, to Jessica—you helped me give this story the life it deserved. Working with you has been wonderful and your friendship is a bonus gift of this publishing journey.

Thank you to all my people who share the love of reading. I'm glad we have one another to talk about all things book related! Our conversations will always bring me happiness.

Thank you to my readers for taking a chance on me and

on this book. I hope Nathan and Adriana's story inspires you to love well and with courage because love is always worth it.

To everyone above, extra thanks for your cheers and support. It meant a lot and helped me to keep pushing forward whenever I felt discouraged or nervous about this journey.

To everyone who helped behind the scenes, thank you for working with me. It truly has taken a collection of amazing and talented people to make this dream a reality. To my editors, Jessica and Laurie—I'm grateful for your insight, expertise, and encouragement. To my cover designer, Josephine, thank you for making such a beautiful, vibrant cover.

Thank you to those who serve in our military and to the loved ones that stand beside them. It is no small thing and your sacrifices are never without notice.

Thank you Lord for making me a daydreamer and not only giving me the passion and ability to write but this amazing opportunity to share my stories. All glory and honor to You.

About the Author

Breanne Andrews lives in Oklahoma with her husband. Reading has been her favorite pastime since childhood and she's always dreamed of writing her own books. When she's not writing or reading, she can be found tending to her chickens, gardening, baking, or hiking and camping. Her goal is to write love stories that inspire hope and joy.

If you enjoyed this book, please consider leaving a review on Goodreads and the site you purchased it from! Goodreads: Breanne Andrews (Author of A Love to Call Home) | Goodreads

If you'd like to subscribe to my newsletter, sign up at my website: https://authorbreanneandrews.com

To connect on social media:
Instagram: @authorbreanneandrews
Facebook: Search AUTHOR BREANNE ANDREWS

instagram.com/authorbreanneandrews

goodreads.com/Breanne%20Andrews%20(Author%20of%20A%20Love%20to%20Call%20Home)%20%7C%20Goodreads